A Sampling of Sleuths

THALIA PRESS
Always Entertaining

Dedication

*We dedicate this anthology to **Susan Slater**, who sadly passed away in May, 2023, shortly before this book was published. Her story included here, **The Totem**, was her final piece of fiction, filling in some early history of the well-loved Native American psychologist from her Ben Pecos Mystery series.*

Contributors

Anne R. Allen
Michelle Bennington
Kate Flora
Lise McClendon
Katy Munger
Gary Phillips
J.M. Poole
Sarah Shaber
Connie Shelton
Susan Slater

Discover a bingeworthy new mystery series

Contents

Twelve Highlanders An' A Bagpipe

A HUBBERT & LIL MYSTERY

Katy Munger

"Go home! Go home! Go home with Bonnie Jean."

The bus full of retirees sang the same refrain over and over as the miles rolled by. TS, who was sitting in the front row behind the driver, was *thisclose* to being driven insane when his Aunt Lil took matters into her own hands.

"Surely Bonnie Jean is home by now?" she suggested loudly as she stood to face the rows of passengers behind her. The bus had long since defeated its suspension system, causing it to bounce up and down on the flattest of surfaces, but that did not bother Auntie Lil. She was as sturdy as a Belted Galloway. Besides, there was no force on Earth that could move her when she was determined to get her own way.

"Perhaps a new entertainment is in order?" she suggested pointedly before sitting down next to her friend Calvin Ewell and resuming their debate on whether the legendary Pict warriors had actually fought the invading Romans in the nude or not, given how much skin their body tattoos had covered. Auntie Lil's stance was that this was nonsense, they had at least been wearing some protection "down there," and probably something that coordinated with their body ink. Calvin thought this was nonsense, but as he was enamored of her, he contented himself with changing the subject.

Their conversation was not as pointless as it sounded. They were on their way to the Highland Games, an annual Scottish cultural extravaganza held each June on Grandfather Mountain in North Carolina. The location was no accident. Besides kicking British butt during the Battle of Kings Mountain in 1780, Scottish immigrants had helped create the Appalachian culture, bringing bluegrass music, quilting, moonshining, and whiskey-making to the mighty mountain range —thus ensuring the success of many a tourist trap for centuries to come.

Naturally, all things Scottish were on the passengers' minds, as was evidenced by what happened next.

"Perhaps I could recite a few soliloquies as Lady Macbeth?" Harlene Bradshaw suggested from her seat near the back of the bus. She patted her improbably red hair and cleared her throat as if to start, but TS jumped in quickly to head her off. Once Harlene got started, there was no stopping her.

"Isn't the Scottish play considered bad luck?" TS pointed out. "Best to steer clear, just in case. I'd hate for anything to go wrong with this trip."

The others nodded their agreement. Not only because having to listen to Harlene overact was bad luck in itself, but also because, as residents of Bonny Bridge Retirement Community, no one on the bus wanted to spoil the premier field trip of the year. Some were returning to the Highland Games for their fifth June in a row. And all were determined to enjoy every moment of the Scottish athletic, dancing, and piping competitions; endless music venues; and food that was most certainly bad for them and so wildly more attractive than the low-sodium, low-fat entrees that the Bonny Bridge kitchen regularly foisted on them.

Just as Harlene was about to suggest she sing *Rose's Turn* instead, albeit in a Scottish accent she was anxious to display, a small Black woman named Clementine, who was sitting with her friends in the middle of the bus, announced loudly, "I need to go potty. When is the next rest stop?"

TS groaned. So far, what should have been a two-and-a-half hour trip had taken a good three-and-a-half hours and counting, chiefly because they'd had to stop every fifty miles for someone to pee. And once the twenty or so revelers had been released at a rest stop, it took forever to herd them back onto the bus. This need for frequent stops was partly because they had started out at the crack of dawn, fueled by far too much coffee, and partly because most of the men suffered from prostate issues.

It was a miracle they had even reached the mountains, TS thought to himself, as the bus gave a groan and tackled yet another incline with a mechanical wheeze followed by a rather alarming backfire that caused the veterans on the bus to duck for cover.

"Did you hear that?" TS said loudly to the driver. The young man ignored him. TS tapped him on his shoulder. The driver turned around, and seeing that he was needed, lifted one earphone up to hear what TS wanted. The heavy beat of hip-hop floated out into the silence of the bus: *"I'm the dirtiest thing in sight. Matter of fact, bring out the girls, and let's have a mud fight."*

"What?" TS asked, confused.

"Wu Tang Clan!" the driver shouted, still in head-phones mode.

Neither the song nor the clan name sounded Scottish to TS, but he let it pass. Besides, he couldn't blame the driver. Anything was better than hearing another one hundred rounds of *I'll Go Home with Bonnie Jean.*

"How long until we get there?" TS asked him. "Miss Bullock needs to visit the lady's room."

"She should wear a pair of Depends!" a retired car salesmen named Horace Grimly shouted loudly from behind him, butting in on someone else's conversation, as usual, and showing no shame at wearing adult diapers. "I can go anywhere, anytime, and my bladder is not an issue. I don't know why more people don't do it. In fact, I'm urinating right now." He smiled in satisfaction.

His seatmate, Desmond Tanner, a renowned civil rights-era lawyer who had spent years trying in vain to convince the other Bonny Bridge residents he had once been prominent, sniffed loudly and inched away from Horace. He had his own thoughts on the matter, but kept them to himself.

"We'll be there in ten minutes," the driver promised TS and put his headphones back on.

"I can wait!" Clementine declared confidently. "I do it in church all the time."

"I don't know why this bus does not have a bath-room," Harlene Bradshaw said loudly, unwilling to give up her bid for center stage.

TS did. It was a refurbished school bus and no amount of paint or onboard potties was going to turn it into a luxury coach. But he wasn't about to complain. He guarded the Bonny Bridge recreational budget as assiduously as Cerberus guarding Hades. The fact was that they did not use the bus enough to warrant replacing it. He took his job as fiscal gatekeeper quite seriously—despite his aunt's frequent attempts to get him to spring for a communal hot tub, swimming pool, cocktail bar, and disco ballroom for "when we are in the mood for dancing."

"Some of us aren't dead yet, you know," she had said when TS rebuffed these ideas.

"They will be if you drag them to disco dancing then throw them into a hot tub," TS pointed out. "The average age here has to be eighty and none of us has the heart of an eighteen-year-old."

As always, Auntie Lil ignored him. She was above the average age and was not about to admit it. When the conversation turned to such things, she tended to zip it.

"Behave yourselves," the bus driver warned as he opened the doors, releasing a steady stream of Bonny Bridge residents into the chaos of a festival well under way. Rather than fight for position, TS waited politely for the others to disembark, staring out the window at the parade of people passing by. He blinked, not sure he was seeing what he thought he was seeing: an enormous man who, in and of himself, resembled a small mountain, dressed head-to-toe in Scottish attire, including a kilt that showed off his tree trunk legs, pulling a large wagon full of black-and-white puppies. Before TS could say anything to the others, a crowd of revelers swept up the old people of Bonny Bridge and bore them away like flotsam on the tide. All except for Horace Grimly, who paused to listen to a garbled message being broadcast over the loudspeaker, then began to resolutely push his walker in the opposite direction.

This was not good. Horace had been showing clear signs of confusion for months. But there was nothing TS could do about it. As usual, he had to stay behind because he was the responsible one. It was up to him to arrange for when and where they would be picked up at the end of the day. By the time he had agreed on the details with the bus driver, every other Bonny Bridge resident had disappeared from sight.

So much for bonding with friends. He hopped off the bus and was immediately jostled by a rather sturdy family intent on reaching the funnel cake stall before anyone else could get ahead of them in the line. TS fell against an anxious-looking young mother with a squalling infant strapped to her chest. When he finally untangled himself, the front of his white linen jacket was marred by a sticky yellow stain that looked suspiciously like a tiny handprint. This would not do. Hurrying after the bus, which had been detained by a crowd of oblivious revelers clogging the road, he knocked frantically on its door.

"Not your thing?" the driver asked calmly as he opened the door to let TS in—but then he stared at TS's stained jacket in dismay, being a rather sartorial gentleman himself.

"I better leave my jacket on the bus," TS explained. "Perhaps white linen was not the best choice of attire for attending an outdoor festival?"

"Ya' think?" the driver answered sarcastically. He stared pointedly at the white linen pants that TS wore.

TS looked down in dismay. His pants were splattered with flecks of dirt. The fabric felt vaguely clammy to the touch. And no wonder. The crowd had carved grooves of mud in the grass and the air was thick with the smell of greasy food. His entire outfit was doomed.

"Tell you what," the driver said. He nodded to a vendor tent set back from the road near the entrance to the festival. "Why don't you hop over there and get yourself a kilt to wear? I'll wait so you can come back on board to change. All part of the service." He seemed so confident of this suggestion that TS felt obliged to take him up on it. Though not without some reservations.

"But I'm not Scottish," he said. "Isn't wearing the kilt of a clan you don't belong to a faux pas or something?"

"You mean like stolen valor?" the driver, who was an Iraq War veteran, asked and TS could not tell if he was kidding or not. "No. Besides, they sell kilts for clans named McSchlitz over there. Last year I saw some dude wearing a tee shirt that said 'The Mighty MacBugs' on it with Bugs Bunny wearing a kilt and playing bagpipes printed beneath that. I'm pretty sure you won't offend anyone."

TS hesitated, but he had made a vow to take a cue from his free-wheeling Aunt Lil, so in the end he went for it. Hurrying over to the clothing tent, he selected a kilt displaying the tasteful colors of the Smith ancient clan—chosen chiefly because the name seemed so common that surely no one would call him on it. Then his eye was caught by a white shirt with immense puffy sleeves and he could not resist buying it as well. And when the vendor recommended a matching sash to wear over the shirt, how could he say no? But by the time he had purchased the outfit and hurried back to the bus to change, he felt rather foolish: he had forgotten to buy appropriate socks. He wasn't wearing shank hose exactly, which he considered a sure sign that one was too old to be displaying one's calves to the public, but it was close. Thank god his socks were black. They'd probably look like knee socks to most people.

The traffic jam finally cleared and honking erupted behind the bus. "I'll see you back here, same place, seven o'clock p.m. tonight. Got it?" the driver reminded him and TS scurried off the bus.

Despite his bravado while buying it, TS suddenly felt silly in his outfit and tried to walk with manly strides to make up for it. If his friends back on Wall Street could see him now, he could only imagine their reaction. But his self-consciousness did not last long. Clementine and her friends, Willadeene and Josette, spotted him within five minutes and came running up with squeals of delight.

TS stared at them in astonishment. All three were sporting kilts, albeit worn in distinctly nontraditional ways. Clementine wore hers over her polyester slacks, while Willadeene had hers draped over one shoulder like a ceremonial cloak. Meanwhile, Josette had fastened her kilt just under her armpits to create a sort of tent that concealed her stomach. "Had to loosen my waist band," she explained to TS. "I had no idea corn dogs were Scottish."

"How very creative," TS murmured, resisting the impulse to point out that corn dogs were most assuredly not Scottish.

"Look at you!" Clementine exclaimed as she surveyed TS from head to toe. "Look at those handsome legs." Her friends laughed their agreement.

Now, TS was good friends with all of them and,

indeed, he had paid their way on the field trip, but he wondered briefly how they could have afforded their new duds.

Clementine answered his unspoken question. "We've got us a new gig," she explained to TS. "Whenever we go up to a stall, people kinda look at us for a little more than is polite, if you know what I'm saying. Then they ask us how we happened to wander upon these here Highland Games. Course, we all know what that means, don't we girls?" Her friends, whose skin was as dark as Clementine's, nodded their agreement. "So you know what we tell them? We say we are black Irish and we took a wrong turn at Donegal! And you know what they do? They laugh and laugh—and then they give us what we want for free! It's already worked three times."

The trio of women held up various souvenirs, ranging from a miniature bagpipe-shaped pocketbook to a quart-size craft beer of Scottish Ale to a ghastly oversized tam-o'-shanter that looked straight out of some 70s-era sitcom with a too loud soundtrack.

"Have you seen my aunt?" TS asked the trio. He knew all too well that an unsupervised Auntie Lil often meant unsupervised trouble.

"I saw her eating sticky toffee pudding earlier," Willadeene offered, pointing at a tent in the distance.

"Yeah, but I saw her at the fish and chips place after that," Clementine said.

"She was eating scones not five minutes ago, somewhere over there," Josette countered, waving toward the entrance to the festival's music section.

TS knew he'd never find Auntie Lil. His legs could not keep up with her appetite.

"You know what you need?" Willadeene said suddenly. TS had no idea what was coming, but he knew he would not like it. "You need some makeup. I mean, you got the look going there, what with the blouse and skirt and all."

"*Kilt,*" TS said firmly but Willadeene was unperturbed. "So what you need now is a little face paint to pull off the whole look. You need to do that Mel Gibson thing."

"She means the Braveheart thing," Clementine explained. "Follow us. I saw that tent earlier."

Before TS knew what was happening, he was sitting in a chair and a thirty-something woman with tattoos up and down her arms was waving brushes around his face and exclaiming at his cheekbones while puffs of Patchouli-scented air assaulted his nostrils. It all happened so quickly that he felt helpless to stop it. In what seemed like mere minutes, she was done and the crowd that had gathered to watch her transform him burst into applause. This filled TS with unexpected confidence and he hopped up from the chair ready to tackle the Highland Games. He shuffled his feet a bit to prove it.

"That's the spirit, Mr. TS!" Clementine exclaimed. "Now follow us. We heard there's a jigging competition going on and we want to take a gander. Isn't that right, girls?" she asked her friends.

Josette nodded enthusiastically. "That's right. We could shake a leg in our day, but I'm curious to know what this jigging thing is all about. We missed it last year because Willadeene would not leave the beer tent."

Swept up by this merry band of women, TS followed them through the crowd, searching for the competitions. As they neared a large tent with a paneled wood floor, the pounding of feet against the hard surface drew them like zombies following the beat of their master's drum. A huge throng had gathered. But as they were in the South, after all, many in the crowd parted to let the old people through. TS hesitated, but the three women were unashamedly opportunistic and grabbed his hand, snaking him through the mob. As they reached the front, TS gaped in astonishment. The floor held the ten finalists in the open jig competition, six of them lithe young ladies who could not have been more than fifteen years of age, and three of whom were likely no more than eight. But the final contestant was the giant man that TS had spotted when they first arrived, the one who had been pulling a wagon of puppies. He was even bigger up close, at least six and a half feet tall and surely weighing well over three hundred pounds. He dwarfed the other contestants and yet…. TS could not believe his eyes. The man had his hands held high over his head in a graceful arc and those elephantine legs of his were leaping and whipping back and forth with an astonishing elegance that made him look every bit as graceful as his younger, and far lighter, competitors.

"Will you look at that Big Bill McGregor go!" one of the observers cried out and the crowd roared their assent.

"The man is a legend!" someone else shouted.

"I heard he won the bagpiping contest yesterday," a man in the crowd offered.

"You should have seen him driving golf balls into the hills earlier this morning!" an excited woman cried out.

"I saw him annihilate the competition in yesterday's haggis eating contest," yet another person offered. "He's in line for the Belter Cup for sure!"

"Who is Big Bill McGregor?" TS asked a woman standing next to him.

Her husband answered for her. "Why, Big Bill McGregor is a legend. He can pipe. He can jig. He can cook. He can drink. He can toss a caber a quarter mile or more, too! I saw him last year. He was the talk of the town. And look at him now! Just look at that man go."

It was true. Big Bill McGregor was whirling and twirling and hopping and stomping. His hands were waving, his eyes were flashing, and his smile was contagious. TS had never seen a man enjoy a jig more.

"Of course, he'll only be good for another hour or so," a more practical observer said loudly. "That's when the beer drinking competitions begin. Big Bill tends to come out of the gate a little fast when it comes to the beer drinking. That will put the kibosh on competing in anything else."

"Did I see him pulling a wagon full of puppies earlier?" TS could not help but ask. He had long since forgotten his face was painted and had no idea that many in the crowd were staring at him in admiration. Why, it was as if William Wallace himself had joined them in the fun.

"He brings a wagon full of puppies every year to adopt out," a woman told him. "Last year, we snagged one of his border collies and it's the smartest dog we ever had."

By now, TS's head was spinning. A giant of a man who could pipe, drink, jig, and loved animals? Now that was a man unafraid to follow his bliss.

The music stopped and the dancers stood panting, trying to catch their breath. That is, all except Big Bill McGregor. He was too busy guzzling a beer that a spectator had handed him. Needless to say, he was the only one on the dance floor doing so, although a few of the older girls looked at him with envy. Meanwhile, it did not take long for the judges to agree that Big Bill McGregor was the winner of this year's open jig contest. A mighty roar went up from the crowd when he was proclaimed triumphant. He received his ribbon with good humor, then celebrated by twirling every one of his competitors in a giant circle. One-by-one, he gripped them under their arms, lifted them up like tiny airplanes on a ride at the fair, then turned them in circles faster and faster as their legs flew up higher and higher in the air. Like a father with a dozen daughters, he whirled each one to great applause and the merriment of all. TS could not remember when he had last seen such joy in action.

"Now that's a real man," a familiar voice said at his elbow. Desmond Tanner stood, staring at Big Bill McGregor. "A gentle giant, as they say. He's like a Scottish Clyde Bellecourt times two! I represented Clyde in 1969, you know." When no one seemed impressed, he looked around for allies and spotted TS. "Is that you, Hubbert? I recognize your shank hose."

"They're socks," TS said grimly. "Have you seen my aunt, by the way?"

Desmond shook his head. "No, but I saw Horace Grimly join the veteran's parade right after we got here. It was on the track that circles the main tents. He fell in behind the slower ones and he's been going in circles ever since, even though the parade ended an hour ago."

He looked TS over again. "Let me guess. You let Clementine and crew do your styling?" Desmond laughed heartily. "They got their hands on me last year. But I must say, your legs are much prettier than mine." And with that, he marched off in search of further diversion, leaving TS wondering whether he should be pleased or insulted.

As he passed the center grounds in search of his aunt, TS noticed that Horace Grimly was indeed still vainly inching along on his walker around a large oval track, enjoying his glory laps as a veteran. Two other quite elderly men had inexplicably fallen in behind Horace and were circling the track with him. TS shook his head and continued searching for Auntie Lil.

Ten minutes later, he found her. The moment he approached the music stages, a godawful wall of sound assaulted him from afar. It sounded like twelve drunken bagpipers and six deaf accordion players were joining forces to drown out a garbage truck. But when he finally made it to that particular stage, it turned out to be a heavy metal band that had augmented their traditional rock instruments with two bagpipers and a single overachieving accordion player. This trio of Celtic rebels were huffing, puffing, squeezing, and strutting their way through what seemed like an interminable playoff of chaotic music and young male ego. Though the bagpipers wore kilts, they had army boots on their feet, skulls on their black t-shirts, and hair that stuck up from their heads in red dreadlocks like rhubarb stalks sprouting in spring. Twins? TS shook his head. This was the least of the weirdness he had seen today.

Within seconds of finding a spot toward the middle of the crowd, the man standing next to TS yelled at him over the noise: "Do you know why bagpipers walk when they play?"

TS shook his head. He had no idea.

"To get away from the sound!" his neighbor bellowed and burst out in incontrollable laughter.

I want some of what he's having, TS thought to himself. Now, where in the deuces is Aunt Lil?

The crowd in front of him had started to undulate like a giant snake slithering through the grass. What in the world? Suddenly, TS saw a wildly bobbing head of white hair heading his way, born along by the outstretched hands of the crowd. He shook his head. It was Auntie Lil, crowd surfing toward him from the front of the stage, with no regard whatsoever for her personal safety. *It's all fun and games,* TS thought to himself, *until someone breaks a hip.*

"Put her down!" TS screamed as his aunt grew closer. When no one noticed him, he clenched his fists, gathered his strength, and shouted with all of his might: "PUT HER DOWN!" The fact that he looked like a Scottish warrior about to attack them with a square-head axe must have inspired at least a few in the crowd to take notice. When Auntie Lil reached him, they gently lowered her to the ground and steadied her until she could regain her balance.

"Just who do you think you are, young man?" Auntie Lil demanded, hands on her hips. The stylish Highland outfit she wore had been designed for a man, not that gender-specific fashion rules had ever stopped her, and it was now more spotted than a dalmatian after a mud bath. A thick streak of grime ran from her forehead down her right cheek.

"It's me," TS said, far more calmly than he felt. "And what in god's name do you think you're doing?"

Calvin Ewell had been pushing through the crowd,

trying to rescue Auntie Lil, and arrived just in time to see her embrace TS.

"Oh, Theodore, I have found my people," Auntie Lil said in rapture. She swept her arms wide, gesturing to the crowd. "This is even more thrilling than the taiko drums I got to play in Japan. You should hear this music. It's full of noise and chaos and life. It makes me feel so alive!"

"First of all, Aunt Lil," TS said patiently. "It would be impossible *not* to hear this music. They're louder than two jets taking off in tandem. Secondly, are you really dressed for being tossed about by a crowd?" He looked at Auntie Lil's kilt pointedly.

"Oh, posh. No one is looking at my old legs and granny panties. Besides, look what I learned!" With this, Auntie Lil bent over and began whipping her head up and down with alarming force, causing her already wild hair to whirl about like a miniature white tornado. TS stared in astonishment at the hairdo this produced. Every strand stood on end, making Auntie Lil look like a giant dandelion. "It's called head banging!" Auntie Lil explained. "A nice young man wearing kabuki make-up and black eyeshadow showed me how to do it."

A nice young man with a deep-seated grudge against his grandmother, TS thought to himself.

The noise from the stage swelled suddenly as the bagpipers finally overwhelmed the accordion player, who dropped to the ground in theatrical exhaustion. The two bagpipers left standing went wild, dueling it out with the guitar player while the rest of the band hopped up and down, swung their instruments around their necks, and generally behaved like savages pumping themselves up for a war party. TS had no idea why people considered the cacophony of sound surrounding him to be music. He himself was partial to Broadway show tunes, original cast albums only. To TS, this was worse than noise. This was assault with a deadly decibel upon his discerning eardrums.

"I can't stay here, Aunt Lil," he explained loudly, then muttered under his breath, "You may already be hard of hearing, but I've got a few good years left in me yet."

"Theodore Hubbert, I am not the least bit deaf. How dare you?" Auntie Lil shot back.

Okay then. Perhaps she isn't quite as deaf as I assumed, TS thought.

"Did you know that heavy metal is nothing new?" Calvin Ewell suddenly interrupted. "The remote Tsimané tribe of the Amazon consider notes that are three steps away on the musical scale—what we call the Devil's Interval—to be quite pleasant! Many heavy metal bands also prefer dissonant notes that lack traditional mathematical relationships. It's really quite fascinating."

TS could not begin to respond to this statement. That was Calvin. He was always interjecting esoteric tidbits of information into conversations, which some people loved and others loathed. TS was somewhere in the middle, while Auntie Lil only encouraged Calvin's habit of professorial mansplaining.

"I had no idea," TS finally shouted into Calvin's ear and the older man nodded sagely. "Let's get out of here," TS added firmly and took Auntie Lil by the hand.

She must have been getting tired as she made no protests and started to follow TS toward a quieter corner. Just then, a change came over the crowd. It was as if an electrical current had started running through it. Some people were turning and staring, while a column of other people formed and headed off toward the center of the festival grounds. Security officers had appeared out of the shadows and were moving rapidly through the crowd in the direction of the same central area.

"Something's going on," TS said, quite unnecessarily, as they were swept up in the crowd and pushed forward faster and faster.

The mayhem did not bother Auntie Lil. As always, the first sign of trouble energized her. Before many seconds had passed, she was practically leading the stampede, the others close behind her. "Hurry up, Theodore," she shouted over her shoulder. "This looks like something big!"

Oh, lord. TS should have known better. Put Auntie Lil and a crowd of more than fifty people together and murder was sure to follow. He did not know if she divined homicidal impulses somehow and managed to be near them when they occurred, or if such lapses in civility were happening around him all the time and he just never noticed unless she was near. Neither possibility assured him.

As they grew closer to their unknown destination, they passed the track surrounding the main tents. Horace Grimly was still plodding along, but had picked up three more followers in his endless quest for veteran's glory. TS could hear wailing up ahead. A large tent had been set up in the very center of the grounds and the commotion was emanating from there. With Auntie Lil acting as point, TS and Calvin Ewell joined forces with an opportunistic onlooker to create a V-shaped wedge, allowing them to pierce the crowd like the fabled Four Horsemen of Notre Dame, parting the throng before them and weaseling their way close enough to see what was happening.

A stout woman wearing her clan plaid from head to toe, along with a bright green sash proclaiming GRAND MARSHAL, stood sobbing in the center of the tent, glancing frequently at an empty wooden stand beside her, shouting for someone to call the police.

"The Belter Cup has been stolen!" a man in the crowd shouted helpfully and a collective gasp filled the air.

"The Belter Cup?" a familiar voice said nearby. It was Harlene Bradshaw, head of the Bonny Bridge Theater Club. Like Auntie Lil, when she saw trouble, she came running. "How awful! I was planning on competing for it." She opened her mouth, as if to start singing *I Love a Parade*, but Calvin Ewell quickly stopped her.

"'Belter' means amazing or fantastic in the Scottish vernacular," he explained. "It's the first time they've ever given out the Belter Club and they were planning to award it to the person who most exemplified the Scottish spirit at this year's games. It has nothing to do with singing."

Harlene looked disappointed, but TS was relieved. He was not sure he could take her singing on top of everything else.

As the commotion at the center of the main tent intensified and security guards arrived to set up a perimeter—talk about closing the barn door after the Shetlands have escaped—Auntie Lil tugged sharply on TS's elbow.

"What?" he asked irritably. All of a sudden, he felt as if he had been poked and prodded and pulled at by the crowd for days.

"Look." Auntie Lil pointed over the heads of the people surrounding them.

"Look at what?" TS countered. "Of what am I looking at?"

"Those young boys running away."

TS followed her gaze and saw a group of five or six boys, perhaps around ten years old, although he was certainly no expert, heading away from the crowd and making a beeline for a forested area on the far side of the running track. "I see Horace Grimley making his tenth lap of the day," TS said, "plus a handful of dimwitted followers and a pack of small humans running into the woods."

"Exactly," Auntie Lil said. "And when is the last time you saw young boys running *away* from trouble when they could be in the thick of it?"

TS stared at her. She had a point. Calvin Ewell knew it, too. The trio took off after the boys, leaving an indignant Harlene Bradshaw behind. As they cleared the crowd and began to walk more briskly toward the woods, they saw Desmond Tanner on the other side of the field, following the same instinct. The quartet met at the edge of the forest, then stopped to regroup.

"This is silly," TS said first. "We don't even know what we're looking for."

"We are looking for the missing Belter Cup," Auntie Little said firmly. "Let everyone else stand around and talk about how someone else should do something about it. We are people of action. Those boys are up to no good. Stand not upon the order of your going, but go at once!"

"Bonus points for quoting the Scottish Play!" Calvin Ewell cried, enraptured.

This time TS did roll his eyes.

"No, your aunt is right," Desmond Tanner told TS. "The behavior of those boys is most unusual. I ought to know. I did pro bono work for inmates of the youth detention center in Raleigh for over a decade. There is definitely something off. We must find out what."

"Nonsense," TS began, but the others had already started moving into the forest and he had to hurry after them to keep from being left behind.

"I told you so," Auntie Lil said a few minutes later as

they burst through a stand of bushes into a clearing crowded with excited nine- and ten-year-old boys, all clustered around a figure on the ground.

"Well, I'll be," Desmond Tanner said, for once at a loss for ten-dollar words.

There on the ground, his arms and legs splayed wide, lay a slumbering Big Bill McGregor. His massive chest and belly moved up and down like a blacksmith's bellows, an enormous snore punctuating each rise and fall. He was more than ten sheets to the wind. He was down for the count—and, there, still gripped tightly in his right hand, was the missing Belter Cup. It lay flat in the grass and a stream of beer tricked out of it onto the ground.

"He stole the Belter Cup!" one of the young boys cried out, having decided that the best defense was indeed a good offense.

"And what exactly is that in your hand?" Desmond Tanner asked sharply, staring at the pint bottle of beer that the boy held. "Let's see some ID," he demanded.

A few of the other boys dared to laugh, but one look from Desmond Tanner silenced them.

"I ain't but ten years old," the boy finally said, meekly handing the beer over to Desmond. "I ain't got no ID."

Desmond took the beer and poured it out in some nearby rhododendron bushes. "Let's have all of it, boys," Desmond demanded, gesturing with his fingers. "And let this be a lesson to you all. Public drinking is a misdemeanor no matter what your age, but drinking underage? Why, I'd be surprised if it didn't land you five years in juvie. You want to miss your high school experience? Is that what you want? No girls? No prom? No being the star of the football team?"

Boy, was he piling it on thick, TS thought. But not without some admiration. If Desmond Tanner was trying to scare these boys straight, he was doing a good job of it.

"We're not doing anything wrong," one of the braver boys protested. "We just saw this man wandering into the woods with a wagonload of beer and followed. We just wanted an adventure."

"Followed him because you were planning to attack and rob him," Desmond suggested in a booming voice. He pointed toward the wagon full of beer. "Why that's Robert The Bruce Scottish Ale from 3 Floyds Brewing Company. Who wouldn't try to steal such a plunder?"

A chorus of dissent followed this statement and now nearly all of the boys looked frightened. Desmond had them where he wanted them.

"How does it feel to be accused without merit, boys?" he thundered. "Yet here you are, accusing this fine man, this best of men, of stealing the Belter Cup." He pointed to Big Bill McGregor and the eyes of every boy widened as they realized his point. "It could be that Big Bill here was simply looking for a suitable vessel for his ale and had no idea what he was taking. I mean, look at that man's size. He deserves a cup worthy of his stature."

TS realized what he was doing and both Auntie Lil

and Calvin caught on soon after. "That's right, boys. It's important to have the facts before you accuse anyone," Auntie Lil chided them.

TS almost choked at this statement. Auntie Lil threw accusations around like confetti. She was the last one who should be....

"We weren't going to mug him. We love Big Bill McGregor. We just wanted to take a look and see what he was doing," one of the boys finally answered. He was small but scrappy, brave enough to speak up, certainly brave enough to defend his honor.

"And steal as much beer as you could when he wasn't looking?" Desmond Tanner suggested, unwilling to turn down the heat.

"Help us empty the wagon," Calvin told the boys, figuring Desmond had scared them enough. "And don't think we're not counting the bottles as we unload them. We'll be back to retrieve the beer, bet on it. And every one of the bottles better be here when we do."

The small band of boys obeyed, their dreams of scoring a pint or two to pass the afternoon away, dying with each bottle they took out of the wagon and placed carefully in the grass.

When the wagon was empty, Desmond Tanner took charge again. "Some of you grab his arms and legs," he ordered them, gesturing toward the stupefied Big Bill McGregor. "And let's have a few of you help me here in the middle."

They all gathered around Big Bill and found a grip. Desmond began to loudly count down from five and when he reached zero, as if they had practiced it first, the assembled crowd huffed and puffed and somehow managed to half-pull and half-push Big Bill McGregor onto the top of the wagon, shoving him into the bed as best they could so that his arms and legs spilled over the sides and his face was turned to the sky. The wagon was barely big enough to contain his Big Bill butt, but it would have to do. Auntie Lil tucked the Belter Cup carefully into a nook between the passed-out giant's thighs and the side of the wagon.

"We're ready to roll," she informed Desmond, as if she were helping lead a wagon train to Utah.

And then, like a triumphant band of Lilliputians bearing Gulliver back to town, the group began pulling and pushing the wagon over the hills, heading back towards the center of the Highland Games. Every boy was needed to make progress over the thick grass and it was slow going. They soon attracted a crowd of followers as they labored along. That turned out to be fortuitous as, one-by-one, the original group members had to drop out to take a breather. Others took their place.

Before long, they reached the track that rimmed the main lawn. Horace Grimly saw them and waved as if they had stopped by specifically to cheer him on. By now, seven other men were following Horace and they, too, graced the group with waves of acknowledgment.

"We're going to need to deal with him when we get back to Bonny Bridge," TS said grimly.

"Agreed," Desmond Tanner said. "But let him enjoy his glory for now."

By the time they reached the central tent, they were all huffing and puffing, nearly every one of them so out of energy they could barely feel elation when they finally pulled the wagon onto its wooden floor.

A silence fell over the assembled throng as they turned to stare at the raggle-taggle parade that had arrived most suddenly in their midst. The Grand Marshal stopped wailing, security guards froze, and three cops who had arrived to investigate stared open-mouthed. The rest of the crowd was too stunned to react. With majestic silence and complete poise, Auntie Lil took her place at the handle of the wagon and began to pull it across the floor, her fellow Bonny Bridge residents helping to push it along.

"We return the Belter Cup to you," Auntie Lil told the astonished Grand Marshall, even giving a small curtsy as if she had just bested Sirs Galahad and Percival to deliver the Holy Grail to King Arthur himself.

The Grand Marshall opened her mouth but no words came out.

"That's Big Bill McGregor!" one of the security guards pointed out. "Arrest him!"

The crowd broke out in boos and protests at this suggestion.

"Certainly not!" Desmond Tanner roared, bringing the crowd to silence. "Who is to say this man did not rescue the cup from the true miscreant and suffer a grievous blow to his head as a result!"

The dubious faces in the surrounding crowd told Desmond that he better adjust his defense and do it fast.

"Who is to say this man did not mistake the Belter Cup for a tankard to drink his beer in?" Desmond pivoted in thunderous outrage. "He had no intention of committing a crime. It was an honest mistake and I say let him be!" The crowd gave out a roar of approval and this inspired Desmond—who had long missed being the center of the spotlight in a jam-packed courtroom—to new heights of oratory. "This man is innocent!" he shouted, flinging one arm up in the air, as if pointing to God for his approval. "And I shall represent him free of charge, if need be, to clear his good name. Long live Big Bill McGregor!"

By now, the crowd was going wild, caught up in the anarchy of the moment and, perhaps, fueled by hours of drinking beer themselves. Half were chanting "Big Bill! Big Bill!" with abandon, while another quarter of the crowd pulled their cell phones out and started filming the chaos, especially when the final quarter of the crowd began accusing the befuddled police officers of manhandling the gentle giant.

"We haven't laid a finger on him," one of the cops protested, looking around in sudden fear.

"And see that you don't!" Desmond Tanner ordered him, still hamming it up for the crowd.

Throughout this entire episode, the Grand Marshall had remained silent, staring from the unharmed Belter

Cup to the snoring, and near-comatose, Big Bill McGregor then surveying the crowd around her. She zeroed in on the many cameras filming her reaction and decided to take the most prudent way forward.

Holding both hands up for silence, she cleared her throat and spoke at the now-hushed crowd. "I have made my decision," she said importantly, ignoring the fact that there were at least four other people on the Belter Cup Committee with her. "And the truth is that Big Bill, I mean, William Foster McGregor, was going to be awarded the Belter Cup anyway. Clearly, he was just claiming what was his, albeit, admittedly, a wee bit early. We shall take no action. He may, in fact, have a section of this tent to sleep it off until the formal ceremony."

With this pronouncement, the crowd mobilized. Volunteers stepped forward to gently transport the huge man to a quieter corner where he could slumber long enough to give sobriety a foothold again. Hoodies were rolled into pillows and placed under his head while three blankets were found in the first aid tent to almost cover the sleeping giant adequately. Some in the crowd offered their jackets to make up the shortfall and, soon, nearly everyone wanted to contribute to his comfort. When all was said and done, and Big Bill had been put to bed, he looked like the pile of coats at an out-of-control New Year's Eve party.

"Braw, but that's a gawsie Scotsman indeed," a man in the crowd shouted out. "By my bahooky, he's the best of men and one that makes Alba look as glorious as it once was!"

Cries of "Big Bill! Big Bill!" rang out once again, followed by, "Alba gu bràth! Alba gu bràth!" filling the tent with Scottish fervor.

Throughout this all, TS just stood there shaking his head. The whole world had gone mad and yet, here he was, right in the thick of it. And with that, a sudden sense of exaltation filled him, unexpected yet exhilarating. Yes, he was surrounded by chaos but, by god, he was part of it—and it made him feel truly and gloriously alive.

"Alba gu bràth! Alba gu bràth!" TS shouted, shaking his fist above his head like the Braveheart he was.

Bring on the years, he thought to himself, *bring on the creaky joints and the aching back along the way. I am getting old, but what do I care?* He feared none of that any longer. Like his Aunt Lil, TS now knew exactly what to do with the years he had left. He would grab life with both hands and hold on.

About the Author

Katy Munger has over thirty years of experience writing crime fiction and is the author of the Dead Detective series; the Casey Jones PI series; and the Hubbert & Lil cozy mystery series. She co-edits *Dark Yonder*, a neo-noir short fiction journal, and is a proud participant in North Carolina's Noir at the Bar reading series. Katy has also contributed to a number of short story collections and was a book reviewer for *The Washington Post's* former *Book World*. She was named North Carolina's Piedmont Laureate in 2016.

You can learn more about the author and her work at **katymunger.com.**

Killer Thanksgiving

Michelle Bennington

Birdie Harper sat in her recliner in the living room, surrounded by boxes filled with pictures, toys, clothes, accessories, trinkets, and piles of old magazines and newspapers. Her house was full of such precious treasures. The people of Miltonville, including family and friends, called her a hoarder, but apparently they didn't know a collector when they saw one.

The wind wailed against her windows. She sipped her coffee and watched the fallen leaves dance across the yard as the sky darkened. Hopefully it wouldn't rain —or snow! The Miltonville Women's Club, commonly known as the MWC, was hosting a Thanksgiving feast for the needy and lonely in the area today. It was one of her favorite events of the season.

She checked the clock on the wall. Seven-thirty a.m. The cooking started at 9:00. Her elder sister, Oda

Dean, had better show up soon. They had to hightail it to the community center to start cooking and serving.

A chill passed over Birdie. Even in her jeans and orange turkey sweater, she wasn't warm enough. She looked around at the ceiling. "Walter? You there? You'd better not be making me cold on purpose."

Her late husband, Walter, died five years ago, but his spirit had remained behind to keep her company—and to sometimes pester her to her wits' end. When Walter didn't answer, she wrapped an afghan around her shoulders and picked up the newspaper. *The Miltonville Times* was fiction disguised as news. Jebson "Jeb" Butterworth had taken over the paper twenty years ago and turned the once trustworthy news source into little more than a gossip rag.

Usually, she enjoyed the semi-fake stories about her friends and neighbors, often wondering which parts might be mostly true. But today she noticed an all-too-familiar-name—Oda Dean Spurlock.

She choked on her coffee. "What!" She was staring at a colorless image of Oda Dean, her husband, Charlie, and their new neighbors Janella and Austin Pickett. The unsmiling lot were glaring at each other over a tree stump. It wasn't the first report of the dispute in the paper in the past six months, but, according to title, the dispute had escalated: *Property Dispute Turns Violent.* She read the first paragraph where Oda Dean supposedly threatened to stab Austin with her hedge trimmers.

The door opened in the kitchen. "Yoo-hoo! You ready for the turkey feast?"

Oda Dean. Birdie scrambled out of her recliner and wove through the piles of stuff to the kitchen. "Have you seen this?" She rattled the newspaper.

Oda Dean wore a teal jacket and a thin brown sweater sprinkled with colorful leaves over her ample bosom. A teal toboggan hat stretched over her graying bob. She swept aside a pile of junk on the table to make space for the bag of breakfast. "I'm not worried about that. Jeb Butterworth is a rotten liar. Always making up stuff about people."

"I thought you and the Picketts had called a truce over your property issue."

Oda Dean jerked the toboggan off her head, causing her hair to stand on end. She jammed the hat in her jacket pocket. Her hazel eyes flashed. "We had—until Austin Pickett cut down my maple tree!"

"He what?"

"Sure did. That tree was a house-warming gift thirty years ago from Momma and Daddy."

"Why'd he cut it down?"

"He wanted to put up a fence. Our other neighbors *never* had a problem with that tree." Oda Dean huffed and smoothed her hair.

"You're telling me he couldn't put his fence just six inches over to accommodate the tree?"

"That's what I said." Oda Dean growled and shook her head. "Anyway, I won't let him spoil my mood for Turkey Feast Day. You got coffee?" She crossed the kitchen and found a clean cup and filled it.

"You didn't really threaten to stab him with your hedge trimmers?"

Oda Dean glared at Birdie. "How can you ask me something like that?"

"Sometimes your temper—"

"*My* temper? *You're* the one who shoved *me* when I tried to go in your back bedroom last month."

Okay, that did happen, but Oda Dean had no business in Birdie's special room where she kept her most prized collections. "You were out of line." Time to change the subject fast before this descended into an argument. "Anyway, Jeb is lower than the scum on a catfish belly."

"Hmmph." Oda Dean stirred cream into her coffee. "You got that right."

Birdie peeked in the bag and extracted an Irene's pumpkin spice donut with a little dance. "My favorite! Pumpkin spice makes everything nice."

"Except you." Oda Dean laughed.

Birdie laughed and delivered a playful shove to her sister's shoulder. "Hurry up. We've got a dinner to get to."

The Miltonville Community Center dining room was decked out with white table linens and fall foliage centerpieces. String lights wrapped around pine garlands hung from the serving table and around the windows.

A local restaurant owned by the Miltonville Women's Club's President Lisa Manning and her husband provided the turkey. Everything else—cornbread pudding, stuffing, fresh cranberry sauce, green bean casserole, mashed potatoes, candied yams, yeast rolls, pies, cakes, and punch—was made the morning of the event in the community center kitchen by twenty MWC volunteers.

By the time the food was served, about a hundred people had packed into the community dining hall, increasing the room temperature by at least a thousand degrees. Birdie and Oda Dean sat at a table in a corner of the room, fanning themselves, and picking at the scrumptious meal they were both too hot to fully enjoy.

But there was always room for dessert and punch. As Birdie and Oda Dean approached the buffet line to select a slice of red velvet cake and wassail punch, Jeb Butterworth came off the line with an overloaded paper plate. His pink jowls jiggled and he lisped slightly as if his tongue was too fat for his mouth when he spoke.

"Good Morning, ladies." His gray hair still stood up in wind-tossed spikes around the bald patch in the center of his head. His square glasses were covered in lint and fingerprints.

Birdie glared at him, a host of colorful words tickling her tongue. How did he even have the nerve to look at them? But knowing Jeb had the power of the pen, and a gullible reading audience, she didn't want to make matters worse. So she offered a flattened, "Hey, Jeb." It felt like her mouth was full of burrs. Unfortu-

37

nately, her mouth kept moving. "You shouldn't have written that story about my sister. You know good and well she didn't threaten Austin. He was the one at fault."

He sniffed and grabbed a cup of iced tea. "Not the way he tells it. She was the instigator for planting the tree right on the property line. He has a right to a fence." He drank from his cup.

Oda Dean interrupted. "Now hold on, mister. I've lived in that house for decades before the Picketts moved in. The Abershires never had a problem with the tree."

Jeb shrugged, his paper plate sagging under the heap of food. "The Abershires didn't want a fence, either."

"Your story was an outright lie." Birdie planted her hands on her hips. "You made it look like there was a big dustup and that Oda Dean had threatened Austin's life, when she did no such thing. You need to retract that story. Lying is no way to run a newspaper."

He laughed. "No can do. That's not the sort of thing that attracts readers. And I've got a business to run."

Birdie glared at him. "Don't you have anything better to do than to stir up trouble?"

He chuckled, popping a bite of turkey into his mouth, speaking as he chewed. "I'm not stirring up anything. I'm reporting as I see it." He nodded toward a table where Austin and Janella Pickett were setting down their cups and plates. Austin glanced around, spotted Oda Dean and Birdie, and headed toward them. "But it looks like things are about to get interesting."

As Jeb walked away, Birdie's fingers itched with the desire to pinch him black and blue. Aggravating man.

"Crap! Austin is looking this way," Oda Dean said, ducking behind Birdie. "Hurry up. Let's get our cake and get out of here."

"We're trapped in this room." Birdie screwed up her face. "Unless you plan on eating this while running to your car, I think he can find us."

By then Austin was already closing in on them.

"Pretend you don't see him." Oda Dean grabbed her cake and punch and beelined to their table.

Austin, a loan officer at the bank, was of equal age and height to his wife, Janella, and wore his sandy, blond hair gelled into a strategically messy bed-head style. His "fresh" scent cologne was strong enough to bloody a nose. He usually had a healthy glow, but today he seemed pale with dark bags under his eyes and a thin film of sweat on his head. Maybe he was coming down with something.

"Good afternoon, ladies. May I sit?"

Oda Dean sulked, poking at her cake, so Birdie answered for her. "Sure. Go ahead."

He pulled out a chair closest to Birdie. "I want to say that I'm sorry for chopping down your tree. Maybe

I shouldn't have done that. I was angry and out of line. I'll get you a new tree."

Oda Dean turned to face him. "Yes, you were out of line. And a new tree isn't good enough. The tree you cut down had a special meaning to me and now it's gone."

He looked down at his hands and nodded. "I understand. I'm sorry."

"I do accept your apology though."

"I had to apologize after I got those bourbon balls. I ate a bunch of them this morning." He patted his belly and suppressed a belch. "Bourbon balls are my favorite. Did Janella tell you that?"

Oda Dean and Birdie exchanged a glance. Oda Dean said, "Bourbon balls? What are you talking about?"

"You left me some bourbon balls on my porch this morning. Had your name on it."

"My name?" Oda Dean shook her head. "I'm sorry, but—"

He winced and rubbed his belly. "Oh man, I guess I've eaten too much today." Austin stood. "Excuse me, ladies. Nature calls. I hope I'm not coming down with a stomach bug or something. I'd hate to miss all this food." He swiped his forehead. "Y'all think it's hot in here?" He stepped away from the table and disappeared down the hall toward the restrooms.

Oda Dean turned to Birdie. "I think he's going crazy."

"Why's that?" Birdie shoved a large bite of red velvet cake in her mouth.

"I didn't make bourbon balls for him. I haven't made *any*. I won't start making bourbon balls until next week to give away for Christmas."

Birdie frowned. "That's weird. Maybe he's confused."

"But he said they had *my* name on the package. Why?"

"Hmm." Birdie drank some punch. "That is odd. It's almost as if someone is trying to stir something up."

"Who? And why?"

Jeb Butterworth's laughter rang out over the other voices. Birdie glared at him. "Maybe Jeb knows something about it. Maybe he has plans to turn this into one of his stories." She stood and nudged Oda Dean. "C'mon. Let's go find out what he's up to."

As they crossed the room to speak with Jeb, they noticed Paisley Creech, sister to the MWC President, Lisa Manning. She was on crutches, wearing a cast on her left foot. She was struggling to maneuver into a chair as her brother-in-law placed her plate and cup on the table. Janella helped Paisley prop her injured leg in a chair.

Birdie stopped and whispered to Oda Dean. "Look at that. Wonder what happened?"

"I don't know. I haven't heard."

"We should say something to her."

They veered toward Paisley. Studious, quiet, and graceful, Paisley was a ballet dancer with the Louisville Ballet. Her dark, highlight-streaked hair was pulled into a tight knot. She wore a long, flowing, floral skirt and fuzzy gray sweater. Paisley smiled, but her brown eyes shone with sadness.

Birdie said, "Honey, what happened to you?"

Paisley's face tightened. "Oh, I had an…. accident." Her smile twisted into a near-grimace. She glanced at Lisa, who stood across the room chatting with someone. "Broke my ankle. Had to have surgery."

"Bless your heart." Oda Dean shook her head. "I hate to hear that. When did that happen?"

"About six days ago."

"Will you be able to dance again?" Birdie asked.

Paisley's eyes watered. Her voice shook. "The doctor says I won't."

Birdie's face wrinkled with concern. "There's always hope, hon. You keep working on it. What are you doing now?"

Paisley wiped her cheek and sighed. "I'm doing the bookkeeping at daddy's horse farm and helping with other administrative tasks."

The Camelot horse farm was one of the most popular tourist attractions in Central Kentucky and had a well-earned reputation as one of the premiere horse farms in the world, offering superior stud services that produced more than its fair share of Triple Crown-winning stock.

"I sure hate to see your foot, but that sounds like a good job while you heal," Birdie added, eager to give the poor girl hope.

Lisa Manning appeared before them. The MWC President had a body carved by yoga and Pilates. She was a nurse at the local hospital and ran the MWC with efficiency, top-notch organizational skills, and a cool, commanding confidence. Her dark, wavy locks were pulled into a low ponytail and she wore a flattering mustard-gold sweater dress with a thick brown belt and knee-high brown boots.

"Hey, ladies. I've heard we're out of rolls and ice. We need more of both. Would y'all take care of that, please?" Her request was delivered as a polite demand that couldn't be questioned. She looked around. "Have y'all seen Austin Pickett?" She dithered. "Janella's looking for him."

Before the sisters could answer, a shriek rang out from the hallway where the restrooms were.

Birdie nudged Jeb out of the way and took off toward the restrooms with Oda Dean and Lisa hard on her heels.

The preacher's wife stood over the lifeless form of Austin Pickett. Lisa dropped to her knees. She felt his pulse on his neck and his wrist. "I can't get a pulse." Her voice shook. "Austin?" She slapped his face. "Austin. Please, you have to wake up." She put her ear to his lips. She looked up, her eyes flooding with tears. "Someone call 911. He's not breathing."

For the third time in two weeks, Birdie paced in the bright fluorescent foyer of the sheriff's department, waiting as Oda Dean was being questioned by the sheriff in connection to Austin Pickett's death. The first time they came in for questioning seemed routine. Birdie didn't think anything of it, assuming that most, or all, of the people present would be questioned about Austin's death. The second time gave her pause. Now on the third occasion, she was worried. It was beginning to look as though Oda Dean was a suspect.

Jeb Butterworth entered the building, whistling. He announced himself to the receptionist.

Birdie said, "Well. I've been calling you. Did you put those bourbon balls on Austin Pickett's porch, trying to stir up trouble?"

He screwed up his face. "I don't know what you're talking about." He narrowed his eyes. "What bourbon balls? Do they have something to do with Austin's death?"

"Not sure. But it seems like the sort of thing you'd do so you can have a sensational story for that seedy little paper you run."

A deputy appeared at the door to call him back. "Jeb, the sheriff is busy right now. But I'll take your questions."

Jeb ran his eyes over Birdie. "I resent your implication, Mrs. Harper. Sounds like you've been hitting the bourbon pretty hard. I'm just doing my job. I'm not a murderer."

Birdie watched him walk away, wishing she could kick him in the shin. She'd aim higher if she could, but she knew her legs didn't kick that high anymore and she'd probably throw her back out if she tried.

An hour later, Oda Dean emerged from a hallway behind the locked glass doors. Her short hair stood on end, her eyes were red and puffy. She dabbed at her nose with a wadded tissue.

The sheriff reached around her to open the door. "I'd recommend hanging around town for a while. We might have more questions."

Oda Dean nodded and said in a watery voice, "Okay. I will. But I've told you everything I know."

Birdie opened her arms and Oda Dean rushed to fill them, breaking down in sobs. "Thank you for coming with me."

"C'mon, hon. I'll take you home." Birdie wrapped her arm around her sister's shoulder and led her out of the building. "How did it go?"

Oda Dean paused on the sidewalk to zip up her jacket. "The Sheriff said that preliminary reports show that Austin might've been poisoned. The sheriff thinks it might be the bourbon balls. Since my name was on the package, I'm the prime suspect. But when they showed me the package, the name was printed on an address label like it came from a company. I would never type out my name on an address label! I'd sign my name. Especially if I'm giving a personal gift to a neighbor.

"Right. That makes sense." Birdie pulled her keys from her pocket. "I hope you told that to the sheriff."

"I did. He seemed to agree with me. But when he asked who I thought would do such a thing, I couldn't come up with anyone. I told him to please keep investigating to find the right person, because I have nothing to do with this."

Oda Dean put a hand over her heart. "But what am I going to do? Austin believed I'm the one who gave him the bourbon balls! And you know Janella is going to tell everyone that my name was on the package."

Birdie's eyes widened. "You know, it's like someone's trying to frame you. Have you made someone mad?"

"No." Oda Dean threw her hands up. "The only person I've had words with is now dead! Do you realize how bad that makes me look?"

Birdie rubbed her sister's back. "Okay. Calm down. There has to be some explanation. We'll figure this out. Somehow."

"And you know what else? When the sheriff showed me the bourbon balls, I asked him to open the box. Even though I knew I didn't make them, I wanted to see them. They definitely weren't my bourbon balls."

"How can you tell? Other than the fact that you haven't made any. What makes yours different?"

"This one was milk chocolate. I always use dark. And there was a large pecan laid across the top of the ball. I *never* do that. All my pecans are chopped to bits, soaked in bourbon, and mixed into the filling."

"Right. So what did the sheriff say to that?" Birdie hugged herself. The air temperature was dropping and the wind smelled like the inside of a freezer, meaning there might be snow tonight.

Oda Dean shrugged. "He just said he'd keep looking into it. But what if he doesn't believe me? Or if he can't find the person behind all this? What then?" Tears pooled in her eyes. "Am I going to go to prison for something I didn't do?"

Birdie looked around to see Lisa and Paisley crossing the parking lot toward the sheriff's station. "Surely that won't happen. The sheriff will get to the bottom of this. Let's go. It's cold." Heavy gray clouds slid across the pale sun.

As the sisters drew near, Birdie could see that Lisa's eyes were puffy and her nose red as if she'd been crying. The whipping, icy wind could've caused that, but she had little or no makeup on and seemed drained. She was dressed in all black.

"Slow down," Paisley called out, hobbling on her crutches.

"Hurry up." Lisa glanced over her shoulder.

"I can't help it. And this isn't exactly my fault, is it?"

"Are you ever going to let me live that down?"

"No. I'm not. If you hadn't sounded that air horn—"

The women stopped short when they noticed Birdie and Oda Dean.

A storm cloud formed around Lisa as she glared at Oda Dean. "How could you?"

Oda Dean blinked. "I didn't do anything."

"Everyone knows you and the Picketts had issues. I saw that article in the paper the other day. And then Janella told me last week that you had given Austin a box of bourbon balls. I can't believe they even let you walk around free."

By then Paisley had caught up to her sister. "Lisa, stop it. We aren't sure of anything. Let's go inside. It's cold. Can you get the door for me?"

Lisa stormed off in a huff. Paisley flashed pitiful, hound dog eyes and muttered, "I'm sorry, Oda Dean, Birdie. She's…. emotional right now."

Lisa held the door open. "Are you coming or not?"

"I've got to go." Paisley lurched quickly forward on her crutches.

Oda Dean pulled her jacket hood up over her head. She whispered, "Don't you think Lisa's acting a little 'off?' I mean, if I didn't know better, I'd think *she* was Austin's grieving widow. Don't you think she seems heartbroken since his death?"

Birdie watched Lisa and Paisley disappear inside. "I think you're right. She does seem a mite too invested." She shot Oda Dean a pointed look. "Do you think *she* framed you for some reason?"

"But why? I haven't done anything to her."

"I don't know, but I think we need to find out."

~

When they reached Oda Dean's colonial-style home on Starling Lane, they were greeted with a warm house and the scent of chili cooking. Oda Dean's husband, Charlie, was kicked back in his gray recliner, watching a college basketball game. In spite of the warm home, he wore a red flannel shirt over a gray thermal shirt and blue jeans. His deer hunting garb lay in a pool of fabric by the door. His salt-and-pepper hair was combed neatly to one side and his dark blue eyes shone from under bushy brows. Charlie wiggled his white-socked feet. "Hey there, ladies. How'd it go?" He craned his neck to look at the clock on the wall beside him. "I made some chili. Have y'all been out to the flea market or something?"

"No, I've been sitting in the sheriff's department, being interrogated by Sheriff Goodman." Oda Dean stomped through the country chic-decorated living room into the kitchen.

"What?" Charlie shot up out of his chair. Though in his mid-fifties like Oda Dean and Birdie, he had maintained his military-trim body. He marched after the women who busied themselves taking out bowls and glasses. "Why were you being questioned? For what?"

"Thanks for making the chili. Have a seat." He sat and she refreshed his glass with tea and ice while Birdie served him a bowl of chili. "I think I'm a suspect in Austin Pickett's death."

Charlie leaned back in his chair and stared at Oda Dean. "You've got to be kidding me."

"I wish I was." Oda Dean sat at the table, putting her head in her hand.

Birdie put a loaf of bread and jar of peanut butter on the table. After all, homemade chili demanded a side of peanut butter sandwiches when there was no time to make grilled cheese. "Someone put a box of bourbon balls, with my name on it, on his porch. He ate a bunch of them and it's likely they've been poisoned. They're still running tests."

Charlie looked up from his peanut butter-smeared bread. "What did the sheriff say?"

Oda Dean recalled her time at the sheriff's office as she made everyone a peanut butter sandwich.

Charlie frowned and shook his head. "If that don't beat everything—"

He was interrupted by the doorbell.

Oda Dean jumped up and raced toward the door. "I'll get it." Birdie followed her, hating to be left out of anything interesting.

Lisa stood on the porch with her mouth pinched into a tight line. The wind swept into the house, cutting into the warmth of the living room.

Oda Dean stepped back. "Come on in."

Lisa crossed her arms over her chest. "No, thank you. I have Paisley in the car. I won't take much of your time. I thought I should come by and tell you that it's probably best if you don't come to Women's Club for the foreseeable future."

Oda Dean put a hand over her heart. "What? Why not?"

Hearing the shock in his wife's voice, Charlie came to Oda Dean's side and placed a hand on her shoulder.

"Well, in light of what's happened with Austin and all, I, as president, feel it's best you don't come anymore. It'd be too upsetting to the other women."

Birdie stepped up. "Now you listen here, missy. I don't care if you're president or not. My sister and I were members of that club before you were even a speck in your momma's belly. You aren't kicking us out of anything."

Lisa raked her eyes over Birdie. "It's probably best that you don't attend anymore, either. We want to be supportive of Janella in her difficult time." She cut her gaze back to Oda Dean. "And since you're a suspect in her husband's murder, you should resign."

"Who said I'm a suspect?"

Charlie stretched his neck to look over Oda Dean and past Lisa. "Is that your car?"

Ignoring Oda Dean's question, Lisa looked back at the white Lexus then turned to eye him as if he had three heads. "Yeah. So?"

He nodded. "Uh-huh. And you're the only one who drives it?"

"Yes."

"Just wondering." Charlie shrugged.

She rolled her eyes and addressed Oda Dean and Birdie. "Anyway, the bylaws state that we need a written or typed and signed letter to make it official. You can mail it in. You have my address." She spun on her heel, stepped off the covered porch, and jogged to her car.

Oda Dean and Birdie gaped at each other. "What are we going to do?" Birdie asked.

Charlie stepped around the women and stood on the porch, hands in his pockets, watching as Lisa's car flew backwards and ripped out of the drive.

"Charlie, get in here. It's freezing." Oda Dean hunched over against the cold wind and held the door knob.

He stepped inside and shut the door. "Her car had a blue sticker on the back. Oval. Had a horse head on it. Said *Bluegrass Iron Horse, 13.1.*"

The sisters returned to the kitchen. Oda Dean said, "So? It's that half-marathon held in Midway every year. She runs all the time."

"I've seen that car over at the Pickett's house recently." He joined the women at the table.

Birdie tore off a chunk of her sandwich and chewed it. "That's no big deal. Janella's in the Women's Club, too. They were probably meeting about something."

He sipped his tea. "Except when Janella was out of town this last week visiting family overnight, that same car was still there at dawn. I saw it when I headed out to track deer."

Birdie buzzed into the Miltonville Community meeting room at the back of the library where the Women's Club held its weekly meetings. The dish of pumpkin spice coffee cake was still warm in her hand and the scent of cinnamon and clove blended with the aroma of old books to create an intoxicating perfume. In any other mood, she might've delighted in the scent more. But not this morning. This morning, Birdie was on a mission. No one was going to tell her she and Oda Dean couldn't go to this meeting or any other meeting. She held her chin high and stepped with confidence in her ballet flats, black leggings, and red plaid tunic, daring anyone to tussle with her. She practically dragged Oda Dean behind her.

"Would you slow down?" Oda Dean carried bags of paper plates, disposable cups, and plastic utensils.

Birdie paused to allow Oda Dean to catch up. Oda Dean tugged at the thick navy cardigan she wore over her lavender turtleneck. "I don't know why they keep this place so blasted hot." She blew out a breath to push a lock of hair from her face. "I don't even want to be here. I should've never let you talk me into this. It's going to cause a big ruckus. And for what?"

Birdie pushed her glasses up on her nose and resumed her course. "They have no right to ask us to leave the club. We haven't done anything wrong and you're innocent of whatever happened to Austin. You might not've liked him, but that doesn't mean you murdered him. The police questioned you. That's it. But they questioned other people, too."

"Yeah, but they questioned me *three* times."

Birdie threw open the door and stepped inside with dramatic flair, scanning the room with a look that dared anyone to question her presence. She sashayed across the room and put the dish down beside the coffee maker. "Oda Dean and I brought some pumpkin spice cake to go with the coffee and tea." This was a test to see where the other ladies' loyalties aligned.

The first bottom to spring up was Bonnie Cutler. She owned the Sunnyside Greenhouse and hosted the Gardening Club's annual flower contest. Bonnie cut a slice of cake with bold, dramatic strokes and stood beside Birdie, looking around the room to see who would challenge her. One by one, nearly all the women rose, except Helen Wise and a couple of other women who were close friends of Janella and Lisa's. The rest circled around the sisters, chittering about the moisture of the cake, how they must have the recipe, and how they felt sorry for Janella, but knew Oda Dean was innocent.

Lisa walked in and stopped short. A deep silence closed over the room. Mouths chewed as eyeballs darted between the sisters and the MWC President.

Lisa stepped aside and motioned toward the door. Her face was washed out and worn-looking, though she was wearing makeup. She wore black pants and shirt under a gray cardigan, looking every bit a grieving widow, though she wasn't. Her husband was alive and well and probably working hard at the restaurant he owned.

She crossed her arms and said to Birdie and Oda Dean, "You ladies have to leave. I thought I'd made myself clear that you should leave our club."

Birdie stepped forward. "You don't have the right or

the authority to tell us what we can and can't do. My sister didn't do anything wrong and neither did I." She pointed at the floor. "And we're staying right here."

Helen Wise spoke up. "She's been questioned by the police in connection to the alleged murder of Austin."

Paisley appeared in the doorway. "Thanks for helping me," she said with a hint of sarcasm as she brushed past her sister. Helen pulled out a chair for her and Paisley plopped down, propping her crutches against the table.

"Lisa was questioned, too, Helen." Birdie crossed her arms. "As was Paisley. So, by that logic, those two should leave the club, too." She held out her hand. "Let's have those resignations, now."

Lisa snorted and rolled her eyes. "I'm not resigning." She passed Birdie and Oda Dean and sat at the head of the table. "I was questioned as a witness, not a suspect. There's a big difference." She placed her phone on the table and opened her notebook.

"Well, say and do what you want, but we're not leaving." Birdie sat at the table. She pulled her sister's arm and nudged her into a chair. "Oda Dean's innocent and all of ya'll know it."

"Not according to this morning's paper." Helen pulled a folded paper out of her enormous purse and slid it down to Birdie.

Birdie's heart sank as she watched the paper slide toward her in slow motion. She hadn't had a chance to read the paper. She'd been too busy making coffee cake and fighting with Walter—or, rather, his ghost since

Walter had been dead for five years. He'd been in a mood to pester. Kept turning the electricity on and off. She almost didn't get her coffee made or her hair dried and curled. On the front page was a large black-and-white image of Oda Dean coming out of the sheriff's office. The title in all caps read: *A WOMAN'S SCORN! Local Woman Questioned for Murder.*

Oda Dean gasped and Birdie winced. This wasn't good.

Birdie rode the crest of her pride. "Jeb Butterworth is a lying toad licker. We do still have the presumption of innocence until proven guilty in this country, don't we?"

Another woman in a velvet floral jacket spoke up. "I have a motion. Can we get on with this meeting? I have a doctor's appointment today. Just let them stay. It's clear they ain't going anywhere and we're killing time."

Lisa lifted her hands. "Fine. Do we have a second?" A hand went up. "Motion carries?"

A chorus of "Yeas" sounded.

Birdie smiled smugly.

"Let's begin." Lisa sighed. "We need to discuss the Shop Local Christmas Village after we hear the minutes from the last meeting. Since Janella isn't here to make the report"—she held up a paper—"I'll read the minutes."

After dealing with old business, Lisa said, "I think we should take a restroom break before we move on to new business. Let's meet back here in ten minutes."

Women young and old jumped from their seats and

headed toward the bathroom. A few ladies moved for coffee and cake, then huddled in a far corner of the room to chat or to check their phones.

Birdie stretched. "I need more coffee." She approached the coffee canteen, which stood near where Lisa's stuff rested. Birdie poured a cup of coffee, set the cup down, and reached to cut a slice of cake, knocking over the cup of coffee. "Crap!" she shouted. "Oda Dean, grab some paper towels from that back table."

As Oda Dean rushed to wipe up the spilled coffee, Birdie pushed Lisa's stuff out of danger but accidentally sent her cell phone tumbling to the floor, causing its screen to light up. When Birdie retrieved it, her thumb touched the screen, accidentally pulling up a photo album. Birdie gasped and turned her back to the other women in the room as she called again for Oda Dean. Birdie couldn't believe her eyes. There was Lisa in a lacy, strappy thing barely covering her lady-bits.

Oda Dean looked over her shoulder. "What's wrong?" When she saw the picture, she gasped, too. She looked closer. "Wait a minute, look at that one." She pointed at a selfie of Lisa kissing a man.

Birdie tapped on the picture, enlarging it.

Oda Dean whispered, "Oh, my stars! That's Austin!"

"You're right. It would explain why she's been so tore up over his death."

"And why Charlie saw her car over at the Pickett house while Janella was gone. Text it to me. Quick. I'll cover you." Oda Dean maneuvered around to shield Birdie.

"She'll know."

"So? We'll delete the thread."

"Okay." Birdie's fingers shook under the pressure of rushing.

Voices sounded in the hallway.

"Hurry, hurry," Oda Dean whispered.

"I am. Quit pressuring me." Birdie sent the image and scrambled to return Lisa's things to the table as Oda Dean rushed to finish wiping up the spilled coffee.

As the other women entered the room, Oda Dean made a loud fuss of cleaning up the mess. "I wish you'd watch what you're doing, Birdie. I can't take you anywhere."

Birdie played along. "I'm sorry. I'm so tired I can't even see straight." She tossed the soaked paper towels and paper plate in the garbage and returned for a fresh cup of coffee and slice of cake.

Birdie sat on spikes for the rest of the meeting, unable to focus or concentrate. She wanted to get out of the room, as far away from Lisa as possible. Oda Dean seemed equally anxious, nibbling on her thumbnail and bouncing her leg under the table.

When the meeting had adjourned, Birdie and Oda Dean sprang from their chairs. They shrugged into their jackets as they headed out the door. Birdie whispered, "We're going to the sheriff's station right now."

Bonnie Cutler followed behind them. "Hey, Birdie, Oda Dean." Her short, chubby body ran toward them on tip toes, clutching her large red purse. The wings of her chestnut hair flew back from her round face.

They stopped in the reading section of the library full of cozy chairs and wooden tables in front of a large picture window that looked out over a copse of trees.

Bonnie's cheek dimples peek-a-booed as she spoke. "I wanted to say I support y'all one hundred percent." She said to Oda Dean, "I know you wouldn't hurt a fly. That Jeb Butterworth is a rotten liar."

"Thank you, I appreciate your support, Bonnie." Oda Dean patted her arm.

"Lisa's too big for her britches anyway, if you ask me. Thinks she's queen of the county. So, I'm glad y'all put her in her place. Especially given the way she treats Paisley."

Birdie blinked. "What do you mean?"

"Oh, she's horrible. Treats Paisley worse than a dog. She's the reason Paisley broke her ankle and had to give up ballet."

"Really?" Birdie leaned closer. "How's that?"

"Lisa was at the house. Her parents were hosting a tailgate party for a football game. Paisley was down at the barn grooming the horses, when Lisa blasted an airhorn for the winning touchdown. It spooked the horse. He reared up and came down on Paisley's foot before she could get out of the way."

Birdie said, "That's awful."

"Why would Lisa do that?" Oda Dean cocked her head. "Everyone knows how skittish some horses can be."

Bonnie shrugged. "She'd been drinking a little. Everyone was. I guess she thought there was enough distance that the horse wouldn't spook. I know Paisley will never forgive her for it." She lowered her voice to a whisper. "In fact, she was so broken up about it that there've been rumors she might hurt herself because she can't imagine life without ballet."

"Poor thing." Birdie shook her head.

They hushed as Lisa marched out of the room with Paisley lurching behind on her crutches, trying to hold her purse. Paisley sneezed and wobbled a little. As she reached for a tissue in her purse, the purse fumbled from her grip, spilling its contents.

"Honey, let me help." Bonnie rushed to pick up the items and shove them into Paisley's purse.

Lisa circled back and held out her hand. "I'll take the purse." She said to Paisley, "Let's go. I need to stop off at the bank and the grocery on the way home."

The women waited until the sisters had disappeared around the stacks. Birdie opened her mouth to speak when she noticed something under a chair. "What's that?" She picked it up.

"Must've fallen from Paisley's purse," Oda Dean said. "Maybe you can still catch her."

Birdie held up a baggie full of dried flower pods. "What is this?"

"Let me see." Bonnie stepped closer to study the baggie. "I'll tell you what that is. Foxglove pods. Why would she have foxglove pods in her purse?"

Birdie and Oda Dean looked at each other.

"Foxglove is deadly. The whole plant is poisonous," Bonnie said. "Maybe she was serious about hurting herself, after all."

"Maybe. Maybe not," Birdie said.

"What do you mean?" Bonnie tipped her head.

Birdie ignored the question. "Can I have those pods? Oda Dean and I are headed to the sheriff's office. I'll turn those in. If Paisley's serious about hurting herself, maybe they'll intervene."

"Sure." Bonnie handed over the pods. "Let me know what happens."

Within fifteen minutes, Birdie and Oda Dean marched into the sheriff's office and insisted on a meeting with Sheriff Harlan "Bulldog" Goodman. Like a bulldog, he was a stubborn, beefy man with a head like a cinder block and bushy russet mustache. They showed him the picture and the pods, and told him about what Charlie had witnessed and all Bonnie had told them about Paisley.

The sheriff leaned forward on his desk. "And you found these foxglove pods on Paisley?"

"Yessir." Birdie clutched her purse in her lap. "They fell out of her purse. And Bonnie Cutler, the greenhouse owner, can verify what these are. "

Oda Dean added, "And didn't you mention to me that Austin might've been poisoned? Maybe that poison was foxglove."

"I'll definitely look into it."

A few days later, the Women's Club gathered again. Birdie and Oda Dean took their place at the table with no interference from Lisa, though she treated them coolly. Typically they met only once a month, but holiday events called for more frequent meetings.

"You covetous, hot-pants hussy. I'll tear your eyes out." Janella Pickett stormed into the meeting in her all-black pants and blouse, mascara streaking down her cheeks, her red hair standing on end. Besides her red eyes and nose, her freckled face was pale as mashed potatoes. She charged toward Lisa, who jumped up and stumbled away from her, tripping over legs, chairs, and purses as onlookers watched the scene unfold with eyes rounded in shock. "You were sleeping with Austin!" she screeched. "How long? A year? Six months?"

An intense silence filled the room.

"W-w-w-ait...." Lisa tripped over a chair, her usual composure vanishing into a trembling voice and shaking hands. She pulled empty chairs out in front of her to slow Janella's progress. "You don't understand—"

Janella threw a chair out of her path. "I understand all too well. I want to know why. And how long. And how you could look me in the face and pretend to be my friend while...." She picked up someone's travel mug full of coffee and flung it at Lisa's head.

Lisa ducked as the mug hit the wall and fell to the ground, the brown liquid seeping into the carpet.

"I had to hear the truth from Sheriff Goodman this morning when he came to my house to question me again about Austin's death."

"I loved him, too!" Lisa shouted. "He said he loved me. He was trying to find a way to leave you, to let you down easy."

Janella froze and struggled to breathe as if she'd been punched in the throat.

A librarian opened the door and the sheriff filled the space. "I'm looking for Paisley Creech."

Paisley ducked her head, her face turning crimson.

Birdie leaned over the table to look at Paisley. "Hon, he's talking to you."

Paisley glared at Birdie with dark malice.

Oda Dean pointed at Paisley. "That's her."

Lisa rushed toward the officer. "What's the matter, sheriff? What do you want with my sister?"

The sheriff and his deputies surrounded Paisley. "Paisley Creech, you're under arrest for the murder of Austin Pickett."

The room filled with a low roar of surprised chatter.

Lisa fell back and batted her eyes in shock. "Wait, what? I-I-I don't understand."

The sheriff explained. "We found traces of digitalis, a poison commonly found in the foxglove flower, in the bourbon balls delivered to his doorstep. We were able to confirm from a neighbor's porch camera that Paisley, with the help of an Uber driver, delivered the bourbon balls to the porch in the early morning hours on the day Austin died."

Janella flopped into a chair as Lisa crumpled against the wall. Lisa said, "Is this true, Paisley? Why would you do this?"

Paisley pushed herself to stand, her face livid with rage. She hobbled close to her sister. "Yes, I did it. Because you took ballet away from me." She pointed at her sister. "You took away the only thing *I* ever loved, so I took away something *you* loved."

As Paisley was being cuffed and led out of the room, Birdie snapped her fingers and waved her hand at Lisa. "Hey there, missy."

Lisa turned a dazed look at Birdie.

"I think you owe my sister an apology." Birdie stood, slinging her purse on her shoulder. "Get your things, Oda Dean. We're going to go see Jeb Butterworth. He's got a retraction to write."

•❖•

About the Author

Born and raised in the beautiful Bluegrass state of Kentucky, Michelle Bennington developed a passion for books early on that has since progressed into a mild hoarding situation and an ever-growing To-Be-Read pile. She delights in transporting readers into worlds of mystery, both contemporary and historical. In rare moments of spare time, she can be found engaging in a wide array of arts and crafts, reading, dance, traveling, and attending tours involving ghosts, historical homes, or distilleries. Find out more about her series at **www. michellebennington.com**. With three different series involving bourbon, hoarders, widows, ghosts, in contemporary or historical settings, you never know what amusement you might find! Connect with her at:

- Facebook
- Instagram
- Goodreads

Fideau Saves the Day

A DETECTIVE JOE BURGESS STORY

Kate Flora

Detective Sergeant Joe Burgess had badly wanted a dog when he was a boy, but circumstances like family stress and poverty had made it impossible. Now, many years on, he was an old grumpy dinosaur, the inside of his head blackened by all the dark stuff he had seen. He was still on the job and he finally had that dog, Fideau the Crime Scene Dog who, despite the ridiculous spelling of his name, was a smart and faithful animal. He'd taken the dog off a monster engaged in trafficking children when the man was arrested. Cops got a lot of pets that way. The man had never deserved such a fine dog. Given the animal's ability to read humans and situations, Burgess wasn't sure he did, either.

Right now, though, it was three in the morning. He'd only been in bed an hour and was clawing some desperately needed sleep from the investigation of a recent homicide. It was not a good time for Fideau, or anything, to disturb him. His job, and the puzzles it presented, often meant he slept about as badly—and rarely—as a newborn.

When the dog nosed the arm hanging off the edge of the bed, Fideau's way of demanding his attention, Burgess pulled his arm away, said, "No, Fideau. Go lie down."

The obedient dog sighed his disappointment and went to lie down on the rug.

Burgess went back to sleep. It was an uneasy sleep, filled with pictures from the crime scene and the many lists of things that still needed to be followed up on. Beside him in bed, his partner Chris, the woman who called herself "Almost Mrs. Burgess" but wouldn't agree to a wedding date, snored quietly. He moved closer to her, enjoying her warmth, and tried to chase his dark dreams away.

Pleasant dreams did not last long. In his dream, he was walking on one of their favorite paths. It was fall, the foliage blazing, Chris striding along by his side and Fideau dashing this way and that as he took in the fascinating scents. He had just taken Chris's hand in the dream when he felt that damp, doggy nose against his arm again.

"Darn it, Fideau," he muttered, opening his eyes to look at the dog. "What is the matter?"

Fideau tipped his head to the side, first one way, then the other, his canine way of saying there was something to be curious about. Then he walked to the closed door, tapped on it with a paw, and came back to the bed.

Reluctantly, Burgess left the warmth of the bed and his pleasant dream behind and got up, pulling on his robe and wiggling his feet into his shoes. He followed Fideau out into the living room. Feeling like someone from the Lassie TV program, he whispered, "What is it, Boy? What's so important you had to wake me up?"

He whispered because, in the other bedrooms, three children—two teens and a tween—were sleeping. There were many reasons not to wake them. Along with the fact, often stressed by Chris, that children needed their sleep to grow, there was the fact that the house was pleasant when no children were squabbling, bustling, chatting on phones, watching TV, foraging for snacks, or playing some awful video game.

Without hesitation, Fideau went to the door and again placed a paw against it. There was something out there that had the dog concerned. It could just be a nocturnal animal. Despite living in the city, there were coyotes, and sometimes deer, and even moose in his small Maine city. Once Burgess had drawn his gun on a curious raccoon. But years as a personal injury detective had given him a lot of enemies. Any one of them might have decided tonight was the night to finally get their revenge.

When he was younger, cops were pretty much untouchable. Now, that was eroding and threats to a cop's family were becoming more common. It had happened to him once before. They had motion activated lights, and he was considering getting a security system.

Burgess drew a slow breath, took in the dark and quiet, and listened, the dog by his side. From outside, there were scuffing sounds, like muffled footsteps on gravel.

Definitely something out there.

Beside him, Fideau gave a low growl.

"Let's go see what it is," Burgess said. He got his gun from the lockbox in the closet, checked it, and put a flashlight in his robe pocket. Then he slowly opened the door.

Man and dog stepped out onto the landing and were greeted by the mingled scents of sawdust and wet plaster. He'd shared the house with downstairs tenants for a decade, their rent helping him to pay the mortgage. Now he and Chris had decided they wanted more space, as well as more privacy, and were having the downstairs renovated to create two bedrooms and a large rec room/living room where the kids could entertain their friends. It was nice to be free of his tenants' complaints as well as their cooking smells.

They'd envisioned a quick renovation. But because the contractor had waited too long to order the sliders to the back yard, the job couldn't be finished. That space was closed off with heavy plastic and plywood, as were the spaces for the new windows.

It left the house far more vulnerable than Burgess liked. Unfortunately, the contractor was a fellow cop doing the work in his spare time, so it was difficult for Burgess to complain. After a few sharp words that had made him miserable, and miserable to live with, he'd left the job of general contractor to Chris. She seemed to enjoy being in charge and was far more charming than he'd ever be. Her charm seemed to finally be getting results. Tonight, though, his castle was too easy to break into.

He and Fideau went down the stairs, guided only by a pale night light. You never wanted to let the bad guys know you were coming. Burgess's steps were quiet. He'd been moving silently through the dark for decades, while Fideau's nails scritched against the wooden stairs. He opened the downstairs door and they stepped outside. In late October in Maine the weather could be extremely variable. Days could go from a mild sixty in the daytime to a damp and chilly thirty-six at night. Clothes that left you steaming at midday weren't enough to keep off the evening cold. Mainers were smart about layering as a result. Tonight, his layers were a tee shirt and a bathrobe. Lucky for him, the robe was courtesy of L.L.Bean and was warm, lined flannel. Only his legs were exposed to the chill night air.

They stood on the granite step, man and dog, both listening to the night sounds. Burgess strained to hear what his dog had heard. The muffled scraping sounds had stopped.

When listening didn't help, Burgess looked down at

the dog to see how Fideau wanted to proceed. Fideau tipped his head to the right, then looked up at Burgess, his ears alert.

"Okay, Buddy. Lead on," Burgess whispered, and Fideau began moving quietly toward the corner of the house past the garage.

Burgess followed, marveling at how quiet the animal could be, even if, being a mostly white dog, Fideau couldn't hide in the dark. He'd only had the dog a few months and was still learning about its talents. What he did know was that the dog could read minds, follow scents, adjust its behavior depending on whether it was dealing with a bad guy or a child, and had decided that Burgess was its person. Chris thought it was hilarious the way the dog had bonded to Burgess. Burgess himself was more perplexed. He was hardly a lovable dog owner.

"But that's just it," Chris had said, when he protested against the dog's attachment. "Fideau knows you need him and there's no way you or any of us can convince him otherwise."

He hoped he was wise enough not to struggle against something he couldn't change. Most of the time. He still struggled against those higher up the department's food chain who were more likely to impede an investigation than advance it. But that was the life. Mostly he'd become adept at being out of the office, if a cop shop could be called an office, where his work couldn't be interfered with.

He sighed, pushed thoughts of work away before his

current case could distract him from whatever was happening here, and slipped around the corner after Fideau.

Like the downstairs, the backyard was a work in progress. Back in the summer, Chris had tried her hand at a few raised beds while Burgess had put a little effort into grass. The result was that the space didn't look quite so much like a mangy dog. Still, there was a fire pit area waiting for the stones to be set, and some outdoor furniture Chris had gotten at a yard sale that still needed to be repaired and painted. There was also a pile of wood that was going to be more raised beds and some fencing that needed to be installed.

On a night as dark as this, he could see none of that. Just dark shapes that loomed, menacing, as he and Fideau made their way through the maze.

He thought he heard something and stopped, Fideau right beside him, pressed against his leg as they both listened.

The sound was faint but he thought it sounded like a small child crying. Sometimes animal noises did sound human. He stayed there, quietly listening, his hand on the dog's collar, while Fideau waited for instructions.

Burgess couldn't locate the sound, only that it seemed to be somewhere in his yard. He released the dog and whispered, "Find, Fideau." Hoping, as the dog moved away, that he wasn't sending the intrepid fellow after a skunk or a porcupine. Dogs, even smart ones, were very unlucky in encounters with porcupines and skunks.

He followed the dog through the maze of chairs, wood and the contractor's equipment toward the back of the yard.

A sudden burst of light from his bedroom window told him Chris had awakened, found him gone, and was getting up to see what was happening.

Ahead of him, Fideau gave a sharp woof and lay down. Somewhere along the line, this dog had been trained to do searches. He still wondered how it had come into the possession of a hateful man who cared nothing for the animal or for anything except pleasing himself and getting money. He solved mysteries for a living but never could solve this one.

He approached slowly, carefully, until he was beside the dog. Just in front of Fideau, there was a small pink bundle. It was sobbing, the exhausted sobs of a small child that had nearly cried itself out.

He bent down and picked it up. A little girl in a pink sleep suit, the kind with nonskid feet. She looked to be about two years old, though he was no expert at guessing toddlers ages. Her face was red and tearstained. Her hair damp from sweat. The suit was soaked through from a soggy diaper and cold from being outside so long. She lolled against him, unresponsive except for the occasional sob. Probably half-frozen.

Pee-soaked or not, he tucked her into his robe, pressing her against him as he murmured reassurance that she was okay now. He headed back toward the house, pausing to pat Fideau's nose and tell him he was a good dog.

As they went back inside, he thought about how easy it would have been to ignore Fideau's attempts to rouse him and gone back to sleep. About what that might have meant for the child.

Back upstairs, he carried her into the bathroom where he turned the taps of the tub on and stripped off the girl's cold, wet clothes. He rubbed her with a towel, seeing that the warmth of the room seemed to be reviving her. Kids could bounce back so fast.

"Mama?" the little girl said.

"Soon," Burgess said. "I'm Joe and this—" because Fideau was right there beside him—"is my dog, Fideau. Do you like dogs?"

"Doggy," she said. "Pat doggy?"

"Sure," he said, and moved aside a bit so she could reach Fideau's head. Fideau lowered his head to the small hand.

Burgess settled her in the warm water, a watchful Fideau beside the tub, then closed the toilet seat and sat while he pulled out his phone.

From the doorway, Chris said, "You thought we needed another daughter?"

"Fideau thought there was something out there that needed my attention. Found her in the backyard. Cold and wet and sobbing."

"He's an amazing dog, Joe. I didn't want a dog but I don't see how we ever lived without him."

"I'm thinking of retiring and giving him my job."

"Cold day in hell," she said. "Besides, we need him here at home."

He called dispatch, identified himself, and told the operator about the girl he'd found. "Anyone report a toddler missing?"

No one had.

He tried not to leap to judgment about parents who were careless with their kids. He'd seen so much of it. Yet he knew that sometimes, while exhausted parents slept, small children escaped from their beds and wandered away. It could be hours before those sleeping parents woke to the shock of a missing child.

"Let me know, okay?"

"Will do, Sarge."

With no relief in sight, he was back to trying to figure out what to do with this child.

From the doorway, Chris said, "I'd go back to bed but it looks like you might need help with this."

It was a long shot but he asked, "You have any toddler clothes? Or a diaper?"

"I've got safety pins and a washcloth. Or dishtowel. And maybe one of Ned's old tee shirts. Big on her but better than nothing."

"That would be great," he said, and Chris went off to gather supplies.

"What's your name?" he asked the girl.

"Ginny."

"How old are you?"

"Two and a haf."

"Do you know where you live?"

"In a house. It's white and has a red door."

It was something. Plenty of kids a lot older couldn't

have told him that much. He probed again. "What's your mother's name?"

"Mama."

"And your daddy?"

No answer. Maybe a divorce situation or a single mother.

"Do you have brothers or sisters?"

"We got a baby. His name Bobert. I come out now?" She held up her arms.

"In a minute," Burgess said. "We have to wash your face."

"Don't like face washed," she said, turning her head away.

"We have to wash your face," he said, dipping a washcloth in the warm water.

"I do it," she declared. "Do it myself."

Definitely in the terrible, or at least assertive, twos. He gave her the washcloth, pleased to see she did a pretty good job on her own. Then he got a towel and lifted her out of the tub.

As he was drying her, Chris appeared, performed her makeshift diaper operation, and slipped a tee shirt over the girl's head. Ned's old tee shirt was a dress on little Ginny but at least she was clean and dry. Her pale skin had turned a healthy pink.

"I washed out her things and put them in the dryer," Chris said. She looked down at the small girl in the oversized blue tee. "Now what do we do?"

"Wait. Hope her parents discover her missing soon

and come and get her. Hope we don't get into a situation where the homelife is unsafe. The parents strung out on drugs or something.

Chris held out a hand. "Ginny, would you like a snack?"

The girl nodded and said, "Where doggy?"

Fideau the mind reader appeared in the bathroom door. The girl lurched toward him. "Doggy," she said. "Pat doggy."

Chris looked at him and said, "We could let Fideau take care of her. He seems to know what to do."

"Not a bad plan. I'd rather not have him rooting through the cupboards for a snack, though."

Little Ginny, her hand on Fideau's soft head, said, "Doggy and Ginny have snack now."

"I guess we have a plan."

Chris got Ginny settled on a chair with a pillow so she could reach the table, and Fideau settled on the floor beside the chair. Dog probably knew that whatever the child was eating, some of it would come his way.

Chris found some goldfish crackers and a plastic glass. "Milk?" she asked the child, and got a nod.

Four in the morning. This was not how they wanted to be spending their time. Burgess was so tired he ached.

The girl was a very precise eater, carefully picking up each cracker, inspecting it, and then eating. Cracker number six, after inspection, was handed down to Fideau. Burgess thought maybe she had a dog at home.

"Bobert is afraid of dogs," she said. "But not me. I wuv them."

Burgess was practically asleep on his feet when his phone rang. Dispatch. "We've got a report of a kidnapping. Two-year-old named Virginia Matheson. About three blocks from your house."

"Probably not kidnapped but wandered away. She's at my house," Burgess said. "Why don't you send the parents here, along with patrol in case there are any kidnapping issues."

Dispatch said they would. Burgess got a name for the mother, Melinda Matheson, and clicked off.

Only moments later, someone downstairs was banging on the door.

"Crap," he said, turning toward the door. "Just what we need. The whole damned family awake."

"I'll get it," Chris said.

Only then did the observant detective notice that while he was still in his robe, she was fully dressed.

"Leave the door open," he said. "Patrol is on the way."

She went quietly down the stairs and the banging stopped. When she reappeared, she was followed by a woman who looked almost too young to be riding her bike off the sidewalk. Long dark hair, a heart-shaped face, and worried blue eyes. She was holding a baby in her arms.

Fast on her heels was a uniformed officer.

The woman paused in the doorway like she was

afraid of what she'd find, her eyes fixed on Ginny, who was still carefully performing her cracker routine. The woman paused as Burgess and Chris introduced themselves, then made a beeline for her daughter.

The officer who'd come in behind her quietly entered the room and nodded at Burgess.

"Ginny. Baby. Darling." She gathered the girl into her already full arms. "I was scared to death. You know you're not supposed to go outside with a grownup."

"Jimmy said it was okay, Mama."

The whole tableau froze at that.

Melinda Matheson said, "Jimmy?" in a way that confirmed he was not someone who was supposed to be near the children.

"Jimmy said come outside to playground, Mama. He taked me out. We walked. I was cold. He drove away."

A very concise description of a kidnapping.

Burgess said, "Who is Jimmy?"

"My ex-boyfriend. Robert's father."

"He doesn't live with you?"

"No way. I was a fool to get involved with him. He's been rough with Ginny and violent with me. I've got a restraining order to keep him away. He was supposed to turn in his keys to my lawyer." She raised a tear-streaked face to Burgess. "He must have kept a set of them. But to do this? To lure Ginny outside on a cold night and then abandon her? That seems harsh even for him."

"But you think that's what he did?"

"Ginny doesn't make things up, Detective. And she can't get out of the house by herself. I've got hooks on the doors well above where she can reach."

A hook that someone with a credit card could probably easily dislodge after he had unlocked the door with his key.

The woman's face was fierce, those blue eyes glaring at Burgess, daring him to disbelieve her. He believed her. Was angry on her behalf that a man she'd presumably loved and trusted had done such a wicked thing.

"I'm sorry this happened to you," he said. "Now you need to tell us where to find Jimmy."

"With pleasure," she said.

Chris had gone to the laundry room and returned with Ginny's pjs and pink sleeper. She held her arms out to the little girl. "Want to put your pjs on so you'll be cozy?"

The small girl nodded and let herself be picked up. As Chris dressed her in warm clothes for her journey back home, Melinda Matheson gave Burgess and the quiet officer information about where they might find Jimmy.

"These are all the places I know about. He moves around a bit. Living with friends. With family. With girlfriends. He's pretty much a parasite."

When Ginny was dressed, the woman turned to go. Burgess realized that she would have her hands full with both children, and that Ginny wasn't dressed for walking. He nodded toward the patient officer.

"Can you give her a hand getting home?"

"Of course, Sir."

Before they left, Burgess had a question. "Do you have a security camera or any kind of surveillance in your house?"

"I do," she said, in a voice that told him she was surprised she'd forgotten to mention that. A missing child would do that. "It probably caught Jimmy in the act. I shouldn't say this, I know, but I'd like to kill him for what he's done. It's just so cruel. I mean, I understand him being cruel to me. He didn't take well to being asked to move out. Parasite, as I said. But to Ginny? She's so little and helpless."

She turned to go, then turned back. "But how did you ever find her?"

Burgess set a hand on Fideau's back. "Not me. My dog. He's a very clever fellow. Insisted I get up and come outside with him."

"Good doggy," Ginny said.

Fideau walked them downstairs, then came back to Burgess, following him into the bedroom as he dressed to go out in search of a man named Jimmy Boudreau, someone who, unsurprisingly, turned out to be well known to the department. So much for a decent night's sleep.

By nine a.m. Jimmy Boudreau, a bit worse for wear after resisting arrest, was in custody, charged with breaking and entering, violating a restraining order, and kidnapping. Little Virginia Mattheson was home with her family. And Detective Sergeant Joe Burgess was at his desk, working on a large coffee, still marveling at the faithful dog who had woken him in time to save a child who might otherwise have died.

About the Author

Maine native Kate Flora is the author of twenty-five books and many short stories. Her most recent Thea Kozak mystery is *Death Sends a Message*; her most recent Joe Burgess is *A World of Deceit*. Her crime story collection is called *Careful What You Wish For: Stories of revenge, retribution, and the world made right*. Her domestic suspense novel, *Teach Her a Lesson*, was published by Encircle Publications in May, 2023. Her true crime works include *Finding Amy* and *Death Dealer*, along with a game warden's memoir, *A Good Man with a Dog*, and a nonfiction book about police shootings, *Shots Fired*. *Shots Fired* and *Finding Amy* were co-written with Joseph K. Loughlin.

Cozy Cottage for Rent

A CAMILLA RANDALL MYSTERY

Anne R. Allen

There are bad dates and then there are I'd-rather-be-home-with-a-case-of-Covid dates. Tonight's had been the latter. All I wanted was to go home to my cozy cottage and cuddle with my cat.

My first mistake had been letting George Grayson pick me up instead of meeting him at the restaurant. He'd been a regular customer in my bookstore for several months—an aspiring writer in his fifties who was some kind of money manager. He had good manners and dressed well, so I admit I hadn't taken the usual precautions one does with a first date. I guess I felt I knew him.

But you never really know somebody until you sit down to a shared charcuterie board and watch him eat all the olives. By the handful. Before you've had a chance to taste one.

It ruins the mood, even if he's taken you to a cute

bistro looking out at the California sun setting over Morro Bay.

Then it got worse. It turned out his divorce had recently become final and he spent the whole evening complaining about his ex, a demanding southern belle named Cinda-Rae. By the time he finished off our bottle of Syrah, I was afraid I'd scream if I heard her name one more time.

As an author of etiquette books, I normally wouldn't open a car door before a man had the chance to do the gentlemanly thing and open it for me. But as soon as his vintage Mercedes came to a stop in front of my bookstore, I have to admit I pushed the door open and jumped out in sheer relief.

I put on a big, fake smile, thanked him, and tried to escape to my cottage behind the store.

"Wait!" He slammed his door and rushed after me. "The books! You said you'd sell my books."

My smile got faker as I kept walking. "Yes. I'll order a couple of copies from Ingram and we'll see how they sell."

"No! I have them in the trunk. Three cartons. Can you take all three?"

"Not now." I kept walking down the gravel driveway.

"But you promised!"

The man was outrageous. One reluctant nod was hardly a promise. He'd obviously been scammed by some vanity press and was deluded enough to think someone might buy his amateurish scribbles. Unfortunately, everybody with a keyboard thought they could write these days. I could hear his Bruno Maglis crunching the gravel behind me, but I kept walking. I gave him another phony smile over my shoulder.

"Sorry. Bathroom emergency." Okay, that was a total lie, but embarrassing things tend to make unassailable excuses. I imitated a laughing sound and took off in a sprint.

When I got to my courtyard, I finally heard no more crunches.

He was gone. I was home safe. Bliss.

Except for the unfamiliar car parked behind my Honda and the fact the screen door to my cottage was wide open.

Maybe my on-and-off boyfriend Ronzo was here. He was supposed to be in New Jersey visiting his sick grandmother, but maybe he'd come back to California early to surprise me. Didn't he know I hate surprises?

I tiptoed inside, closing the screen door behind me, and tried to work up a cheery smile to greet him.

But instead of my amorous Jersey boy, there in my living room was a strange woman, wearing flannel pajamas, colored sort of a peachy-pink.

The place smelled of garlic and oregano. Probably from the empty, gooey pizza box abandoned on my coffee table.

"There you are!" The woman looked at me as if I were a particularly unpleasant species of vermin. "The towels need to be changed. They don't look dirty but they smell like Chanel Number Five, so I can tell some woman has used them. And I don't think you've changed the bed sheets either."

"Um…." That was the only noise my mouth would make. The woman was tall and square-jawed, with dark, close-cropped hair. She looked like a drill sergeant in pink pajamas. This was all too absurd.

"And some cat got in here. My husband is allergic to cats. He threw it in the bushes."

"Buckingham? You threw my cat in the bushes? Is he all right?" If this deluded woman had hurt my cat, I was going to call the police.

"How should I know? You're going to get a terrible review from us. I'm sure you know that, with the way you leave things all over the kitchen counters. And where's our breakfast? There's nothing in the fridge but a couple of English muffins and a rotting avocado. We're going whale watching in the morning, so we have to get an early start. Bring us some toast and eggs by 7 AM. Oh, and I don't eat gluten, so the toast has to be gluten free."

Okay. I had to be calm but authoritative. I took a deep breath.

"Ma'am, you've made a mistake. This is not a vacation rental. It's my home, and I need to take a shower and get some sleep. I've had a rough day, and I need to get up bright and early to open my bookstore. Check your app and get the right address."

Her drill sergeant face reddened. "We made a mistake? No, girly, you made a mistake lying about this place. It looked like such a find—a cozy cottage, only a few blocks from the beach. But you're so bad at house-keeping, no wonder it was cheap."

I took a step back. Her breath smelled like stale wine. She'd probably been wine-tasting, a major tourist activity around here.

"Ma'am, you've got the wrong address. You need to contact the people who manage your rental. How did you get inside? I know I locked the door."

"Duh. The key was under the pot of geraniums just like you said." The woman reached for her purse on the dining table and pulled out her phone. She fiddled with it for a moment, then stuck the phone in my face.

"There's the picture. Tell me that's not this place."

Dear Lord. There was my cottage, in all its 1920s beach-cottage cuteness. Who could have got back here to photograph it? And how did they know where I keep my spare key?

Someone in the bedroom let out a curse.

"Hey bitch, that damned cat has been in here. I can't sleep when I can't breathe. Where's that nose spray?"

A man stumbled out. He had long, dyed-blond hair and a ravaged face like an aging rock star. In fact, he looked exactly like an aging rock star. What was his name?

Mick McVeigh. Frontman of that grunge band, Bitter Vetch. Wasn't he dead? I thought all the grunge rockers were dead.

The "bitch" gave him a dismissive sigh.

"Mick, I told you it's in the bathroom. In the case next to the sink. Open the window to air out the room."

The man made a fist as he stumbled toward us. I didn't know which one of us he planned to hit. I cringed as he lurched toward me.

"Who the hell are you, blondie? You look like a librarian. Are you a librarian?"

I had dressed in a conservative vintage DKNY suit so George wouldn't get any wrong ideas. I probably did look like a librarian. Maybe Mick didn't hit librarians. I had to hope so.

"She's the maid. And she's going to get us some clean towels." The woman gave me a nasty scowl.

"She can get an effing lightbulb for the lamp in there. It's burned out."

Okay, playtime was over. I had to get rid of these ridiculous people.

"No." I spoke in as firm a tone as I could muster. "I'm not a servant. I'm the owner of this cottage. You've been scammed. You need to leave. Right now."

Mick swiveled back to me, his face purple. He wasn't much taller than me, so his eyes bored directly into mine. If eyes really could stare daggers, I'd have been dead.

"Scam? You're the scammer, blondie. We paid in advance for this place. And you're the one who's going to leave."

He twirled me around, grabbed me by the upper arms and physically lifted me off the ground. He kicked the screen door open, set me down on the top step and pushed. I fell on the bricks that paved the courtyard, trying to break my fall with my hands.

The woman was screaming obscenities at Mick.

"Now we'll never get clean towels!" was the last thing I heard before the door slammed.

I lay there a moment, too dizzy to stand. My hands felt raw where they'd hit the bricks. Something warm oozed from my right knee. Buckingham appeared and meowed. He rubbed his furry black and white face against my cheek. Sweet little guy. He knew exactly how I felt. He'd been thrown out the same way.

I managed to get to my feet and stumble across the courtyard to my car. I was sitting in the driver's seat before I realized I couldn't go anywhere. Their rented Buick SUV had me parked in. I was too dizzy to drive anyway. I pulled my phone out of my purse to call 911, but hesitated. If I called the police, there would be a scene, and it would last forever, and I'd never get to sleep. I'd prefer not to deal with them until morning.

First, I'd call Plantagenet. My best friend. He and his husband Silas had a big house with one of those lovely foam mattresses in the guestroom.

"Camilla darling!" Thank goodness. Plant was in a good mood in spite of the late hour. "How was the date with Mr. G.Q. tonight?"

"Awful. But in contrast to what's happened since, it was almost not vomitous." I went on to give him a semi-coherent synopsis of the evening.

"So you were beaten up by David Lee Roth and

now you're imprisoned by a rented Buick? Are you bleeding? Do you need to get to a hospital?"

"Not David Lee Roth. Mick McVeigh. From Bitter Vetch. Yes, my knee is bleeding." I could see a blood stain spreading on my slacks. "And my hands, a little."

"I'll be there as fast as my little Ferrari can go. Meanwhile, call 9-1-1. This is a matter for law enforcement."

I didn't call 911. I sat there in a state of semi-catatonia until Plant arrived. He was a little angry with me, but I agreed to summon the police first thing in the morning.

He and Silas were kind, giving me chamomile tea laced with brandy while Plant tended to my wounds. Just a skinned knee, scraped hands, and some purpling bruises where Mick had grabbed my arms. I'd be okay in a day or two.

The memory foam mattress helped.

In the morning I called the Morro Bay police station and talked with a nice woman named Lonnie about the scam victims who'd taken over my home. She knew me by name, since I'm a local business owner, and said they'd seen a rash of vacation rental scams. I told her the officers had permission to enter the premises to evict the deluded visitors, and she reassured me my home would be vacated in time to open the store at ten AM.

But at 9:30, when Plant drove me home, we saw police cars—and even an ambulance—parked on the street in front of the store and in my driveway. We had to leave the Ferrari halfway up the street. Yellow police tape barred our way into the driveway, which I was relieved to see was now Buick-free.

A lot of law enforcement people seemed to be over-reacting to a petty crime.

So were the press. Reporters and TV camera people milled around the front of the store. A policeman barred them from entering, and I supposed he'd keep me out too. Somebody said my whole property was designated a crime scene.

It took a few minutes to get anybody to tell us what the crime was. Finally, a local TV reporter told Plant that a body had been found in bed in the cottage—the body of a man. With long, blond hair. He'd been shot at close range. They were trying to identify the body now.

Wow. It was sad, but I had to admit I wouldn't grieve for the man.

"It's Mick McVeigh," I told her. "From the grunge band Bitter Vetch. I'm sure his wife will identify him."

The reporter looked at me as if I'd recently arrived from Alpha Centauri.

"What gave you that idea? This isn't a celebrity. It's some unhoused person who wandered into a woman's home after he'd been shot."

"His wife would be angry if you called him home-less. They paid to rent the house. Unfortunately, it wasn't for rent. Is she all right? Was she attacked too?"

"What wife? There was only one person in the house." The reporter still seemed to think I was a sadly uninformed space alien.

When we finally got past the other reporters to talk to the policeman guarding my store, he said we couldn't go inside, but a detective would want my statement. We couldn't get in anyway because three large cartons blocked the doorway.

Book cartons. Labeled with the name of a notorious vanity publisher. Oh, dear. George must have unloaded his books after I escaped.

When I explained it all to Plant, he gave an inappropriate laugh.

The policeman harrumphed. "Are these your boxes, sir? They shouldn't be left out here as a temptation for porch pirates. We could put them into the store after forensics checks the place."

I explained who I was and thanked him, but Plant had already pulled open the top of one of the cartons.

"*The Dark Chaotic Heart*? What is this, a sci-fi romance?"

He held up one of the paperback tomes. The cover looked a bit like the swirly opener of an old black-and-white episode of *Dr. Who*, except a muddy gray heart had been substituted for the police box.

"I'm afraid it's some sort of memoir." George hadn't suggested it was anything as interesting as science fiction.

"Can I take one?" Plant thumbed through the pages. "How much are you charging for them?"

"For you, not a penny." I rolled my eyes. "In fact, if you can get all the way through it, I'll buy you dinner."

A determined looking man in khakis and a bad

sport coat pushed through the gaggle of reporters and camera people toward me. Obviously the detective.

I answered his questions as he entered it all into his iPad.

"So your story is a guy thought he'd rented your house and when you told him he had the wrong house, he threw you out? And you think he was a rock star?"

I nodded. I guessed that was as good a recap as any.

"He looked like Mick McVeigh, and his wife called him 'Mick' so I'm pretty sure that's who it was."

"A wife? What wife? You saw a wife?"

"Absolutely. She was wearing pink pajamas."

The detective, whose name seemed to be Ramirez, gave me the same skeptical look I'd had from the reporter.

I kept trying. "She really was there. But she must have left in the rented SUV." My voice sounded whinier than I intended.

"Do you have the license plate number of this SUV, ma'am?" I feared Detective Ramirez didn't believe a word I was saying.

"No. But I think the frame said 'Hertz'. It was a red Buick."

Detective Ramirez wrote something on his iPad, but made no eye contact.

Plant could see my increasing frustration and asked the detective if he might take me home, in light of my injuries.

When Detective Ramirez finally understood that the deceased had been violent with me the night before, his expression went from just-the-facts-ma'am robot to fierce investigator.

"Do you own a firearm, Ms. Randall? Did you use it to protect yourself from the man who assaulted you last night?"

I didn't like where this was going.

After I convinced him that I did not own or have access to a firearm, he let Plant whisk me off, with my promise I'd be available for further questioning.

As we drove back to Plant's house, we tried to sort out what was happening. He'd gleaned some information from a couple of the reporters. The man had been found in bed (my bed!) with a bullet wound to the back of the head. There had been no signs of forced entry.

Or of the woman in pink pajamas. No sign of anybody but Mick in the cottage.

At this point, I didn't much care who had shot him. I just wanted my house and store back.

And a nap. I needed to lie down and process all of this. But as soon as we got home, my cell phone rang. It was Ronzo, my Jersey boy.

"Mick McVeigh?" He laughed as if this was hilarious. "You killed Mick McVeigh, the nastiest guy in rock and roll?"

After a moment of stunned silence, I asked him how he heard the story. Even the police didn't know the identity of the corpse. Maybe that reporter I'd talked to had believed me after all. Ronzo was a music blogger, so it made sense he'd be one of the first to hear.

"But who said I killed him? You know that's absurd."

He laughed again. "Twitter. It's all over Twitter. Somebody attached a photo of you from your socialite days and you look really hot, so it's going viral. Mick looks like he's been sleeping in a dumpster for ten years. Coke takes its toll. So what happened?"

I tried to give a quick overview of the situation, but Ronzo kept laughing.

He quieted down when I mentioned the woman.

"That's probably his wife, Roxanna DeWitt. She's a piece of work. Used to play bass for a couple of Jersey bands before she ended up in rehab on the west coast. That's where they met—Mick and Roxy—some fancy rehab place. Her family's got a buttload of money. Do you think she killed him?"

I was glad he'd voiced what I'd been thinking.

"He was pretty awful to her and called her the b-word. She was cursing at him when he threw me on the ground. Maybe she snapped."

"The police must suspect her. They always like the partner for a domestic homicide."

I sighed. "The detective seems to think I made her up. She must have packed her bags, carefully tidied the place, then drove away in their rental car."

He took a quick breath. "She has a rental car? They can use that to trace her. You've got to get the police to understand she was there in your house and you spoke to her. No doubt in my mind that she killed him. Probably self-defense. He's abused all his girlfriends. I read he was shot with a Ruger LCP. That's a real small gun a woman might carry."

Plant didn't agree about going to the police with Ronzo's information on Roxanna DeWitt. For one thing, I didn't know for sure the woman I met was Roxanna, and I had no way of proving a woman had been in my house at all. Plant had seen the rented Buick, but there was no way to prove Roxanna had taken it.

Silas's advice was that I should call his lawyer. He said if I'd been named a suspect, even if only on Twitter, I shouldn't talk to the police without legal representation. Bad news. Lawyers cost money.

But I needed that nap first. And some aspirin for my painful wounds. I thanked them both, turned off my phone, and escaped to the guest room's lovely foam mattress.

It was getting dark when Plant roused me from a sound sleep.

"Sorry, darling, but your public is waiting. It's time to give a statement to the press. They're wreaking havoc on our landscaping."

I brushed my hair, touched up my make-up, and tried to smooth out the wrinkles in my bloodstained "librarian" outfit. I hoped the police would let me get into my house—at least for a change of clothes—soon.

When I walked into the living room, I could see through the front window why Plant was worried about the landscaping. All their drought-tolerant succulents were bent and broken as crowds of reporters and camera people covered the front yard. Silas was outside trying to calm them down.

"They don't all think I killed Mick McVeigh, do they?"

I hoped Plant would reassure me, but he didn't. He took my hand and led me out the front door to the porch. Immediately microphones and cameras came at me. Cameras. Great. And there I was, looking like a librarian on a bender.

"This is all a mistake." I spoke in as loud a voice as I could muster. "Mick McVeigh and his wife were scammed into thinking they'd rented my house. When I asked them to leave, they threw me out. Then somebody seems to have shot Mick in the head. And his wife Roxy disappeared in a rented Buick SUV. This is a tragedy, but has nothing to do with me. That's all I have to say at this time."

A roar of new questions came from the crowd.

I was grateful when big, burly Silas stood between me and the reporters and hurried me back toward the door.

"That's all folks!" he said. "Camilla has made her statement. Now go home."

He and Plant propelled me back into the living room. Silas closed the drapes to shut out the scene, but we could still hear their roars.

"Unfortunately, we may need ear plugs."

"I have a better idea." Plant gave a sly smile as he sauntered over to the stereo and Silas's impressive vinyl collection.

"I think a little Bach played by E. Power Biggs might give them a 'Come-to-Jesus' moment."

The opening notes of the pipe organ practically blasted me out of the room. Plant motioned for all of us to go to the kitchen in the back of the house.

"Let's have a nice family dinner back there, shall we?"

"I'll make my mac and cheese with lobster," Silas said. "And let's not turn on the TV news. We can stick to Netflix tonight, and you'll probably be out of the news cycle by tomorrow."

Unfortunately, the news wasn't much better the next morning, although the reporters were gone. Apparently, my mention of Roxy had backfired, and now the investigators had to check my house for her prints and probably wouldn't release it until evening.

Silas escaped to his office in town. Then Plant said he needed to work on his new screenplay and disappeared into his study.

I tried to get the bloodstain out of my grimy DKNY slacks without much success. Luckily Plant had an old jogging suit in the guestroom closet I'd borrowed before. Then I had to deal with the dozens of voice mails and texts from reporters who wanted to know why I killed Mick McVeigh. One wanted to know how long I'd been having an affair with Roxy DeWitt.

Around lunch time, Plant rushed into the guest room and asked if I knew anybody named Lindy-Mae. He said he'd been reading *The Dark Chaotic Heart*, and it seemed to be a *roman à clef*. George had cast himself as the lead, bestselling author "Giorgio Galliano." There was a New York socialite-turned-bookstore-owner named "Carmella Randolph," who bore an uncanny resemblance to yours truly. And the villain was somebody named Lindy-Mae.

"Cinda-Rae, her name is. His ex. He hates her." I laughed. "So is the book readable? It's not awful?"

"Oh, it's awful. In a compelling sort of way. The man is a lunatic. But I think I know what got your cottage listed as a rental. Lindy-Mae did the same thing to get revenge on Carmella—took a photo of her house, put it for rent online and told people where the key was."

"Why? What had Carmella ever done to her?"

"Got Giorgio to fall in love with her, apparently. He's obsessed with Carmella. He's been stalking her for years. Lindy-Mae blames her for her marriage break-up."

"Years? But the real George has only lived in Morro Bay for a few months." This information bonged in my head like last night's organ music. George was obsessed with me? He'd been stalking me? That might explain why his wife knew where I kept my spare key.

"Does Lindy-Mae want to kill a rock star by any chance? Somebody named Hick McFay or something?"

"No. But I think it's time you called the police again. This is important information. At least about the rental scam."

On the phone, Lonnie was polite, but didn't seem much interested in Cinda-Rae Grayson. Apparently, after they'd discovered Roxanna DeWitt's fingerprints all over my cottage—and a set of bloody pink pajamas in the trash—they found her staying at an upscale hotel nearby. Detective Ramirez was interrogating her now. Obviously Lonnie thought the case was all sewed up.

But the good news was I could go home. I couldn't find Buckingham, but I figured he'd come out of hiding once all the strangers were gone. The cottage was a little discombobulated, and they'd taken the bedding—just as well. I wouldn't have wanted to deal with the blood—but the mattress looked unsullied.

I put on fresh sheets, had a blissful shower, and even managed to open the bookstore for late afternoon traffic. Regular customers rushed in, eager to know "what really happened."

I appreciated their concern, but by the time I closed up at six, I was beyond exhausted—and worried about Buckingham. I searched all his hideouts in the shrubbery around the courtyard. I even phoned the yogurt shop next door. He sometimes managed to get in there and beg for treats. But they said there was no sign of him.

I put some salmon in his bowl and opened the kitchen window. His sense of smell was pretty amazing when it came to his favorite foods.

I fed myself some microwaved enchiladas, opened a bottle of chardonnay, and tried to relax. I had my home back. I could tidy things tomorrow. What happened with Mick and Roxy was tragic, but it had nothing to do with me.

As I drank my second glass of chardonnay, somebody knocked on my door. I almost hoped it was the police, so I could tell them about Cinda-Rae Grayson and her vacation rental revenge.

But when I opened the door, there was George himself, looking dapper as ever, wearing an incongruous smile.

"I heard about your troubles." His faux-friendly tone had a disturbing edge. "What a nightmare having the cops all over the place. Were you able to save my books? I left them in front of the store. But the next morning police and reporters were everywhere and I couldn't see them."

I thought I ought to be polite and offer him a glass of wine, since I had one in my hand. But oh, dear, now I knew he'd been stalking me, I didn't feel terribly safe around him. I supposed I should be a bit sympathetic. Dealing with his vindictive ex must have been awful. I wondered if he suspected she might have killed Mick McVeigh.

I put on my Manners Doctor smile. "It's all terribly tragic, isn't it? But your books are safe, and I've put three in stock. My friend Plantagenet is reading it now. He says it's compelling."

George sipped chardonnay and looked thoughtful, but his expression darkened.

"Plantagenet Smith peaked ten years ago with *Wilde in the West*. He hasn't had a hit since he won that Oscar. So I'm not sure I care about his opinion. And I know you never planned to sell my books."

I tensed. That was too rude for me to tolerate under normal circumstances. But I needed some questions answered.

"Can we talk about your character Lindy-Mae?" He must have suspected his ex's vacation rental scam. "Plant wondered if your ex rented out my cottage the way Lindy-Mae did with Carmella's house in your book."

George let out a derisive laugh. "Of course. I would have thought that was obvious."

"Do you think she knew she was scamming a rock star?" I probably didn't need a third glass of wine, but I poured one anyway.

George's tone turned from snarky to outright hostile.

"Oh, so you're a rock star now? I saw those photos of you on Twitter. You looked like a slut."

I put down my wine glass and worked at staying calm.

"What? No, of course not. I'm talking about Mick McVeigh, the murder victim. I'm sorry you didn't like that Versace dress. It was very much in fashion, but that was twenty years ago."

"Versace. Versace." George spoke in a sing-song, mocking voice. "You really think you're better than me, with your designer clothes and a Countess for a mother. But I heard her title was bogus, anyway."

This man seemed to know everything about me. I tried to speak in an even tone.

"Everything about Count Braganza was bogus. He

went through my mother's entire fortune before she died."

I was only a few feet from my phone, which was in my purse on the coffee table. I needed to get Plant and Silas here. Now.

George's face settled into an angry scowl.

"You don't remember me, do you? I was a waiter at one of your mother's soirees at Randall Hall. You were nice to me then. My boss chewed me out for spilling some canapes and you took me aside and said he'd been rude. Then you kissed me."

Dear Lord. This was ringing a distant bell. He'd been in tears, poor thing. There was so much drama swirling around the Hall when the Count was in charge.

"I kissed you? I must have had too much champagne. Some of Mother's catering people had dreadful manners. I'm sorry you were treated badly."

"Sorry? Oh, you'll be sorry all right. I need to make a clean break from the sorry past."

Now George seemed to be imitating a villain from a Lifetime TV movie. Time to get this lunatic out of my house.

But he was on a roll. "You've been leading me on all these years. I was sure when you divorced that TV news guy, you'd see the light. We were meant to be together, you and me. I could see it in your eyes. That's why I moved us to Morro Bay. Cinda-Mae hated the fog. That's why she despised you."

Okay, we were in crazy-town now. George must have been running a fantasy about me in his head for years and couldn't tell it from reality. This had to stop. I eyed my purse and faked a laugh.

"Despised? Past tense? So she's over it now she's had her revenge?"

His voice went flat. "No. Cinda-Mae's dead. Went off a cliff at Big Sur a couple of days ago. Something happened to the brakes on her Kia. I needed to get rid of old baggage."

I somehow managed to keep from screaming as I stood and grabbed my purse.

But he was quick. He grabbed my arm and yanked the purse away.

"Did you think you were going to call your police friends?" He pulled out my phone and turned it off. "Not a chance. Nobody's coming to your rescue tonight, and no other blondes are going to be in your bed, looking like you in the dark. You really should have changed that lightbulb. And not left the window wide open. I need to get rid of old baggage. Start a new chapter in my life."

I tried to breathe normally. Okay, George killed Mick McVeigh, thinking he was me. Because we had the same hair color. And because George's fantasy of me was "old baggage." I edged away from him.

A couple of bangs on the door startled us both. I yelled "come in" in a cheerful voice. I didn't care who it was. Beelzebub and a few demons would be welcome.

In stomped the big teenaged kid from the yogurt shop next door—holding Buckingham.

"This little guy sneaked into our back room. He was asleep under the old strawberry boxes."

George's face contorted in rage.

"Get out! This isn't the time for a booty call. She doesn't want you, fat guy!" He reached into a pocket and drew something out.

A nasty little gun. He waved it at the poor young man.

Buckingham gave a yowl and jumped from the boy's arms. He made an impressive leap onto George's chest, claws out.

Now the yowls were from George. He dropped the gun, and the quick teen picked it up and pointed it at my attacker.

"Nice little Ruger LCP Max here, dude. My mom says these things hold twelve rounds. Insane for a little concealed-carry pistol, isn't it? Ms. Randall, you wanna call 9-1-1?"

I did.

Later, when the local TV people were asking us questions about the night's dramas, the young man, whose name was Matteo Lopez, basked in his well-deserved hero status and thanked his mother, who worked at the local gun shop.

The police didn't let Roxanna DeWitt go until morning, poor thing. But it turned out the red substance on her pajamas was tomato sauce from the pizza box Mick threw at her. That had been the last straw that drove her to leave and move to a hotel. She'd been as shocked by Mick's death as anyone.

Two days later, the corpse of Cinda-Rae Grayson was found in her Kia, submerged in the ocean off Highway One near Big Sur.

After he finished George's book, I rewarded Plantagenet with a charcuterie board at the bistro where I'd gone with George. As we shared olives, I asked him what he thought I should do with the books.

"A bonfire would be good." He gave me an impish smile. "I did give Detective Ramirez several copies, but the rest—get rid of them. The sex scenes are, um, disturbing. And the rest is sheer lunacy."

Buckingham was waiting when I got home. I made tea, fed him some salmon, and turned on the local TV news.

The reporter said Roxanna DeWitt was staying at her parents' home in Connecticut, and they asked for privacy at this tragic time.

George Grayson was being held without bail on two counts of first-degree murder. He was pleading insanity.

Matteo Lopez had been offered a college scholarship by the local Rotary club.

"Yes. Karma does exist," I told Buckingham. He yawned, jumped up on my lap, and purred.

About the Author

Anne R. Allen is the author of twelve funny mysteries and two how-to books for writers. Her bestselling Camilla Randall Mysteries series are a laugh-out-loud mash-up of mystery, rom-com, and satire. She also has a collection of short stories and verses called *Why Grandma Bought That Car*, which has been translated into French, Italian, and Spanish, and is the co-author of *How to be a Writer in the E-Age...a Self-Help Guide*, written with Amazon #1 seller, Catherine Ryan Hyde. Her latest nonfiction book, *The Author Blog: Easy Blogging for Busy Authors* was named one of the Best 101 Books on Blogging and one of the Best Books on SEO by Book Authority. She's also a contributor to *Writer's Digest* and *Writer's Market*. Anne shares her award-winning writing blog with *NYT* million-copy seller, Ruth Harris, at Anne R. Allen's Blog...with Ruth Harris. Visit **annerallen.com** for more information on the author. You can also find Anne on Facebook, Twitter, LinkedIn, and Bookbub.

A Tale of Two Vineyards

A BENNETT SISTERS MYSTERY

Lise McClendon

H e hadn't intended to disappear.

Pascal d'Onscon wasn't afraid of anything. He was a Frenchman, after all, and a vain one at that. And why not be proud? Frenchmen had survived the guillotine, the Prussians, Hitler, the Kaiser, crazy kings, powdered wigs, and satin breeches. They had known famine and torture and humiliation at the hands of enemies. But in the face of something he could only call an infatuation, he shook. His hands actually trembled.

He understood men. He worked with them, drank with them, played pétanque with them. Women, like his two sisters and one ex-wife, were a mystery. He didn't try hard to understand them, that was folly. French women in particular were sly like foxes. They could appear one way and transform into something much more sinister. Better to just steer clear.

He knew almost nothing about American women.

So it was best to make himself scarce. Remove from the field of play. Take a breather. Let his pulse return to normal. She was, after all, under village arrest. She wasn't going anywhere, her passport seized.

His boss in Paris had come with a request at the right moment: Pascal was needed in Toulouse. In his role as a wine fraud detective he had proven his worth to the agency many times over, sussing out liars and tricksters who dared to undermine the integrity of the precious nectar of the vine. If he had wanted to stay in Malcouziac, his boss would have okayed it. But in this case, he was glad to leave.

He owned a small cottage in a village outside of Toulouse, his only permanent residence in his peripatetic job. It was past time to check on it. The agency rented him a room in Malcouziac, in a medieval stone building where the ground floor had been converted to a pharmacy. His room upstairs was dismal and primitive but had running water and electricity thanks to the pharmacy below. It looked out over the vineyards surrounding the hilltop village, another plus. Locking it up for his trip seemed perfunctory. Off he went.

He found his motorcycle parked in the city lot, strapped on his helmet, and headed south. He loved to ride his motorcycle. It made him feel wild and free in a way that he obviously was not in his everyday life. He was no longer young, having turned forty a few years back. He had a government job. He was a responsible citizen. He obeyed, and made others obey, the law. He was not wild and he was not free, but on his bike—as

Americans called their *motos*—he let it rip. The roar of the engine was thrilling.

When he arrived at his cottage with its overgrown lawn and peeling paint, a shutter flapping in the wind, he was simply tired. His ass hurt. His back ached. He had a headache from squinting into chrome. He swung a leg over and dismounted but it took five minutes to get the feeling back in his feet. Two hours on his motorcycle had aged him by twenty years. *Merde*, he was getting old. His back especially reminded him. Soon he would be lucky to play boules with old men. He glowered at the machine and threatened to sell it.

He had the day to kill here at his cottage, so set about fixing the shutter and chopping back the grass and vines. He wasn't much of a homeowner; in fact he hadn't been here for six months. The kitchen was a disaster of dead crickets and mouse droppings. When his neighbor Irene stopped by, he was glad to stop cleaning.

"I see your moto," she explained. Irene raised goats and made cheese at the farm next door. She was a hale and hearty seventy, somewhat cranky but with a good heart. For some reason she liked Pascal. He didn't question her regard, simply pulled her in for three *bisous* and a hug.

When he stepped back, feeling a twinge in his back, she frowned. "You work too hard, Pascal." She eyed the yellow plastic gloves on his hands. "I will send my daughter. She is home from college."

He stripped off the gloves and snapped them on his

thigh. "I can clean, Irene. But some help would be nice, thank you. I will only be here overnight though. Off to a job in Toulouse."

They discussed the goats, her pride and joy. She walked him to the backyard where she pointed out Maisey, Petal, and Zsa Zsa. The baby goats, the kids, were adorable. She could hardly wait for them to arrive, her eyes twinkling as she talked about them.

"I must get my car out of the barn to make room."

Irene blinked. "But—but you moved it a month ago." She swiveled to look around the house. "Where —mon Dieu. Was that not you, Pascal?"

They walked to her barn where Pascal had stored his old BMW for the winter. When had he put it inside? February, he thought. Just before that job near Narbonne. The space was empty, not even tire tracks. Some bastard had stolen his car. He put his hands on his hips and hung his head.

"I'm so sorry, Pascal. Je suis désolé. I thought you came for it. I saw the man drive it out. He looked like you." Irene patted his shoulder. "You have the insurance?"

"Who would do this?" Pascal said angrily. "Who knew it was in here?"

Irene shrugged. "Perhaps someone in the village? There are some lads."

"I should not have left it so long unattended. It is my fault, Irene." He calmed his voice. "Do not be anxious. I will find this thief."

Irene insisted on feeding him. Déjeuner was the least

she could do. He ate the warmed soup and crusty bread, drank a dram of her wine, and excused himself. Returning to his cottage, he jumped on his motorcycle and went for a drive around the village backstreets. As he suspected, no BMW in any open shed or garage, nor parked in plain sight. His old green sedan, with its massive engine and ugly sunspots, was gone.

When he returned to the cottage, Louise, Irene's daughter, was finishing the bathroom. "Not too terrible," she said, grimacing. She refused to accept any money which annoyed Pascal. "Maman says she lost your auto. She feels terrible."

He tried to reason with Louise, and Irene through her. They felt responsible. There was no talking them out of it. Only one way to get this guilt off them, and that was find the damn car. How many green BMWs of that vintage remained on French roads? He would find out in Toulouse.

The wine fraud agency, officially inside the *Institut National des Appellations d'Origine* but with liaison officers like Pascal who worked with other agencies, had a small office in the city. Upstairs in a modern office block, so different from the Belle Époque Paris headquarters, Pascal was greeted the next morning by a fellow investigator, Mathis Cochet. They knew each other from a case two years before, a massive scam of Côte de Rhône wine. Almost the whole agency had worked that case.

"We are together on this thing?" Pascal asked,

pulling out a chair by the desk Mathis sat behind. "What is it exactly?"

Mathis, wiry and black-haired, not yet thirty, opened a folder on the desk. He sighed. "Not much of a case. I don't know why they pulled you off whatever you were doing."

"The surveillance continues. Nothing happening at the moment. Let me see." Pascal held out his hand for the folder. He spun it around and skimmed through it. Mathis was right. It was a disagreement between vintners. Probably just a rivalry. These things popped up constantly and were difficult to untangle. He closed the file. "What do you suggest?"

"We go talk to the two old *grincheaux*."

Pascal stood up. "Can you drive? I'm on my moto."

The domaine of the first *grincheau*—a perfect word to describe the curmudgeon who ran the place—was called Château Lemaigre. The old man burst out of the *maison*, wearing a red apron and brandishing a broom as a weapon. He was yelling incoherently. The detectives stayed in Mathis's car until he wore himself out.

Pascal was first to exit, keeping the car door between him and the old man. "Monsieur Lemaigre? We are from the fraud agency. We've come to hear your complaint."

At which point the old man threw the broom to the ground and put a shaky palm to his forehead. He waved them inside the house, shuffling through the doorway.

Mathis took the lead then, using his charm on the man, proposing a drop of wine to calm the nerves.

When the bottle shook in his hands, Mathis took over the pour, giving each of them a taste. They sat at a bruised pine table strewn with breadcrumbs. A jumble of produce was piled in the sink. Pascal saw no evidence of a woman. Did the old man do everything himself? He had to be eighty. Pascal thought about his own bachelor cottage. Enough to make anyone a *grincheau*.

After the proper interval, Mathis began a soft questioning. Monsieur Lemaigre, in control of his temper now, explained that his brother was using the domaine's name on his own vintage, his own bottles, without permission.

"Your brother?" Mathis asked.

Lemaigre waved a hand impatiently. "He has no right to use it as a vintner. This domaine has been in the wine business for sixty years."

"And your brother's vineyard?"

"Two miles to the west."

"I mean," Mathis asked, "how long has he been in business as a vintner?"

The old man scratched his bald scalp, displacing three or four hairs. He shrugged. "No idea." His eyes cut away. He did know.

"When did you take over here?" Mathis asked.

"Nineteen-sixty-two. I've been working hard every day before and since."

"I'm sure," Pascal said. "All by yourself?" He glanced around the kitchen.

Lemaigre's head bobbed. "My wife died fifteen years ago. I hire workers when I can."

Mathis glanced at Pascal then back at the gent. "Are you aware of the social services for—for *les Français?*" '*Of a certain age*' went unsaid.

"I don't need charity," Lemaigre huffed. "I do just fine."

Pascal made a note under the table to call Social Protection. The man needed someone to check in on him at the very least. Family wouldn't be volunteering, apparently. Mathis brought the discussion back to the brother. "What is his name, this brother?"

"Adolphe." He grinned, his face crinkling and exposing a lifetime of dental neglect. "Like Hitler."

They got directions to the brother's vineyard and promised to write up a report of the complaint soon. Pascal dodged his question of 'when exactly.' No one in the Republic promised paperwork at a certain time. "The complaint must be investigated completely," Mathis explained. "That is the only way."

Back in the car, Mathis checked his wristwatch. "*Déjeuner?*"

Pascal agreed to lunch in the small village nearby. There was little on offer but a bakery that made sandwiches, so they took what they could find and ate outside under a plane tree along the road. Then it was off to see Hitler.

The brother's winery, called Domaine Lemaigre, as opposed to Château Lemaigre, looked well-cared-for and prosperous, if equally small. There was a tasting room, freshly painted, with blue shutters. They parked in front of the building and waited for the owner or staff to appear.

"I wonder how old this one will be?" Mathis whispered. Pascal had found that most wineries were run by old men, although more sons and the occasional daughter were taking over now. A middle-aged man with a hard sunburn and straw-colored hair, wearing a blue coverall, exited the house, wiping his mouth on a colorful *serviette* before greeting them.

"Monsieur Lemaigre?" Mathis asked. He nodded, wary. "We are from the Wine Fraud Unit. Your brother has lodged a complaint. I wonder if we can talk inside?"

The man looked stunned. He stepped back as if to avoid a blow. "My brother?"

Mathis glanced at Pascal, who added: "You are Adolphe Lemaigre?"

His shoulders dropped. "Ah. No. That is my father." He glanced behind him. "He is not well."

"Can we speak inside?" Mathis gestured toward the tasting room and the three men tramped over to it. Cool, musty air bathed them as they entered. They settled at a round table at one side of the bar.

"What's he done now?" the younger Lemaigre asked, crossing his arms. He introduced himself was Jean-Loup. He asked to be called Loup. He despised the pretentiousness of double names.

"He says he has the rights to the winery name, Lemaigre," Mathis explained. "Do you know anything about that?"

Loup sighed. "He's been complaining about that for

years, ever since my grandfather split the land between them. We have completely different labels, different varietals, different wines."

"When was the land passed down?" Pascal asked. French inheritance tangles were common. The tales he'd heard.

"*Grand-père* died around 1960. It took some time, they say, to separate the hectares and divide things up."

"What was the vineyard called under your grandfather?" Pascal asked, pen poised. Had they not thought about the confusion of the similar names?

"Simply Lemaigre, Vintner." Loup looked away, frowning. "I might as well tell you." He sighed, laying his hands flat on the table. "My grandfather was German. He called his wine a Spätburgunder, what we call a Pinot Noir. He left Germany to come here, in the twenties."

"Did he return to Germany during the war?" Pascal wondered aloud.

Loup nodded. "He was made to leave. My name originally was Wolfgang. And my father's was Adolphe. He used his middle name, Léopold. Not much of an improvement if you ask me."

"But your last name, it is French, yes?"

"A translation. Our name was Alosen. The fish, like a shad? Known here as *le maigre*. This is common knowledge. My father didn't want anyone to know but it was impossible to hide. Everyone has long memories and *grand-père* was proud, perhaps too proud. My father changed our name to match the vineyard. I am telling no secrets. I am sick of hiding. It is all in the past." He balled his fists on the tabletop. "I was born in France. I *am* French."

Pascal glanced at Mathis. The younger man didn't look at him.

"Did he fight for Germany, your grandfather?" Mathis asked, eyes widening. The World Wars were still an open wound in France.

The vigneron slumped in his chair, his anger gone. "He did." Loup's voice was sad but resigned, his eyes moist. "*Messieurs.* He was a Nazi."

The issue between the brothers over the names of their vineyards, so similar but not unexpected, as it had once been one larger vineyard, went unresolved. The son was told what his uncle was told: investigations would proceed.

In the car, driving back to the city, Mathis was incredulous. "I can't believe he just said all that. That his grandfather was a Nazi, that he gave his son Hitler's name. I find that—horrifying."

Pascal had seen worse over the years. He was rarely surprised by people. Was he cynical in his 'old age'? *Bien sûr.* "When did he return to France?"

"Sometime after 1945. I wonder if he bought the land before the war."

"Or got it cheap when it was all burned out. Or maybe left his wife and children here to tend it? If the sons are elderly now, they must have been born before the war." Pascal glanced at Mathis. "Did the old man not want to meet, or was he really ill?"

"Senile, according to Jean-Loup," Mathis said. "Gone in the head."

It was convenient to hide behind such ailments to avoid confrontations with angry relatives and representatives of the Republic. Another Social Protection call perhaps. He jotted that down and a note to look up names, death dates, and property deeds on the two vineyards.

They were stopped at an intersection outside the city. Pascal looked up just in time to see a green sedan speed by, going north. "That's my car," he shouted. "Follow it. Go, Mathis." As the younger man hesitated, he told him: "It was stolen. Go!"

Mathis hit the accelerator and cranked the wheel left. The BMW was almost out of sight, at the top of a hill. "Catch him, Mathis," Pascal growled.

Mathis punched the gas again and his auto shuddered. "Okay, but how will we stop him?"

He had a point. This was not a patrol car. They had no siren, no flashers, no spike strip. Plus Mathis's little Renault was no match for the BMW. By the time they reached the top of the rise it was out of sight. Maybe left behind that hedgerow. Maybe right around that bend.

Pascal tapped the dash. "We've lost him. You can turn around. At least I know his territory."

Back in Toulouse, Pascal left Mathis at a desk,

researching the history of the Lemaigre vineyards. Pascal found an empty office and used his mobile to contact Social Protection about the brothers. After several transfers he spoke to a woman who said she would take down their information and pass it on.

"Two old *grincheaux*," Pascal explained. "One living alone. Higher priority perhaps, but the other one has health issues associated with aging. He lives with family."

The clerk, Sophie, had a lovely voice. It reminded him of Merle's voice, with a musical quality, soft yet confident. "So, Sophie, can you tell me if there have been home visits with any officials—to the two vineyards? It appears the brothers have been feuding for some time."

"Easy enough," she said, clicking away on a keyboard. "Yes. There have been two visits, both within the last year. Both for Léopold for health checks. The other one, Bernard, nothing. He is a bit younger."

"What are their ages then?"

"Eighty-six and seventy-seven. Perhaps one born before the war, one after?"

"Bernard needs a periodic visit, Sophie, if you can arrange it."

She would get him on a list. Léopold already had a social worker. She promised to confer. Pascal hung up, wanting to talk a little longer. It was ridiculous, how much he missed Merle's voice.

He shook himself and called the *gendarmerie* to report his car stolen from a goat barn. A bit embarrassing, but not so much now that he was sure he'd seen it. The woman who took down his details didn't have anything about her that reminded him of Merle. Just as well. He wanted to ask her to research how many green early 90s BMW sedans were on the roads in France but she hung up abruptly.

Next he called his automobile insurer who told him he must have the police report before he could file a claim. Good old circular bureaucracy. He called the *gendarmes* back and asked to have a report of his stolen vehicle sent to him via email.

Just before five Mathis stood in front of the desk with a sheaf of papers. "What have you found?" Pascal asked. "Sit."

Mathis handed him the paperwork and cleared a pile of journals from a chair so he could sit down. He sighed. "History of the vineyard, before and after it was split." He glanced at the papers. "Take a look."

The first page looked like a scan of an old deed. It was dated 1906. "What's this?"

"The *grand-mère*'s family bought the land in the early days of the century. It stayed in her name until her death."

"Which was when?"

"Nineteen-forty-three."

"During the war? Was she killed?"

Mathis shook his head. "Childbirth, it appears. Birthing Bernard."

Pascal frowned. "In forty-three? So the old man didn't go fight with Hitler?"

"Or came back for a quick visit?" Mathis finished for Pascal. "Apparently not."

Pascal eyed him. "Our Bernard is—"

"Not a Lemaigre." Mathis raised his black eyebrows.

Oh, merde. A fine mess. "Does he know, you think? I don't think we should be the bearers of that news."

"Maybe it's the reason for the animosity. Perhaps the father blamed Bernard for the death of his mother. That happens, I've heard."

Too much conjecture. "But the land was in the wife's name." Pascal peered at the second deed. "Geneviève Crépin. So her estate goes to her children, Adolphe and Bernard. Whether or not they have the same father. So we keep that quiet. It's not our business."

He shuffled through the documents. The death notice for Sören Alosen. The Nazi as he would be known later. Born somewhere in *l'Allemagne* and died in France, at a hospital in Toulouse, in 1961. No cause of death given. He was fifty-six years old. "Any actual evidence that he fought for Hitler?"

Mathis had been thorough. Or curious. He had found a short newspaper account, in German, of the death of Geneviève Crépin. According to the article, she gave birth to a boy then died three days later. Her husband, Sören Alosen, was away, serving in special forces for the Third Reich. Pascal's eyebrows rose. "Does that mean he was an SS officer?"

Mathis shrugged. "Probably."

"Just as well she didn't survive, she would have been branded a collaborator. Can you imagine growing up in France with a father everyone knew was not only a Nazi but the worst type?"

"No." Mathis had reddened with anger and Pascal remembered he was Jewish.

"It's a wonder he wasn't arrested for war crimes."

"Maybe because he didn't try to hide it? He was very generous to charities in the area, it says in his death notice. Maybe he rehabilitated his reputation. They didn't even mention his service under Hitler in his own obituary."

Pascal stacked the documents. "Anything else I should look at?" He handed the pages back.

Mathis flipped to the last page and plucked it out. "This one."

Pascal skimmed the document. This police report was more recent, dated October 2006. Concerning the younger brother.

"***Gendarmes* were called to the home of Bernard Lemaigre**, outside the village of l'Aussounnelle, approximately 23:00. Upon arrival two officers found M. Lemaigre sitting outside the house in his dressing gown. He was distraught and speaking rapidly. Officers calmed him and understood that something had occurred in the house in relation to his wife. Madame Lemaigre was found in an upstairs bedroom, unresponsive. Ambulance services were called. They arrived approximately 1:00. Medics were unable to resuscitate Madame.

Officers encouraged Monsieur to dress then took him to the gendarmerie in Pibrac. He called his daughter in Paris. They took his statement and released him. He was given a ride home."

"What happened to Madame?" Pascal asked.
"On the reverse," Mathis replied.

"Statement of Bernard Lemaigre. October 8, 2006. *Ma femme et moi* —my wife and I—we argued. It was at dinner, which she prepared very badly by the way. Her usual. The argument was nothing unusual. Some words, of course. But no blows, no spits, no violence, nothing. She went to bed early. I decided to sleep in my daughter's room. I didn't want to argue any more. I stayed up for a while, cooling off, having a cognac. Then I went upstairs to sleep but saw the light was still on in my wife's bedroom, *our* bedroom. It was very late. She had gone up several hours earlier. I pushed the door open slightly to peer in. Make sure she wasn't crying, as you do. I saw her as you found her, sprawled on the coverlet. No pulse. I called the emergency line. You know the rest."

"Not very distraught by then, apparently." Pascal sat back. He handed Mathis the page.

"What do you think? He didn't mention a daughter at the vineyard."

Pascal shrugged. "Maybe they no longer speak."

"Because she blames him for the mother's death?" Mathis speculated. He was full of speculations.

"Possible. Or he's a *grincheau* that she can't abide. Did you find out her name?"

"Not yet. I was more concerned with the wife's death. It was ruled accidental, no known cause. That seems odd."

Pascal frowned. "How did she die then? Stroke? Heart attack?"

Mathis shrugged. "No post-mortem."

Pascal told him to do a little more digging tomorrow. Find the daughter and whoever examined the body of Madame. "Probably nothing. After all these years."

How it related to his brother's vineyard was a mystery. But Pascal had always followed his instincts, even when they led him down random paths. He left Mathis at his computer and found a bistro nearby for dinner. It was early, not yet dark this near the solstice. The streets were full of students and tourists and office workers, ready for a bite of delicious cuisine, a glass of wine, and a laugh to put the shine on another warm summer day.

As he mopped up the juices on his plate with the heel of the baguette, Pascal felt a pang. It was sudden, and slightly painful in his chest, and he sat back, catching his breath. What was it? He swallowed the bread. Around him couples ate and drank, as usual.

And as usual he was alone. This had never bothered him, at least for many years. He enjoyed the uncomplicated life, free of drama, chores, responsibilities, hysterics.

Free, also, of companionship. The sounds around him—chatter, laughter, the clinking of glasses—dimmed for a moment and he realized what the pang was.

He was lonely.

That evening he drove back to Château Lemaigre. He wondered about the old man, who technically wasn't terribly old, still in his seventies. He acted like an old man though—suspicious, obnoxious, and meddlesome. Exactly the type of man Pascal's own father would have been, had he not died early, at sixty-one.

Perhaps, he thought as he drove down the dirt lane and parked by the *mas*, that was why Lemaigre irritated him. Pascal had done his best to not end up bitter and sour like his old man.

He got off his moto in the twilight. The sky had faded from orange to purple in the hills beyond the vines. The thought jumped into his mind, rather insistently: *I am not my father.* But really, how different was he? Yes, his father had married twice and had four children by the time he was the same age as Pascal was now. Like old Lemaigre, he had missed the war but felt its effects. But as a man, how was Pascal really different from *le père?* In the old photos they looked so much alike. The thought unsettled him.

Bernard Lemaigre didn't answer the knock. Was he

still toiling in the vines? All the windows were dark. Pascal checked his wristwatch. Nine o'clock. High time for sleep for old men.

In the office the next morning, Pascal found Mathis at the computer, looking far too lively for the hour. Pascal had gone back to his cottage last night, managed a little sleep, then was up with the goats. He was now nursing a coffee from the machine in the outer office and cursing its small size as well as the pain in his back.

"Ah," Mathis said, glancing at him then back to the screen. "I have found the daughter." The printer began to whir in the next room and Pascal walked over to retrieve the printout.

The form was a revenue bill in the name of Corinne Botrel. She had a Paris address at the time of the bill—ten years earlier. Pascal walked back to Mathis. "Nothing more recent?"

The printer came to life again. When it finished, there were three new sheets for Pascal. A birth certificate for Corinne naming her mother as Éliane Lemaigre and her father as Bernard Lemaigre. On the next sheet Corinne applied for a name change to Botrel in 2007. The last sheet was another application, also quite dated, for a spot in an *école maternelle*, the state-supported nursery school, for a child named Lola. Only the mother's name was on the application.

"Where is this *maternelle* then?" Pascal waved the sheet at Mathis.

"Close by. Pibrac."

"Still nothing in the present?"

Mathis shook his head. "Perhaps she changed her name again?"

"Let's take a ride," Pascal said, pulling his leather jacket back on.

In Mathis's Renault, Pascal remarked, "Do you find the timing interesting? Corinne changes her name around the time her mother dies. Was she waiting for that moment? Did she have something to do with her mother's death? Does she know something about Bernard? Perhaps to punish him? We only have the old man's word that he called her in Paris. She could have been anywhere. At home even."

The *école maternelle* was attached to a primary school on the north side of Pibrac. New neighborhoods had sprouted up since Pascal was last in the area. Mathis told him it was overflow from a nearby town with many aviation companies headquartered there. The sounds of the schoolyard, so similar everywhere, floated over the low brick buildings. They found the office and when the director of the *école maternelle* was located, they showed their identifications. Her eyes widened as she led them into her office and shut the door.

Mathis turned on his charm, explaining why they were here, simply looking for an address of a former student's parent. "Madame Corinne Botrel. Or perhaps Lemaigre, as she was known."

The light of recognition shone on the director's face. "Ah, yes, Corinne. She's not in any trouble, is she?"

Pascal smiled reassuringly. "No trouble at all. Just some loose ends we're tying up with her family vineyard."

The director, an energetic fiftyish woman with a bob of auburn hair, rose from her office chair and walked back into reception. In a moment she returned with a file card in hand. She frowned at the card as she returned to her chair. "I see she was officially Corinne Botrel, yes. I forgot that." She smiled at the men. "The last address I have for her is Domaine Lemaigre, near l'Aussounnelle, I believe."

Mathis nodded then squinted at her. "*Domaine*, you say. Not Château?"

She flipped the card for them to read. Definitely Domaine Lemaigre.

"Her uncle's vineyard then," Pascal added. "Not her father's. The names are confusing. So similar."

The director smiled professionally. "I don't know, monsieur. All I have is the card."

They thanked the woman and were back in the Renault in record time. "Now what?" Mathis asked. "She lives with the uncle?"

"Could she be taking care of him in his infirmity?" Pascal asked. He didn't think that was it, but who knew?

"Maybe the director wrote it wrong. It happens."

"There was no woman living with Bernard. He is alone, I'm certain of that."

Mathis turned the key and backed out onto the street. "It's all very cozy, isn't it."

Pascal lowered his sunglasses. "Time for a chat."

They reached Domaine Lemaigre before noon, driving into the quiet courtyard again. It occurred to Pascal that this brother, Adolphe *aka* Léopold, had inherited the original vineyard's house. As the older brother probably, but had that been a sticking point? Had Bernard only received the land and vines for his half?

Again, no one appeared to greet them or give them a taste of product. The investigators walked to the door of the large farmhouse, built of stone at least a century earlier with a heavy wooden door and an iron knocker. Mathis employed that, rapping loudly. Soon footsteps could be heard and the door creaked open.

A young girl stood there, about twelve or thirteen, Pascal guessed, with long blond hair cascading over her shoulders, blue eyes, and a sweet face with freckles. She eyed them silently.

"Mademoiselle," Pascal murmured. "We are wine fraud detectives from Toulouse. We spoke to Jean-Loup the other day. We've returned to have a word with Corinne, if she's available."

No look of surprise so Corinne *did* live here. The girl hesitated then said, "I'll see. Wait here." She shut the door.

Mathis turned to survey the vineyard, which was planted right up to the house on at least one side. He stepped over to examine the grapes and was sniffing them when the girl returned. She frowned, glancing at Mathis. She turned to Pascal. "Wait there, in the tasting room."

The men took up chairs in the tasting room and settled in. Mathis did more observing inside. "Do they do tastings? Perhaps with the old man's illness, they've stopped doing so?"

Pascal ran a finger through the dust on the round table. "Business is down, for sure."

They didn't wait long. A few minutes passed before a tall, blond woman pushed through the door. Her face was tanned by the sun, and aged as well, if Pascal was any judge of these things. She could be anywhere from thirty to fifty. She wore a dirty apron over a shapeless blue dress with ties at the collar. Her hands were rough and chapped. Her hair was pulled back haphazardly. She looked tired, with dark circles under her eyes. She barely smiled at them as she sat down, as if expecting an interrogation.

"Madame," Pascal began. "I am Pascal d'Onscon, and this is my partner, Mathis Cochet. We are wine fraud investigators. Your father, I believe, is Bernard Lemaigre?"

She shrugged and crossed her arms. She still had said nothing.

Pascal continued. "He has filed a complaint against his brother for using the name Lemaigre on his bottles. Are you aware of this?"

She finally spoke. "The complaint? Yes, Loup told me."

"What is your view then, of the dispute?"

"It is stupid. It is nothing new." She squirmed for a second and recrossed her arms.

"Have you spoken to your father about it?" Mathis asked.

"No." She pressed her lips together.

"Do you speak to your father?" Pascal asked gently.

Her eyes darted toward him. "Not often."

Pascal wanted to ask about her mother's death but it seemed too soon. She was wary. "And what is your role here at Domaine Lemaigre? Do you work here?" He glanced at her work apron. She nodded silently. "Taking care of your uncle?"

She winced. "Léopold is not related to me by blood. You are aware, I'm sure."

"How is Léopold? Is he well?" Pascal asked.

"No. He is far gone, if you must know. The doctor says he has weeks at the most."

"My condolences to the family." Pascal leaned forward. "You say he's not related to you by blood. Is he related some other way?"

She exhaled and looked at the ceiling. "He is my father-in-law in a way. Jean-Loup and I—we are not married but it is France after all. You can figure it out."

"He is your cousin, yes?" Mathis struggled to keep his voice neutral. "Your first cousin? And the girl, she is your child with Jean-Loup?"

Corinne set her jaw. "We are half-cousins, if it's any business of yours. My father and Léopold were half-brothers, a fact that didn't come out until their father died. It was a bit of a shock to all of them."

Pascal sent Mathis a warning look. "We became aware of this, Madame. I'm sorry to bring up painful memories."

Corinne huffed. "Painful? No."

"Your father, he didn't spread the news far and wide about Léopold being only a half-brother when he found out?"

"I suppose he did. I wasn't born yet."

"How did your parents meet, madame?" Pascal asked.

She frowned again. "Why? My mother is dead."

"A tragic loss to you, I'm sure. My sympathies." She frowned. He continued: "Do you think your grandfather was aware of Bernard's parentage—he must have been if he was away during the war and his wife had a child."

"By all accounts he was a bitter, horrible man, and, yes, a Nazi. I'm sure he knew. He was many things, I'm told, but not stupid."

"Yet he withheld that information from your father and Léopold."

"Loup says his grandfather wanted to keep the vineyard for himself. His name was never on the documents. Our grandmother owned the property." She seemed to relax finally, letting out the family secrets. "The sons were old enough to take over but he didn't want them to. Especially Bernard, of course."

"Because he was not his son?"

She shrugged.

"Your father told you this? Did your mother also know?"

"Of course."

"When did your parents marry?"

She paused to think. "Around 1970, I think."

Pascal glanced at Mathis. It was his turn. "We read the police account of your mother's death. We're terribly sorry and don't mean to pry into your private lives."

Corinne raised her eyebrows. "But—?"

Mathis tried to look even sorrier. "*Pardon*, madame, but the animosity between the brothers has brought a small light onto those proceedings. If you don't mind, we'd like to ask you a few questions about the event."

She sighed. "*D'accord.*" She glanced at her watch. "But I must go to the house soon."

Mathis smiled cordially then launched in. "The statement your father made said he called you that night, and that you were in Paris. Is that true?"

"I was in Paris. But he did not call me. Jean-Loup called me."

"Did you question your father or anyone else about the events of that night?"

"What does this have to do with the name of the vineyard?" she asked angrily.

"We are just trying to understand the dynamic between the two families, madame. That is all."

She glared at Mathis then spoke again. "I talked to my father after I got over the shock. He said my mother died, alone, in her room. He would not allow an autopsy. He said he wanted to honor her for religious reasons, but I was not convinced. They quarreled like mad idiots, constantly. Certainly my mother felt trapped. I left home as soon as I could."

Mathis sat back and looked at Pascal, passing the baton. "Do you think there was foul play?" Pascal asked. "That someone harmed your mother?"

"Someone? You mean, my father? I would not put it past him. Somehow he convinced everyone he was a blameless old fool so there was no investigation at all."

"What did Jean-Loup tell you, besides that your mother was deceased?" Pascal asked.

"That night? Not much. But later Jean-Loup told me there was bad blood between the brothers," she said without emotion. "That he suspected my parents were arguing about Léopold. That he spent a good bit of time over there with my mother."

She looked into Pascal's eyes, begging him not to make her spell it out, that her father suspected an intimacy between her mother and his half-brother. He nodded. "I see."

"Could Léopold have been at their house that night? Maybe your mother called him?" Mathis speculated.

"It's possible. But he wouldn't have harmed her, I'm sure. Before all this, before his decline, he was a—what do they say—a teddy bear. Very sweet tempered. My father must have got his charming personality from whoever *his* father was. But at least he wasn't a Nazi."

"Did both brothers change their names to Lemaigre after your grandfather died?" Pascal asked.

"Before. They wanted to shame him. Show independence, tell the villagers there was distance between them and the old Nazi. So when Léopold turned twenty-one, he changed his name and petitioned the court on Bernard's behalf, too." She looked up. "I changed my name as well. I know how they must have felt."

"How does your father feel about you joining this family, here, with your uncle?"

Her eyes flashed angrily at Pascal. "I don't care how he feels. I'm sure he concocted this little exercise for you because he wants to provoke me or Jean-Loup. But he is dead to me."

"Madame," Mathis said softly after her words faded. "*Juste une idée.* It is not too late to reopen your mother's case. To find out perhaps if she was killed by—poison for instance."

She rubbed the heels of her hands into her eye sockets and sighed. "*Merde.* There is nothing I'd hate more." She stood up. "I know he killed her. I just can't prove it." She turned and walked out.

The two men walked in silence to the Renault. As Pascal snapped his seatbelt on he muttered, "*She* can't prove it but I know someone who can."

They drove down the country road toward Toulouse, ruminating on their next move. Pascal stopped Mathis with a tap to his arm. This intersection was where they saw the BMW.

LISE MCCLENDON

"Will you indulge me, Mathis? Go on a car-finding mission?" Pascal raised his sunglasses. "No high speeds required. In fact the slower, the better."

Mathis followed instructions, turning left onto the larger, but still two-lane, road. At the top of the hill he slowed. "Which way?"

"Left." The car pointed down a hedge-lined narrow road. "Slow down at the lanes."

Mathis poked along, taking his foot off the accelerator at each gate so Pascal could try to get a look beyond. They drove that way for five miles without success.

"Turn around. Let's try the other direction," Pascal instructed.

Retracing their route, Mathis turned left at the main road. It wound off to the right, past a large villa and more vineyards, then an orchard of walnut trees, a sheep pasture, and more grapevines. "More prosperous over here," Pascal noted.

"Maybe they can buy their own cars," Mathis said with a smile.

They traveled on almost seven miles when it happened. An old green BMW sedan appeared at the opening of a wooded lane, poking its nose out like a lizard testing the air. "*Mon dieu.* The luck. Keep going," Pascal said. "But slowly." Mathis crept along at twenty kilometers per hour. "Not that slowly," Pascal whispered. "Don't be conspicuous."

They passed the car, idling at the edge of the roadway in the drive. Beyond the car was an ancient wrought iron gate hanging crookedly and, in the distance, a farmhouse. The driver's face was obscured by shadow; only the knuckles of his hands on the steering wheel were visible. As soon as they passed, the BMW turned out into the road and sped away in the direction of Toulouse. Mathis kept driving away until Pascal stopped him.

"Okay. Well done." Pascal scribbled it into his notebook. "He's changed the plates. Now turn around somewhere."

Mathis turned the Renault around in the weeds. At the driveway where the BMW had appeared, Pascal asked him to stop. Once out of the car, Pascal took several photos with his phone of the mailbox, the gate, and the house. Over the arched gate were rusted letters that were hard to read. Mathis squinted into the sun and made out 'Villa Blanche-Rose.' Pascal walked up to the open gate and snapped a few more photos of the unkempt yard, overgrown hedges, and limp field of weeds and lavender. He returned to the car.

"Good work, *mon ami*," he said, snapping on his seat belt again. "Back to the city."

After Mathis parked his car behind the office complex, Pascal told him they would go the *gendarmerie* first. "Two inquiries: Madame and the BMW."

But, being Frenchmen, they realized it was time for *déjeuner*. No one would be in their offices, at least not the

people they needed to speak to. So they took themselves
to a small bistro on a side street that Mathis frequented.
The staff knew him by name and brought him a cool
glass of Sancerre without his ordering it. Pascal ordered
one as well and they had a pleasant, if rushed, meal.

"We will split up, eh?" Pascal told Mathis as they
pushed through the modern doors of the *Police Nationale*
building. They showed their warrant cards to the man
at the front desk and were directed through to the
offices beyond. "You go to the brigade liaison. They
have one here, I assume?" The brigades were small
groups of detectives that moved around the country to
solve suspicious deaths and other heinous crimes, with
headquarters in Paris and satellite offices around the
country.

"I know the man," Mathis said. "He works with
BRI."

"I'll find someone to report about my car." Pascal
glanced about at the desks, then at the line of offices on
the sides. Mathis walked away. Pascal asked the first
person he found where he should report a sighting of
his stolen vehicle. The woman, short and dark and
young, in a *gendarme* uniform, straightened and stood at
her desk.

"I believe I can help you, monsieur."

After he had filled out the form, transferred the
photos to the gendarme's email, and given every last
detail he could think of, he thanked the woman and
went in search of Mathis. He sat across a desk in a side
office with the nameplate of E. Clérico: BRI on the

door. BRI was the acronym for the *Brigade Recherche et d'Intervention*, or Investigation and Intervention Brigade, a department that investigated all sorts of serious crimes, from human trafficking and gangs to burglary and murder.

"*Messieurs.*" Pascal nodded. He offered his hand to the detective and introduced himself. There was no second chair so he leaned against the wall to listen to the explanation Mathis was giving. It appeared he had just finished. Clérico sat back, arms crossed, looking unconvinced.

"I was just telling him, d'Onscon, that quite a bit of new information has come to light," Mathis said, his voice betraying a nervousness. Perhaps he was younger than Pascal imagined. Or had never come across a possible murder before. Pascal hoped he had not been too generous with his speculations.

Pascal began: "That's right—detective, is it?"

"Lieutenant, monsieur. In the BRI here in Toulouse." He was a stout man with a closely-cropped head of brown hair, jowls, and small eyes. "This case has been closed for fifteen years. It would take more than a few cross words between relatives to open it, as I explained to your colleague."

"*Pardon*, lieutenant." Pascal put his hand on his heart and tucked his chin. This humility stance sometimes worked. "We are but wine fraud investigators. Wine is our business but we are inquisitive by nature. It is in our blood and our training. We were called in to mediate a dispute between two brothers over the labels of their wines. As we dug into the controversy, we uncovered what we believe may be a suspicious death." He paused, letting that characterization of Madame Lemaigre's death settle.

"Quite suspicious," Mathis muttered.

"The animosity between the families is profound, monsieur," Pascal continued. "They each inherited half of their late father's vineyard, although in truth it was their late mother's."

"One brother had a different father," Mathis interjected.

"And one brother got all the structures, it appears. But the inheritance is not the issue. It has come to light that the wife of one brother was perhaps too close to the other brother. This was suggested by family members. Madame argues with her husband, perhaps about her liaison with the brother, and within hours she is dead. No known cause. No post-mortem. How could it be natural or an accident? There is not a scratch on her. It is worth at the very least some interviews, *oui?*"

Clérico made a disparaging noise. "For what purpose? A disagreement between brothers or a marital spat is hardly proof of murder."

Pascal shrugged. "You will never know unless you do some digging yourself. I'm sure you too are inquisitive. This is indeed new evidence, monsieur. A woman who could be your own mother has died mysteriously. Why no post-mortem? Send your thoughts up the chain of command. Give the woman a chance at the justice she deserves."

"All right." The lieutenant slapped both palms on his desk and stood up. "I will look at the old records and see if there is anything to send on. *Merci, messieurs.* You have done your duty." He waved them out.

On the sidewalk, Mathis hung his head. "Well, we tried. I doubt anything will come of it. How did you make out with your stolen auto?"

"Much better. I expect it returned very soon." Pascal slapped the younger man on the back. "But what are we going to report about this Lemaigre winery business?"

Back in the offices of the Wine Fraud Division, they discussed the issues. They looked up the applicable laws on labeling. And wrote a short report to their superiors that there was no crime in naming your wine similarly to your neighbor's, whether he is your brother or not, if there is no intent to deceive the consumer. The labels were not at all similar. And there appeared to be personal issues behind the request for an investigation.

Pascal slept on the sofa at Mathis's tiny flat in Toulouse that night. In the morning he proposed to the younger detective that Mathis buy the motorcycle that hurt his back and nether regions. He was done with it. They agreed on a price and both were happy.

Just before noon that day, Pascal received a phone call. His car had been recovered and the thief arrested at Villa Blanche-Rose, an abandoned estate where he had been squatting for many months. He was a known offender who had been hiding there. It might be hard to get rid of a tenant in France, legal or illegal, but let him steal a car and it is over in a flash.

Driving his BMW out of Toulouse that afternoon Pascal didn't head toward his cottage. He just wanted to be back in the Dordogne. His crazy obsession, his infatuation with Merle, had not abated. It would not do. He had to go back and deal with it, somehow. But one task remained: he called his neighbor, Irene, as he drove.

"I am in my auto, Irene. It has been recovered."

She nearly screamed with relief. "Oh, I am so glad. It is fine? No damage by the dirty thief?"

"It appears he loved it as much as I do."

"Will you have dinner with us tonight to celebrate? My cousin Jacques is joining us. He sells the *crottins* for me at markets. You know him."

"Ah, tell Jacques *allo* for me. Have a wonderful dinner *en famille*. I must go back to my assignment in the Dordogne."

"And what is this assignment, Pascal?" Her voice turned cagey and sweet. "Does it involve a *femme fatale*?"

Pascal laughed, turning onto the toll road and hitting the gas. At least the thief had taken care of the car. Even the oil level was good. The old BMW roared forward.

"Ah, Irene, there is always a *femme* involved for me." He laughed again because it was not true for many years but now, remarkably, it was true.

It would take the French bureaucracy several months to order the investigation into the death of Madame Lemaigre reopened. Bernard was very vocal in his opposition but in the end he lost that battle, and raised a few eyebrows in the process. Another month or two and the body was exhumed. A post-mortem on the remains revealed a high dose of tranquilizers, enough to render a woman her size unconscious. Enough to kill her? Maybe not. But the *policiers* and the Republic charged Bernard with homicide and planned to show that he had drugged and smothered his wife after he found she was unfaithful to him.

Unfortunately, Léopold could not testify. He had lost his memory long before. He died in his sleep a month after Pascal and Mathis visited the winery.

Bernard Lemaigre professed his innocence right up to the day he was convicted of manslaughter and sent to prison for eight years, what would probably be the rest of his life.

Corinne and Jean-Loup reunited the two wineries, creating a new label for the new vineyard. They named it after their daughter, Lola, formally Félicité, and their grandmother, Geneviève, skipping the troublesome generations. Vignoble Félicité-Geneviève was announced with a large wrought iron sign displaying the letters 'F' and 'G.'

Pascal was not aware—*bien sûr*—of these events that would enfold when he drove back to Malcouziac that bright summer day. There was, as yet, no sense of justice served, only a hope of it. He parked in the city lot outside the walls, spent fifteen minutes examining every nook and cranny of his beloved auto, looked under the hood, checked the trunk for contraband, polished the chrome, and finally locked it up.

As he strode through the narrow stone gate of the old bastide wall he thought of Merle and felt a lightness to his step. What would happen? He had no idea and yet he couldn't stop smiling.

——◄•●•►——

About the Author

Lise McClendon is the author of numerous novels, short stories, and articles, including the Bennett Sisters, Jackson Hole, and Swing Town mystery series. Her latest Bennett Sisters mystery is 'Here There and Everywhere.' Her short story, 'Forked Tongue,' was included in the Anthony-winning anthology, *The Obama Inheritance*. She has served on the national boards of directors for Mystery Writers of America and the International Association of Crime Writers/North America. She is on the faculty of the Jackson Hole Writers Conference. Get a free Bennett Sisters French cookbook at **www.lisemcclendon.com**. Follow her on Facebook, Amazon, and BookBub.

Inventions Can Be Murder

A CHARLIE PARKER SHORT STORY

Connie Shelton

I f I hadn't given Sally a ride to work that day we might never have been dragged into a new investigation in the first place. But the moment we pulled onto the street where our RJP Investigations offices reside, it was clear from the hubbub that something bad was going on. An ambulance was backed into the driveway of the place directly across the street from ours, with two patrol cars angled to the curb, lights strobing their red-and-blue flashes all over the place. But the two vehicles that concerned me the most were the wagon from the Office of the Medical Investigator and the plain gray sedan I recognized as belonging to Kent Taylor, Homicide Detective with Albuquerque PD.

I slowed to a crawl and edged my Jeep into the driveway at RJP. The neighborhood is a mix of residential and commercial, with most of the latter being small offices such as ours. My brother and I bought the gray and white Victorian house and converted it several years ago—Ron being a licensed private investigator and me being the accountant for our partnership. Sally Bertrand is our part-time receptionist. It's one of the larger places on the block, and most of the neighboring houses are still single-family homes, including the one with all the action across the way.

I turned to my spaniel pup in the back seat. "Freckles, be a good girl and wait here." Sally and I climbed out of the Jeep, just as the ambulance left, in time to spot Detective Taylor heading toward his car. Okay, I know it's really none of my business but I couldn't resist crossing the street to ask him what was going on. Understand, Kent and I kind of have a history, as he has arrested me on an occasion or two and has repeatedly requested that I not butt into his active homicide investigations. Call me a slow learner.

Taylor turned as I approached. "Charlie." He gave Sally a brief smile.

"Don't chase me off just yet, Kent. Come on, obviously something's happened and it's right here. I have to know."

"Well, you don't *have* to, but I can give you the basics so you'll leave me alone." He tossed his jacket into the car, as the early morning chill was disappearing into a full-blown glorious September day. "We got a frantic call from a woman who claims she and her boss were guests here, she got up this morning, discovered him downstairs in the kitchen, half dressed and dead."

"They don't call homicide unless it's ..."

"I wasn't finished. EMTs showed up first, couldn't immediately establish the cause of death, so the OMI and I got the next set of calls. Ernie's in there with the victim now. I gotta get back."

"I'm pretty sure the resident is an older woman who lives alone here," I told him. "Were the guests related to her?"

"I'm still taking statements, but that's not my impression. The victim is a professor from the UNM campus up near Taos. His assistant is pretty shaken up, so I'm getting the story in bits and pieces."

"Professor Elbert Lindsay?" Sally's voice came out as a croak.

Taylor's gaze darted to her. "You know him?"

"My husband and I attended his lecture last night at Popejoy Hall. He's brilliant. Oh my gosh, you're saying he's dead?"

I turned my attention toward her and saw that her face had gone white as a sheet of paper. Her many freckles stood out like ginger-colored dots, and even her blonde hair seemed paler than normal. Her lips were trembling and tears had begun to pool in her eyes.

"Sally? Maybe we should go in the office and get you some water."

She shook her head. "How did he die? I just can't believe this."

Taylor pulled out his little spiral notebook as I took Sally's freezing cold hand and rubbed it. "What can you tell me about this lecture?" he asked.

She stared toward the front door of the house where a gurney was being wheeled out.

"He spoke about new innovations in epilepsy treatment. Our oldest son is having some—anyway, Professor Lindsay is one of the leading experts, doing a summer stint of teaching for UNM ... I think it's just for this summer, and he's leaving to go back to Boston in a week or so. *Was* leaving." She swallowed, hard.

"Was there any kind of disagreement or disruption during the lecture?" he asked.

"No, the evening went well. The professor took questions afterward. I didn't get the chance to speak directly with him, but his assistant was gracious and visited with me. Oh! You said his assistant discovered his body. Was that Ainsley Jones? She was so sweet to me. Could I...?"

Without really waiting for permission Sally ducked past Kent and rushed up to the covered porch of the blue house. The gurney was in the driveway now and a young woman with blonde curls, wearing yoga pants and an overly large t-shirt, had just stepped out of the house. She stared after the covered body through shell-shocked eyes.

"Ainsley! It's Sally, from last night." The two hugged each other, rocking side to side.

Kent seemed torn between heading up there after Sally and just giving them a moment.

"You didn't answer her question, Kent. How did the professor die?"

He shrugged. "No outward signs of violence. My

guess is the medical investigator will find it was a heart attack or stroke or something. It just seemed strange to him, and that's why I was called. The victim was in the kitchen, seemingly in the middle of making a cup of chamomile tea, but his pants were down around his ankles. Weird. You either walk around in the house in your boxers, or you have the pants on. Why were they down? And I found three cups in the sink, with traces of coffee in them. Someone other than the older man and his assistant were present but I can't get much out of her. Maybe she'll say something to Sally."

My mind raced through a bunch of possibilities as to why a man might be in the process of removing his pants, but most of those actions wouldn't take place in the kitchen of someone else's home. I glanced up at the porch as Ernie Tafoya, the medical investigator, and his assistant pulled away from the house. Sally and Ainsley Jones were still on the steps, talking quietly.

Without actually conferring about the matter, Kent and I strolled toward them and he suggested we all sit down. Ainsley and Sally took the porch swing. Taylor and I settled into a pair of wicker chairs opposite them.

"You'd never guess Dr. Lindsay was famous," Ainsley was saying. "He was very quiet, somewhat reclusive in his personal life, lived alone, worked in his laboratory most of the time. This summer program in New Mexico was unusual for him, I gathered. He mentioned to me on the plane flight out, back in June, that he was giving himself the trip as a bonus for having made a breakthrough in his research."

"What was he working on?" Kent sat with pencil poised above notebook.

"It's something complicated," she said with a sigh. "I don't really understand it."

"His lecture last night was about new developments in the treatment of epilepsy in kids." Sally turned toward Kent. "My son's condition hasn't responded well to medications, so we're looking at options."

"It's some kind of device, he's been working on in his lab," Ainsley said. "All very secretive until he gets it patented, I think."

"I loved what he had to say, but must admit I didn't understand half of it," Sally admitted.

Kent stood. "Well, it's irrelevant until the medical investigator comes back with his ruling. Based on our conversation when I arrived, it's sounding like a probable heart attack or something like that." He turned to Ainsley again. "I'm sorry for your loss."

He gave me a look, like *take it from here* before he walked down to his car and got inside. He's a good detective, not so great with hand-holding or dealing with someone's grief. I felt for the assistant. Here she was in a strange city, far from Boston, her boss just died, and she didn't know what to do.

"Let's walk over to our office," I suggested. "We've got coffee or tea, and I brought blueberry muffins my neighbor sent with me."

Sally wrapped an arm around Ainsley's shoulders as we left. Both of them seemed a bit dazed, still. I got the muffins out of my car, went inside, and set the kettle to heat while Sally went to her desk to call about the status of her minivan at the repair shop. By the time we settled at the kitchen table with mugs of tea, I noticed both of them had a little more color in their cheeks.

"I should probably make some calls," Ainsley said, "but I just don't know how to begin. Everyone he worked with will be devastated, both in Boston and New Mexico. Well, okay, maybe not the lady at the bakery in Taos—they had words. Ugh, I need to drive back up there to pack my things. And his things, I suppose. There's no one else to do it."

"At least the summer term already ended. There won't be staff and students expecting him back in class there." I realized that wasn't a very caring thing to say, so I switched paths. "Did he have health issues?"

She shook her head sadly. "No. That's the thing that makes this so unbelievable. He had a complete physical three months ago and passed all the tests brilliantly. He was an older man, yes, but healthy."

"Sixty-three is hardly ancient," Sally interjected. "Um, I remember it from the program. Same age as my dad, and he's out on the hiking trails every weekend."

We all nodded silently. I helped myself to a second muffin.

Ainsley's phone rang and she fished it from her pants pocket. Frowning at the screen, she answered. "Oh, yes, Mrs. Guthrie. You are? Oh. Right." She listened and hung up. "She's heard about Dr. Lindsay. She's home now, so I'd better go back over there." She rose from her chair and gave a nod toward the front of the office.

I was embarrassed to admit I didn't even know the name of the woman who lived directly across the street. I'm terrible. My sleuthing mind, however, did put it together that Ainsley was not related, or particularly close, to the neighbor. She wouldn't have addressed her so formally.

"Clara Guthrie is the one who organized last night's event, isn't she?" Sally asked. "She introduced Dr. Lindsay on stage."

"Right." Something about Ainsley's demeanor said there was more.

We all figured that out as soon as we watched the younger woman cross the street, where Clara Guthrie met her on the porch and proceeded to address her with animated talk and a shaking finger in her face. Sally and I looked at each other, incredulous. The young woman's boss had just died, and she was getting chewed out. No sympathy?

I grabbed the doorknob, ready to blast over there, but Sally put a hand on my arm. "She's like that. She'll settle down."

At least Ainsley had an escape. Her rental car was gone from the driveway when I looked out again, ten minutes later.

~

Three days went by, during which I did my normal accountant thing, billing clients, making bank deposits, and other such mundane tasks. Ron had been in and out. He does a lot of background checks for corporate clients these days. The market for private investigators to track wayward spouses has largely gone away now that people spy on their partners with tracking apps, and everyone has a phone camera to catch them in the act. I, for one, am glad for the loss of that type of business.

I was loading my purse, my little spaniel Freckles at my side, when Sally showed up at my office door.

"Ainsley Jones is on line one. She says she's spoken with Kent Taylor and wants to pass along what he told her."

I raised an eyebrow, questioning.

"It was a heart attack, apparently. But if you could just talk to her?" Sally ducked away before I could come up with an excuse.

"Ainsley—I hope you're doing all right?"

"I don't know. Did Sally tell you, the police have ruled Dr. Lindsay's death was natural causes."

"She said, yes. She told me you had talked with Detective Taylor."

"Yeah, see, that's the thing. His department isn't going to investigate."

"Well, it's hard news to digest, but sometimes an otherwise healthy person can simply have a heart attack."

"I really believe that's not the case. There's more to

it, I'm sure."

How can you be so sure? I wanted to ask but it seemed callous to ignore her feelings. "I can call Kent and see if there's something he's not telling you. Although, don't be surprised if he won't tell me either."

"Thanks, Charlie. Anything you can learn will help put my mind at rest. Meanwhile, I'm back in Boston. I just threw all of the professor's things into his suitcase and brought everything back here. Since he has no immediate family, and his personal possessions will be collected by a cousin, I think I'd better take a few days to separate out his work papers and figure out what to do. It's just so sad that he was on the brink of this breakthrough and I don't want to see all of his work lost."

It was sad. I told her I'd get back if Kent Taylor offered any new information about her boss's death. But when I phoned him, Taylor's input didn't change anything.

"The MI's office made their ruling. I asked about possible poisoning, allergic reactions, all of that. Ernie told me he personally reviewed the other pathologist's reports. They ran the standard tox screens for drugs and poisonous substances. Didn't find a thing. Sometimes a person's heart just stops. It could have been a sudden onset heart attack; he didn't find the kind of damage that would indicate a chronic condition. Sorry, I don't have any more than that, and I do have a full caseload right now. This one just doesn't merit a lot more of the department's attention."

I thanked him and hung up. Ainsley was still in the denial phase of her grieving; at some point she would come to terms with it. I stuffed my phone in my bag, switched off my computer, and called out to Freckles with the magic word 'go.'

An hour later, I was watching the dog race around our small neighborhood park, chasing a tennis ball that I'd already repeatedly thrown, when my phone buzzed inside my pocket.

"Charlie, we can't let the police drop the case," came a breathless voice. Ainsley.

"Unless there's something to grab Taylor's attention—"

"I found something in Dr. Lindsay's notes. He'd received a threat. It's a note and I don't recognize the writing. It says 'You'll never get credit. The device is mine.' What do you suppose that means?"

She had *my* attention.

I asked if she'd passed this new information along to Kent Taylor and she said he wasn't answering his phone. I agreed to give it a try if she would send me a picture of the note, but two calls to him during the next twenty-four hours went unanswered. I showed the note to Sally, but she didn't know what it meant. The professor hadn't shared any specifics about a device, and for all I knew the note could be referring to something completely outside his professional work.

Sally was having none of my justifications. "It can't be a coincidence," she insisted. "The man is working on some kind of breakthrough medical technique, he hasn't yet patented his device, and suddenly he's dead? At the very least, I'm going to suggest that Ainsley make sure all his papers and laboratory are secured from anyone who might get to them."

"Good idea. Ask her if he'd brought this medical device with him—either to work on it while in Taos, or whether he had it with him here in Albuquerque."

I suddenly remembered the three mugs in the sink at Clara Guthrie's house. Ainsley had said the event organizer had joined them after the speech for coffee. What if Clara had tampered with the brew? She'd certainly seemed to have some harsh words for Ainsley the next morning. I'd need to ask her about that. Still—the thought bugged me— Kent said no toxins showed up in the report. Hmm.

Then there was the woman at the Taos bakery Ainsley said had argued with her boss. Who was that, and could there be any connection to the threatening note?

All this was running through my mind as Sally spoke to Ainsley. I had so many questions, I held out my hand for Sally's phone and took up the conversation. I asked about the professor's invention and she wasn't certain whether Dr. Lindsay had brought the medical device to New Mexico with him. She agreed to check his safe in Boston.

"No one in the scientific community knew about it," she insisted. "I feel sure about that. Dr. Lindsay was very protective of his work."

"Who from Boston might have come here to confront him, to give him that note?"

"I honestly can't think of anyone." A hitch in her voice gave away her emotional state.

"Okay, give it some thought. Meanwhile, you mentioned his having words with someone at a bakery in Taos? Was it Sweet's Sweets, by any chance?"

"Yes! Amazing that you know the place."

"It's kind of a legend, and one of my favorites." I couldn't imagine anyone there being less than gracious with a customer, so I asked her to give me the details. Then, "What else happened that I might check?"

"On the drive from Taos to Albuquerque, there's a stretch of the road that passes through a little community and he got a speeding ticket there. It was a tribal officer and the professor got a little belligerent with him. He's not used to dealing with the laid-back style in New Mexico. I can't see how that's of help."

Nothing out here seems to move quickly enough for people who are used to a big-city pace. But, I couldn't see how a traffic violation could follow the man to a residential house a hundred miles farther down the road. I asked Ainsley to send me a picture of the ticket, if she could find it. At the very least it would have the officer's name, if we needed verification.

We ended the call and I quickly jotted notes about everything she'd told me. The bakery connection was interesting, and I saw it as the perfect excuse to visit one of my favorite places in northern New Mexico. A glance at my watch told me it was still early enough in the day to make the drive and arrive before closing time.

I'd worked up an unhealthy sugar-binge craving by the time I made the turn just south of the Taos Plaza and pulled into the parking lot in front of Sweet's Sweets. It was nearing four p.m. and the idea of a cup of English tea and a few cookies was stuck in my head.

The dark-haired young woman behind the counter was familiar to me from my previous couple of visits, and she greeted me with a smile.

"Our favorite customer from Albuquerque!"

I was amazed she remembered, although I have to admit I've ordered a couple of pricey custom cakes over the years.

"I'll tell Sam you're here." She left me to browse while she walked through a curtain into the kitchen.

Samantha Sweet and I met quite by accident at a resort spa in Santa Fe, and I almost immediately knew there was something different about her. Not one for woo-woo magical healing, I still couldn't deny that a nasty bump on my head completely went away when she grabbed my hand to help me up off the ground. I kind of let that aspect of the friendship go, once I discovered she's the most talented baker in this stretch of the Rockies.

Now, she walked out of the kitchen, wiping her hands on a towel, her white baker's jacket smudged with a touch of chocolate on one sleeve. She brought me into a quick embrace and I immediately felt my road-weariness disappear. I asked if she had a minute for a cup of something together and we took seats at one of the three empty bistro tables in the shop.

"Dr. Lindsay? Yes, he's been in quite a few times this summer. I don't remember any kind of an argument. Jen—do you?"

Her employee brought us a plate of assorted cookies, shaking her head. "Oh wait. I do remember ... That lady lawyer, the one with the streak of white in her hair ... she got into it with him over the last éclair in the case one afternoon. He'd already asked for it and she practically pushed him out of the way. I could tell he really wanted it, but he was a gentleman and gave it up. I made it up by slipping him an extra slice of the pumpkin cheesecake at no charge—one for him and one for his assistant. He got the better end of the deal."

"A lawyer? Did you get the sense they knew each other?" I asked.

"Maybe. You know, I do think this woman teaches some courses at the UNM campus. They could have met there."

"Still, it sounds minor," Samantha said, handing me a mug of tea and setting hers on the table.

"It was. Once the woman flounced out of here, the atmosphere relaxed a lot. I remember a hippie couple who chatted him up and they congratulated him on keeping his cool."

"Did they seem to know him? Sorry, I know I'm

grasping for ideas." I explained about Elbert Lindsay's death and why I was looking for clues. They both expressed shock that he was gone.

"They might have," Jen said. "He gave them a lift when they left. I think I heard them say they were taking the bus somewhere, like maybe Las Cruces?"

"Ainsley Jones, the professor's assistant, told me the argument happened the day before he went to Albuquerque to deliver an important lecture."

Jen shrugged. "No idea about that. I do remember he and the assistant had their heads together over some papers. Maybe it had to do with the speech."

I could easily check that out. Sam excused herself, saying she had a big cake to finish and deliver, and we ended the visit with one of those 'great to see you again' exchanges. I had Jen box up the cookies, plus a slice of cheesecake that I would probably devour once I got home. Or it might accidentally disappear during the drive, since it would be past my dinnertime by then.

One more quick stop on my way out of town, at the UNM campus south of town where Lindsay had taught this summer. But I quickly discovered how quiet things could be after hours. The janitor had no clue what I was talking about.

The drive home only gave me time to brood. Was there some kind of slow-acting toxin that could have been slipped to the professor, something would not have stopped his heart for several days, something that wouldn't show up on a standard screening by the medical investigator? I might be able to research that, but how would I know whether the pushy female lawyer or the now-unavailable hippies could have somehow administered it?

I shook my head and helped myself to another cookie from the box on my passenger seat. None of this speculation seemed very likely. The one person I kept coming back to was Clara Guthrie, the event organizer. The woman's actions seemed fishy, and I hadn't yet interviewed her in person.

It wasn't terribly late when I got back to Albuquerque but I was weary from the drive and the thoughts churning in my head. Sweet little Freckles had ridden along, happy enough to go anyplace with me, but I could tell she was eager to be out of the car too. We pulled into the driveway at home. Drake's truck sat there, and the warm glow of lights beckoned me.

"I've got some soup on the stove," he said. "Make you a cheese sandwich to go with it?" He really is the best husband ever.

I had to confess that I'd spoiled my appetite with sweets on the way home. "How about if we walk Freckles down to the park together? Maybe I'll be hungry when we get back."

I filled him in on my day, and he told me about the photography crew from National Geographic he'd been chartered to fly over some of the more spectacular red rock formations on Navajo land. It had been a full day for both of us, and it wasn't long after having our quick bowl of soup that we fell into bed.

By eight o'clock the next morning I was back at the office. It was Sunday and the place would be quiet, a perfect time for me to go over what I'd learned yesterday. I wanted to know whether Ainsley had any luck figuring out the note she'd found among Dr. Lindsay's personal things, and to ask a few questions about what I'd learned in Taos.

"A woman lawyer? Oh—you must mean Priscilla Gatti," Ainsley said. "Yes, I remember that day at the bakery."

"I got the impression there was some ongoing animosity between them?"

"I only met her at the beginning of this summer, but after observing her for three months I'd say Ms. Gatti has ongoing animosity with a lot of people." A sigh. "Maybe that's not fair. She's just a very prickly woman who seems to walk into every situation looking for a fight. Nitpicking conversations, an ardent feminist who comes off as a man-hater. I don't know if that's true—I heard she has a husband. Poor guy. It always seemed that her male colleagues would suddenly switch direction when they saw her coming down the hall."

"So, she probably didn't have a personal interest in Dr. Lindsay's work?"

"She taught a couple of pre-law courses, he was in science. Their fields of work didn't overlap at all, as far as I knew."

Sounded as if the bakery encounter was nothing but an example of the woman's obnoxious personality.

"At the bakery, they said the professor gave a ride to some hippies who were there at the same time?"

There was a pause. "Oh, yes. Interesting couple. It was a short ride, just a mile or so to the bus station, but what I got from the conversation in the car was that they were taking a gap year, vagabonding around the Southwest, staying in hostels, hitchhiking some. They'd been in northern New Mexico and Colorado for most of the summer and were headed south. We marveled a little, after we dropped them off, at how they could live for a year with only the possessions they could carry in a backpack."

I had to laugh. "I couldn't do it."

"Me neither. I feel like I'm roughing it in an RV."

"So the professor didn't know them before that day?"

"No, I'm sure he didn't. And they didn't express any interest in his work. I think you can scratch them, and Priscilla Gatti, off your list of suspects."

It was kind of what I was afraid of. And I was back to Clara Guthrie, the woman across the street. I mentioned that I'd seen Clara talking to Ainsley that morning after the professor's death. "Can you tell me what that was about? She seemed kind of forceful."

"She was pretty charged up about the police having been to her house. Wanted to know if they searched the place and why I let them in."

"What!"

"Yeah, as if I wouldn't let them in after discovering my boss dead in her kitchen."

"You said she had been there the evening before, after the lecture, right?"

"Yes, she got us settled into the house, earlier in the day, but everyone was wide awake, kind of feeling the adrenaline after the lecture, so we all went back there together. She made coffee—decaf, she assured us—and we visited a while."

"Anything unusual in the discussion? I'm just wondering whether Clara maybe had developed a thing for the professor... I don't know, sort of a starry-eyed crush or something?"

"Um, maybe a bit of that. Of all the committee members who put the event together, she was the one who pushed to take charge, offered her home to us, hung near his elbow all evening."

"Was there a relationship of some sort—professional or otherwise—between them?"

"I could look for clues among his things, but I was under the impression that they'd maybe met once or twice before that evening. Phone calls, emails, maybe..."

"If you could check those for me, that would be good." It still didn't feel quite right. I couldn't see a woman becoming possessive of him quite that quickly. There was more to this whole story, but I was hitting a lot of dead ends.

I reminded myself that I still hadn't actually interviewed Clara Guthrie. Surely I could learn something there. I left Freckles in her crate in my office, went downstairs, and walked across the street. Clara's car was in the driveway, and she answered almost immediately after I pressed the bell.

"*What?* What do you people want?"

Not exactly the gracious woman she'd been around Dr. Lindsay. "Well, first, I came to offer condolences."

She cooled, maybe two degrees.

"I do have just a few questions, if you don't mind, about the evening before the professor's death."

"And this is your business because…?"

"I—we—have been asked to look into it." I hoped my nod over my shoulder gave the impression that RJP Investigations was fully behind this. "Since you organized his lecture venue and offered your home for him to use, which was very gracious indeed, maybe you can tell me if Professor Lindsay seemed worried about anything? Whether he felt at threat at all?"

Something shifted in her expression. Her anger toward me *was* masking grief. She stepped aside and let me in. Her home was laid out similarly to our offices, parlor on one side of the entry hall, formal dining room on the other, a staircase leading to the second story.

"He seemed edgy, keyed up about something. I knew Elbert years ago when I was a student in one of his classes. Even though he was only five years older than I, he made it clear that a relationship would not be appropriate."

"Now—when you knew he was coming here—did you hope to rekindle that old feeling?"

She nodded. "But he didn't even remember me. I shouldn't have been surprised. A man as handsome as he was, many female students over the years must have developed feelings for him. But it hurt."

Motive.

"Did the two of you talk about it?"

She shifted her weight to the other foot. We still hadn't taken seats, and I was now feeling too edgy to relax.

"I... I'll admit it, I flirted a bit. He showed interest. I flirted some more. After the lecture we three came here. I made coffee, slipped a tiny sleeping pill into Ainsley's cup so she would get tired quickly. She did, and she went upstairs without finishing her coffee."

The hair at the back of my neck rose. "Did you put something into the professor's cup, as well?"

She stared with wide eyes. "*No!* Absolutely not. I *hoped* I'd get him up to the bedroom, not *harm* him in any way. We began kissing, embracing. I told him I'd be willing to come to Boston if that's what it took to be together. We were standing near the kitchen sink and he suddenly collapsed. I had no idea what to do. He just sank to the floor and within a minute he was gone."

"You didn't call for an ambulance or anything?"

"He was dead. I couldn't believe it. He'd unbuckled his belt and his trousers had slipped down to his ankles. I couldn't pull them up, give him some dignity. All I could think was that it would harm his reputation if we were discovered together in that position. I panicked, locked up the house, and went back to my sister's place."

Momentarily stumped, I stared at her. Down in my pocket, my phone rang and I saw it was Ainsley. I asked Clara to excuse me, then dashed out the front door and took the call.

"Charlie, you'll never believe what I found on the professor's phone."

My mind was still reeling a little from Clara Guthrie's admission, and I had to ask Ainsley to give me a moment to get back into my office. The two-minute walk across the street and up the stairs cleared my head a little.

"Professor Lindsay received an offer for his medical device," she said when I asked about the new information. "It was for $14 million dollars!"

"Seriously?"

"Yes, an email from one of the biggest pharmaceutical companies. It starts out to say 'This is to confirm our conversation earlier today... document attached...' When I opened that document, it's a contract. They were serious."

No wonder Lindsay had seemed edgy, excitable. He wouldn't want to talk about the deal until papers had been signed, money received, announcements made. But when it came to motives, I'd guess a $14 million device would trump unrequited love from a former student. Clara's admission had seemed genuine; now I believed her.

"Ainsley, would anyone else from the university in Boston know about this offer?"

"I don't see how. It came in two days before his death."

"But the device… others knew about that, surely."

"Very few. His field of research was well-published, of course, but he'd kept the actual medical device and its development very much under wraps."

"Good. That narrows our field of suspects. Tell me the names of everyone you can think of who knew about it."

There were two. And one of those was familiar to me.

Before calling Kent Taylor or the Office of the Medical Investigator, I knew I'd better have my research in order. I went online and looked up Dr. Max Criglee, the unfamiliar name Ainsley gave me.

Dr. Criglee practiced in Taos, New Mexico, according to his profile piece on his own website. A leader in diabetes research and treatment innovations, he was actively working on a transdermal delivery system for insulin so patients would not have to endure the daily agony of traditional injections. I went to his LinkedIn profile where he had followed a number of other prominent researchers, including Elbert Lindsay. When another within his circle commented on Lindsay's work, Criglee responded, "Yes, I've read all his published pieces."

A quick search of Lindsay's name showed me he had, indeed, published in several of the most respected medical journals. So Criglee was well aware of everything Lindsay had chosen to make public. What he didn't know was the extent of the research on the professor's new device.

And where would he be able to learn about that?

Through his wife, the Taos attorney, Priscilla Gatti.

The lawyer, teaching at the same campus for the summer as Lindsay, could have surely found ways to gain access to information. She might have even somehow seen the email with the offer from Big Pharma, or perhaps she overheard the phone call when Lindsay himself received the news. The connection was there.

My hands were shaking a little as I started to dial Kent Taylor's number, but then I stopped myself. There was one more bit of evidence that Ainsley might be able to find for me.

"Do you still have Dr. Lindsay's things with you?" I asked. She confirmed. "Can you look at the clothing he was wearing during the lecture?" My mind was racing over possibilities. "His dress shirt or suit jacket, to start with."

"Um, sure. Give me a minute."

I could hear papers rustling as she must have set them down, footsteps across a wooden floor, some other background noises.

Movement at my office door grabbed my attention. I looked up to see the face I'd just been researching online. Max Criglee stood there. *Oh shit.*

"Hang up the phone," he ordered. The hand that had been down at his side now held a gun, aimed at me.

I raised my hands, pretending not to have heard his instruction, praying Ainsley would figure things out.

He stared me in the eye. "End the call. Now."

I cut off Ainsley, fumbling a bit as the list of recent calls showed up and I touched Kent Taylor's cell number, dragging a loose paper napkin across the screen to hide it from view. I hoped this scheme would work, since I couldn't risk breaking eye contact with this deranged doctor again.

"How did you get in here?" I practically shouted, covering any sounds from my phone and trying like mad to stall for time.

"Ms. Parker, how silly of you to leave the front door unlocked when you're in the office all alone."

"Okay, that's true," I admitted in a lower tone. "But why are you even in this neighborhood? Dr. Lindsay's lecture was days ago. I know you attended it."

"I had a few questions for the lovely Clara Guthrie, your neighbor."

"Like what?"

"Just clarifying a few points about the time she spent with the good professor that evening after the program."

I had a sickening thought. "Did you harm her?"

"Oh, no. I was just about to stop at her house when

173

I saw you go over there. I knew you would ask the questions for me. Word of your snooping around in Taos has already gotten out. All I had to do was wait out of sight and find out what you learned."

I gave a quick glance down at my phone. Stupidly, I had also covered the screen from my own view so I had no idea whether Taylor had picked up, my words were going to his voicemail, or if a connection had even been made.

"You came after the professor's research notes and hoped to get your hands on the new medical device he invented, didn't you?"

The look on his face revealed a lot. "Forget it," he said. "I'll ask the questions. What did Clara Guthrie tell you?"

I hedged and stalled and stammered as much as I could get away with. His hand on the pistol grip wasn't firm at all—not an experienced target shooter, that's for sure. I let him think my wide-eyed stare at the gun was due to fear, but in fact I checked to see whether he'd released the safety (he had, darn it) and whether I could tell if there was a round in the revolver's chamber (most likely there was—it appeared fully loaded).

But if it came right down to it, I could probably make a sudden move and get it away from him. This was a soft, pudgy guy, not one who spent hours at the range.

Still, even the pudgy ones get lucky, and I hoped I wasn't betting my life on this. *Keep him talking, Charlie.*

"It was some kind of toxic substance, wasn't it?"

Play to his ego. "It must have been very effective, delivering it through that transdermal system you've been working on, huh."

"It's a good system. A small gel-like substance contains the insulin and gets absorbed into the skin within an hour."

"But it wasn't insulin you gave him, was it? What did you use that acted so quickly but didn't show up the next morning when the body was discovered?"

"Nice try. I don't have to tell you anything."

"So what now? How will you get me out of my own office, out onto the street, and then what—you'll kidnap me? Hold me hostage in exchange for Dr. Lindsay's invention?"

As I talked, I listened like crazy for any sound of approaching police cars. A car passed on the street below, but I heard no sirens, no shouts, no imminent raid on my behalf.

"Oh, I already have the research materials, the patent application, the prototype. My wife took care of that. That fool Lindsay shouldn't have been quite so secretive. No one will now know it isn't my work."

"But he received an offer from a company—" Uh-oh, that was a mistake. He clearly hadn't known about the most recent communication Lindsay received.

I watched the barrel of the gun waver, straighten, waver again, his finger on the trigger the whole time. Adrenaline rushed through me. Which direction should I go?

And then I heard the faintest sound from downstairs.

"Upstairs! In my office! He's got a gun!" My shout was so loud it took Criglee off guard and he made a quarter turn.

And I pounced. With a twist I didn't know I had in me, I wrenched his wrist, bending it backward so he dropped the pistol. He hadn't cocked the hammer and, thank goodness, it didn't go off.

Ron appeared in my doorway, followed immediately by Kent Taylor. Both had weapons drawn and it was an easy takedown to get Criglee in handcuffs. I finally breathed again.

"How did you figure it out?" Sally asked me, later that afternoon.

She had come over to our house as soon as I called her to let her know that Lindsay's killer was caught. We sat outside under the gazebo with Ron and his wife Victoria while Drake stirred up some sangria and poured glasses for all.

"Kent will have to figure it all out for sure, but I'm thinking that Criglee approached Dr. Lindsay at the end of the lecture, as I'm sure many others did, and shook his hand. Somehow, maybe with the other hand, he stuck one of his transdermal patches on Lindsay's wrist, forearm, somewhere. I don't have the details. Maybe the patch had a peel-off backing and he somehow removed it unnoticed. Maybe he actually let some of the toxin get on himself but then cleaned it off somehow. From what I read online about this system he invented, the gel-like substance stays on the skin for only a few minutes and then gets absorbed, releasing the medication. Or in this case, the toxin."

"But Dr. Lindsay wouldn't have noticed it?" Drake asked.

I shrugged. "For insulin, it's supposed to be an absolutely painless method, so maybe he never felt it. Criglee admitted to me that the toxin he used would be absorbed quickly and take effect within an hour or so, but would be completely out of the system within eight hours. Since the professor wasn't discovered until the next morning, it's no wonder the MI didn't find anything."

"So how will this ever be proven?" Sally asked. "No weapon, no toxin…?"

I held up my index finger. *But wait—there's more.* "During my online research about Criglee's patch, I actually read some of the fine print. While the gel gets absorbed into the skin, it can leave residue on clothing. It's recommended to be applied to uncovered skin until it goes away. I asked Ainsley Jones to preserve the professor's clothing from that night and warned her not to touch the shirt or jacket cuffs, just in case any toxin remained. She reported that she found two little smudges, and she's going to ship the items by overnight express to Kent Taylor."

Drake raised his glass and we clinked them. "So it

looks like your newest case is a wrap," he said, leaning over to kiss me.

———◄•●•►———

About the Author

Connie Shelton is the author of more than 50 books, including the bestselling Charlie Parker mysteries, the Samantha Sweet cozy paranormal mysteries, and the Heist Ladies series. She's known for a light touch when it comes to sex and violence in her stories, but is much more lavish with food and chocolate. She taught fiction and non-fiction writing courses for six years before developing her own novel writing course, Novel In A Weekend. In the early 2000s she was a frequent conference speaker and a contributor to *Chicken Soup for the Writer's Soul.* She now lives in northern New Mexico with her husband and dogs. Get a free book when you sign up for her newsletter at **connieshelton.com.** Follow Connie on Amazon, Bookbub, Facebook, YouTube, Pinterest, and Twitter.

One Night in Brownsville

Gary Phillips

Brownsville, Texas is landlocked. But in the southern corner of this border city, known for the infamous railroading of Black infantrymen in the Brownsville Affair of 1906, there's a seventeen-mile channel that empties into the Gulf of Mexico. Barges moving large mounds of scrapped steel and iron derived from ships motor regularly along that channel. Belo Resources is among the five ship-breaking facilities dispersed toward the terminus of the channel. Ship breaking is the major economic engine of Brownsville.

These days, the politically correct, media-massaging term Ernesto "Ernie" Carraja and the other workers at Belo had been taught to say is ship recycling. Even in the red meat state of Texas, there is some notion of being seen as environmentally conscious as long as it doesn't undercut profits. Though his bosses, including Whit Barrison, would guffaw at placating them tree hugging tofu lovers as symbolized by the populace in the state capital, the blue city of Austin. Yet ironically Belo had recently been sold to a Silicon Valley, green type named Noel Komsky, who also owned, among other holdings, a professional soccer team.

Working on a skeletal third shift past one in the morning, Carraja reflected on these matters as he used his oxyacetylene torch to finish cutting through the hinges of a floor safe welded to the B deck. He was in what had been the captain's quarters of a decommissioned Merchant Marine freighter called the SS Hugh Mulzac. Carraja turned the valve on the torch off, killing the flame, and set the apparatus aside. He also removed his blackened cowhide gloves.

A warm breeze blew across his face as he lifted the goggles off his eyes to inspect the results. Deftly using a pry bar, he inserted the chisel end in the gap between the safe's door and frame. He grunted with exertion and popped the door off. It thudded heavily to the metal flooring.

"Nice work," a voice said in Spanish.

A surprised Carraja stared at the newcomer. He was dressed in dark workingman's clothes, thick-soled shoes, and a ribbed mask over his face with only a cut out for eyes. Held in one of his large-gloved hands was some kind of compact dull-finished weapon. The armed man stomped on the two-way radio the workers used for communicating in the ship. Carraja had left his on a built-in shelf by the hatch.

The taller man's form was framed in the doorway to the quarters, lit by lights strung along the upper portions of the bulkhead. He stepped further inside. Sweat coated the part of his face visible inside his mask.

"What do you want?" Carraja said in English. His words came out harsher than he meant.

The intruder pointed with the extended barrel of his weapon. "That."

Carraja looked into the safe. Inside were two stacks of money, bound with rubber bands at intervals, and a metal box about the size of two shoe boxes lashed together. It wasn't unusual to take apart safes on ships; everything was readied for the smelter. But he'd been given specific instructions by his immediate boss Barrison: Anything he found in the safe, don't tell the others on the crew and turn the contents over to him. But a man with a gun overrode any such order. He bent to remove the cash and box and hand them over.

"Fucker..." A man's curse echoed from within the freighter. Whatever else he was going to say was interrupted by a burst of what Carraja momentarily took for loud, angry wasps. He then realized why the intruder's gun had a long barrel. There was a silencer screwed into the end of it to dampen the sound of gunfire.

"Shit," a masked O'Conner cursed, quickly pivoting from the welder about to hand over the goods. His next motion was to shoot out the row of overhead lights.

In a sibilant tone he commanded in Spanish, "Slide

your cell phone to me." Carraja didn't protest. He took his smartphone out of his pants pocket and did so.

"If I were you, I wouldn't leave this room just yet," O'Conner said, this time in English. "In fact you might want to close the door and latch it shut."

"Okay," came the worker's reply in the half-gloom. There were electric lights on stands on the sandy ground outside the ship, illuminating portions of the rusting hulk. Some of that light filtered through the missing sections of the hull.

O'Conner moved off silently. Behind him he heard the door, hatch, whatever the hell they called them on boats, hiss close. He speculated about what had gone wrong, while foremost concentrating on staying alive and eliminating the threat. He didn't think any of the bound workers had gotten loose.

The corridor was dark enough, though there were patches of spill light. O'Conner undid the strap on the Ingram and lashed the weapon across his torso, freeing his hands but keeping the assault rifle in easy reach. He went forward, listening and breathing shallowly. Nothing. He was almost at the end, having ducked below a row of glassless portholes. The hatch here was open and let unto a lighted corridor, perpendicular to the one he was in. Finger on the Ingram's trigger, he took a chance and looked out, left, right, then pulled back in. Again no sound or sensation of another's presence.

When the four of them had descended on the beached freighter, they knew there would just be seven at work this early morning. The four thieves knew there'd only be one of the seven tasked with the safe. Maybe he was even promised a cut.

"The first week they get a ship in," Starks had said, "involves pumping out the oil, diesel residue, and whatever other sludge is in the ship." They were in the Kris Kristofferson suite at the Baystar, a refurbished 1920s-era brick hotel overlooking Sunrise Boulevard in Brownsville. Singer-actor Kristofferson was a lauded native son.

Starks tapped a finger on the blueprint unfurled before them on the table, anchored on its edges by various objects including a .38 Special snub nose revolver. "Holes are cut out of the sides to let in air and light, some of the bulkheads and portions of the bow are also removed, then them boys go to town."

"Aren't these hombres gonna be scattered all over the ship stripping it apart?" Hanson asked. "How do we know we got them rounded up and accounted for?"

Starks smiled, exposing a yellowed bicuspid. "They don't usually authorize a third shift. Whit has the other six on to cover the real reason, his man down in the captain's cabin. Once he's done and taken care of how he's supposed to deal with the box, they plan to knock off.

"Anyway, the way it works is, they move through together, probably be bunched mid-ship."

"Probably?" Hanson interjected.

"Even if they aren't," Starks said, drawing out each word slowly, "that's why there's four of us, in case we need to fan out quickly and gather up the flock." He smiled, pleased with his simile.

Drayton, who'd brought O'Conner in on the job, observed, "Even before you get your cherry popped down in these parts, they hand you a gun. Some of them boys might be packin'."

"Don't you worry," Starks replied, "we'll have us some serious heat."

Hanson and Drayton seemed satisfied. O'Conner had more questions and asked them.

Too bad he hadn't acted on his instincts and shot Starks when it crossed his mind earlier tonight, O'Conner regretted. He was certain Starks was the problem. The closer they'd gotten to pulling the job, the more solicitous he'd become. Never a good sign in a thief. Back at the portholes he looked out but saw no figures on the ground, only the looming shadows of the piles of scrap and the marsh area beyond where they'd parked their vehicles. The metal was grouped ferrous and non-ferrous, Starks had told them.

Having no choice, O'Conner moved further into the ship. What he hoped was that Starks would figure he had the box and was trying to escape with it. He needed to keep him away from where it really was. He came to some metal rungs set in the corridor and ascended. He paused just below an opening and slowly came up. O'Conner stared into the vacant eyes of Hanson. His masked corpse lay at the edge of the hatchway, sideways in the corridor. The hatch had been removed. O'Conner knew it was Hanson from his linebacker build going soft. His torso had stopped leaking blood when his heart had given out. Hanson's weapon lay near him, minus its magazine.

About to push the body out of the way, O'Conner's hand froze in place. He frowned, withdrew his hand and leveraged himself through the opening without disturbing the body. He stepped over Hanson and taking a knee, examined the corpse, using the confiscated smartphone's flashlight function. Sure enough, Starks had boobytrapped the dead man.

Preoccupied, O'Conner inadvertently touched another part of the phone's screen and an image sprang onto it. The picture was the welder with two young children, girls, seven and nine, he estimated. All of them smiling. He put the phone away, making sure the ringer was off.

Starks had lodged a flash-bang grenade in the dead man's arm pit. The pin was pulled. The cylindrical device gave off heat, light, and sound in a five-foot radius, causing temporary blindness and deafness. Apparently Starks had come better armed than the rest, O'Conner concluded. Moving the body would have jostled the thing, causing the lever to release and it would have gone off. It wouldn't kill him, but was designed to disorient the target.

O'Conner removed the device, keeping the release lever depressed. He took out one of Hanson's boot laces and wound this around the mini-canister to secure the lever. He crept forward with it. Starks had to be nearby to hear the blast and no doubt spring from hiding. He wouldn't want to waste time. Probably planned to wound O'Conner, then grind the barrel of his Ingram into the ragged hole to make him tell where the box was. *That's how I would have done it,* O'Conner assessed.

The end of the passageway let out into yet another corridor. Here the dismantling of the ship was evident and large sections had been cut away. Gaping holes looked into stripped rooms or dark metal caverns. In this area, there was only one light, halfway down, overhead in the center. Close to where he stood was still intact. There was a hatch on either side of the hallway. Starks had to be in one of the rooms, ready to rush out for his reward. O'Conner meant to oblige him.

But before he could toss the grenade behind him, Drayton appeared at the other end of the honeycombed passageway. He had his mask off. He was pale as bleached linen but held onto his Ingram. O'Conner drew back into shadow. The wounded man came forward on unsteady legs. His side glistened wetly. Starks hadn't put him away as he had Hanson.

O'Conner watched, tucking the confiscated grenade into his back pocket. Drayton paused, gathered himself, and went forward again. He also knew or suspected that Starks was behind one of the hatches ahead. He was only going to have one chance to get it right. As he got closer, O'Conner could see a small, tight smile on the other man's face. Stopping again, Drayton grimaced as he bent over. He straightened up holding several small, odd-shaped pieces of loose sheeting in one hand. He threw these along the corridor and screamed in pain.

The hatch to the right cracked open on surprisingly quiet hinges. Drayton waited. O'Conner waited. The hatch opened more. From the angle where he was, the hatch blocked Drayton's vision. But from where he was hidden, O'Conner could see it was Starks. He was still partly inside the recess, his body not yet a prime target. He would be one very soon for a ready O'Conner.

But Drayton got anxious. *Must be wearing out fast,* O'Conner surmised. The wounded man unleashed a volley, figuring to at least strike Stark's lower extremities exposed beneath the edge of the hatch.

The hatch slapped back with a clang. From the recess of the hatchway, Starks emptied bullets into Drayton. His body jiggled and jerked from the impact of the high velocity rounds ripping bloody trails through him. Just as quickly, the suppressed gunfire stopped, and Drayton's corpse collapsed onto the grey decking as if boneless.

O'Conner would have to chance stepping out to get the shot. He did so but Starks was keyed up now, sensing the other man was nearby. He fired at O'Conner, falling back into the hatchway. O'Conner had also dropped back and wasn't hit. He couldn't chance Starks out-maneuvering him and getting back to the captain's cabin. Mouth compressed tightly, he strode to the open hatchway. There was blood under his boots. Drayton had gotten a piece of Starks. O'Conner went through.

This was a short passageway and the only way out was up, topside. O'Conner proceeded slowly up a set of iron steps, the night sky above the opening. There were

drops of blood on the steps. Just as he was about to
stick his head out it occurred to O'Conner where Starks
was. O'Conner had also studied the ship's plans.
Toward the rear of the freighter—aft was it?—was
another way to the captain's cabin. Hurriedly he
reversed his course.

Too late, O'Conner got back to the darkened
corridor outside the once captain's quarters. He could
tell the hatch was open and he heard cursing. He
slowed. A light shining from within the room snapped
off. Assault weapon lashed around him, O'Conner put
his back against the bulkhead and inched forward in the
near dark. He froze. He'd heard a rustle of clothing.
O'Conner lay on the metal floor and slid forward, his
Ingram held GI-fashion as he used his elbows for
propulsion.

Starks' gun erupted, spitting rounds into the
corridor in a sweep. Pinging ricochets echoed off the
metal, some near the still, prone man. The suppressor
eliminated any gun flash so Starks' location in the room
was still not certain. But the safe would be the best place
to hunker behind, O'Conner reasoned. It got quiet
again.

Crouching, he unwound the boot laces, and tossed
the flash-bang grenade he'd taken off Hanson's body
into the cabin underhanded. He aimed it where he
remembered the safe was located. O'Conner averted his
eyes as it went off with a boom, intense white light
flooding the room. Starks bellowed and fired his
weapon blindly.

"Think you're clever?" he challenged, shooting impotently again.

O'Conner squinted as the light started to fade. He zeroed in on a mass that was taking shape in the bright essence and fired his Ingram. There was a clatter and more cursing. The light subsided but O'Conner used the smartphone again. Starks stood blinking at the side of the safe, a hand to the blood spreading across his chest. The Ingram was at his feet.

"Fuck you," he growled at O'Conner.

The last robber standing pumped bullets into Starks' heart. The double-crosser's body folded in on itself as he dropped to the B deck. O'Conner saw what Starks had seen, the torch man had managed to weld the safe's door partly back in place.

"I figured I could run," Ernie Carraja said behind him.

O'Conner turned, gun barrel first, the light from the phone illuminating the worker.

"Hoping you'd leave. I could maybe sneak back and keep the money for myself, say you took it." He looked wistful then continued. "But one of you, whichever one was left alive, would come after me and what good would that be?"

"Get the safe open," O'Conner said.

Carraja put a portable light and stand in place and soon had the safe's door off again. He took out the two stacks and the black metal box, then set them down.

O'Conner picked up the box and cradled one of the stacks in the crook of his arm. "The others are on C deck, toward the front of this tub. Alive and tied up. One of them has a goose egg behind his ear, another one a sore jaw."

Carraja couldn't take his eyes off the untouched stack. Were all the bills hundreds?

"You might want to hide that somewhere before you call the cops." O'Conner lingered in the doorway, crinkles flashing at the edges of his eyes framed in the mask's opening. He pivoted about and left.

O'Conner didn't return to the Baystar. The suite and the adjoining one had been secured under a false name and a credit card with money behind it in that name. But when the police conducted their investigation, four supposed out-of-town businessmen commanding those rooms were likely to raise suspicions, particularly if only one of them returned in the wee hours.

He drove the older model Corolla used for the job an hour inland toward McAllen. O'Conner stopped once to buy and eat a fried chicken sandwich with waffle fries at an all-night knock-off Chick-Fil-A. Afterward, he paid cash for a room at a highway motel called the Skyview. Several eighteen wheelers were parked on the wide expanse of gravel fronting the check-in office.

In the room he forced open the metal box and stared at what was inside. Starks, who'd set up the score, had said this was supposed to be about smuggled diamonds. What O'Conner held was an old notebook of some sort. The item was leather bound, stuffed with lose pages. From one of the nearby rooms, a plaintive *narcocorrido* about drug lord El Chapo Guzman played low. He leafed through the diary, an eyebrow going up now and then as he skimmed the entries, written in precise, block lettering. There were also diagrams, formulas, and sketches of pigeons as well.

He unfolded a loose sheaf of onionskin paper taped together to make an 11" by 17" sheet. It was a drawing of some sort of a futuristic-looking tower, notations festooning the paper. A name for the thing was printed in that precise lettering below the drawing. It was a name O'Conner recognized primarily as that of a boutique car company. But he knew, too, that it was the name of a person, a historical figure.

"Hmmm," he mused, leaning back from the tiny desk he sat at in the cheap wood-paneled room. Folding his arms, he stared blankly at the framed image over the desk, a velvet painting of a beaming Shaquille O'Neal riding a unicycle while juggling basketballs shaped like skulls. O'Conner twisted off the cap of the plastic pint bottle of vodka he had with him and took a sip.... then another.

Whit Barrison paced as he smoked in front of the public bathroom at Boca Chica Beach east of Brownsville. Families were out on the sand or in the water enjoying themselves. Laying on the sidewalk at the corner of the men's room—the women's was on the other side of the squat structure—was a greasy sleeping bag, sans homeless occupant. He eyed this hostilely and not for the first time since his wait began three ciga- rettes ago. He looked around at the scrape of footsteps on the concrete pad.

"You Barrison?" the newcomer asked. He was over six feet and had close-cropped hair with grey creeping in at the temples.

"What if I am?"

"I hear you want a job done."

"You a cop? You wearing a wire?"

The other man lifted his shirt to show a reasonable set of abs. "We can go inside there and you can feel me all over if you like," he intoned. "Get frisky and shit." His expression was flat, devoid of emotion.

Barrison developed a sour look as he stubbed his cigarette out. "No, that's okay."

"Word is you're offering a finder's fee for locating this guy, this guy who was part of a string you put together to take down some swag from a junked boat."

"Freighter," Barrison corrected.

"You work for the outfit, right? The ones handling the freighter."

Barrison swatted at a mosquito buzzing his face. "That's not your concern."

"You got a lead on this guy?"

"Something like that. My source told me he lives in California."

"L.A.?"

"No. Someplace they call Riverside. He plays at being Mister Suburbs."

"You know all that, why don't you go get him yourself?"

"I don't do that." He made it sound as indignant as he felt.

"You want the goods back? No matter what it takes?"

"Yes."

"What if I go get this guy, and keep what I get for myself?"

"You might find some cash, but that's peanuts compared to the thing you need to retrieve. A diary."

The stranger smirked. "You one of those weird dudes into My Little Pony? This some kind of collector's item?"

"You're a regular Kevin Hart, aren't you?" Barrison considered another smoke but didn't take his pack out. "This diary, this journal, it's one of a kind. Look, I'll front you five thou for expenses and I guarantee you a sweet payday if you get it back." He added, "If it means you take care of this guy, this O'Conner, there's a bonus in it for you."

"That's what you and Starks worked out, was it?" the man standing across from him said.

The ruthless glint in Barrison's eyes evaporated as his jaw became unhinged. He realized who the stranger was.

"A three-way split? Starks to do the heavy lifting. Recruit the crew, knowing all the time you two would stiff us?"

Barrison spread a hand before him. "Goddammit,

O'Conner, it wasn't my idea to do a double-cross on top of ripping off the——" He caught himself. He wasn't going to give that name away. "Look, that shit was Dickie's doing. He got greedy. I've got the connection to realize real money for that journal. We can be partners on this, okay?"

"No. You're a liability." O'Conner removed the .38 Special with the suppressor tucked behind his back in his waistband. He grouped two into Barrison's chest. The routing manager of Belo Resources exhaled loudly, stumbling forward. O'Conner caught him and eased him down into the sleeping bag. He left the dead man wrapped up beside the restroom. Back in the Corolla, he drove west on Highway 4 from Boca Chica and on through Brownsville. Along the way, he rubbed off the dry rubber cement-like coating he'd put on his fingertips to obscure his prints.

Noel Komsky severed the call. What a relief. At first, with the dead robbers at his Belo facility, he was worried what Barrison might say to the authorities. After all, one of the deceased, Starks, had a record and was Barrison's brother-in-law or some kind of relation, however they constituted family in Texas. He'd gone to Barrison in good faith when he'd come out here to Seattle for a mini-retreat. Komsky knew about Barrison's background, the information gleaned from the kind of research he routinely did on new personnel when making an acquisition.

The only way to get a decommissioned government ship for recycling was to be on their approved facilities list. They weren't sent overseas to places such as Chittagong in Bangladesh for cheaper costs as private ships were allowed to do.

Belo Resources was on the list. It had taken years and money, heartache and hope, but Komsky finally had a line on Nikola Tesla's fabled Journal of Speculation and Formulations. The one in which, over the years, he had documented in meticulous notes, schematics, and the like his greatest concepts from intergalactic radio to workable lasers powered by gold no larger than a baseball. And who knew what all else. For geeked-out techies it was the Holy Grail— let alone that those ideas might garner billions.

Tesla died in 1943, living modestly off his patents, unlike his rival Thomas Edison, a ruthless and relentless self-promoter, who'd amassed millions. The papers the electrical genius left behind in trunks in hotel rooms were seized and secreted away by the Office of Alien Property at the behest of J. Edgar Hoover. This despite Tesla being a naturalized U.S. citizen.

For decades, it was believed the journal was among the confiscated papers. Turned out it wasn't. Where had it been and who had hidden it, no one really could say. Once its disappearance was known, fraudulent versions surfaced but were invariably dismissed. Until this one. Komsky had gotten a line on it through intermediaries, one of whom had the wherewithal to bestow a tentative authentication on the item based on photographs of some of its contents. For through whatever series of circumstances, involving murder and double crosses Komsky was certain, the artifact had wound up in the safe of the Mulzac.

Now Barrison was dead as well. No doubt at the hands of the thief who'd gotten out alive that night. The good news for Komsky was that Barrison, under suspicion by the cops, couldn't talk. The bad news was the journal was now nowhere near his grasp, where he could physically examine it, and was now in the possession of that thief.

If that guy didn't know exactly what he had, Komsky understood the thief knew it had value. That man would certainly find out what it was and determine its worth in certain circles. Would the thief contact him and demand a sizeable ransom, Komsky wondered? Or would he offer the journal to another party? He stood at a window overlooking a typical drizzly day in Seattle. He sipped on his wheat grass smoothie as he contemplated the journal's fate.

Ernie Carraja lifted his goggles to inspect his work. He and the other six had been questioned by the police. He'd made sure to cut away his welds from the safe door before that. It was plausible to explain the masked man putting a scary-looking gun on him and making off with the cash and metal box. But trying to explain sealing the safe, then taking off the door again, that would point to him as an accomplice. And now Barrison was not a worry. He must have been in on it too, Carraja guessed.

Well, he had no plans to buy a fancy car or blow the money on big-breasted strippers. Though such notions were tempting. It was over $40,000, not really enough to run away for long on anyway. But enough to make a sizeable down payment on his girls' college fund. For a moment, he regarded a plaque riveted to a bulkhead done in brass relief. It was a portrait of the man the ship was named for, Captain Hugh Mulzac. Those determined eyes looking back at him reminded Carraja of that robber's steely glare. He shook off the feeling and slipped his goggles back into place. He cut through the plaque as he resumed dismantling the ship.

"What're you reading?" Gwen Gardner asked O'Conner. She was fresh out of the shower, crossing through the living room carrying a cup of coffee. She wore a loosely-tied kimono robe, a towel around her wet hair.

He regarded her for a moment, pulling his thoughts together. "Some might say it's science fiction.... or maybe the blueprint for fantastic inventions." He was sitting in an easy chair in their townhouse, early morning sunlight streaming through the windows. He'd been up before light, absorbed in his study of Tesla's journal. He held it up, slightly shaking the cracked leather-bound notebook. "It's the speculations and formulas of Nikola Tesla."

Gardner knew what her old man did on occasion, him being semi-retired and all. Usually she didn't want to know how a job of his went. This time, hearing the famous man's name, she did. Setting her coffee on an end table, she sat on his lap, grinning at him.

"Tell me all about it, big daddy."

They shared a laugh.

About the Author

The son of a mechanic and a librarian, Gary Phillips has published various novels, comics, short stories and has edited several anthologies, including the Anthony-winning *The Obama Inheritance: Fifteen Stories of Conspiracy Noir*. *The Washington Post* and *Booklist* named his most recent novel *One-Shot Harry* as one of the best mysteries of 2022.

O'Conner the professional thief in this story also appears in the novel *Warlord of Willow Ridge*, as well as *Culprits: The Heist Was Just the Beginning*, a linked anthology co-edited by Richard Brewer that follows the characters in the aftermath of a heist gone sideways. *Culprits* was optioned (and changed) and the miniseries is set to air on Disney+ UK. Learn more about Phillips and his work at **gdphillips.com**.

The Totem

A BEN PECOS MYSTERY

Susan Slater

I 've decided it's better to learn life's lessons while young than not to learn them at all. Perhaps, one is never too young to be faced with the decision between right versus wrong—if one chooses correctly.

My lesson started innocently enough. I was ten the summer I found the skull. It was certainly not something I had planned, so was it fate or, as my grandmother would say, "my spiritual destiny"? It didn't seem to be such a momentous thing at the time. It was dusk. My favorite time of day when the light of the moon would peek over the Jemez mountains, and as I waited would finally spill across the rapids of the river making a shiny path on top of the water.

In my child's imagination I made up stories about following the path. Surely it led to someplace magical. My childhood preceded Minecraft, Roblox, and watching the Meta Universe through special goggles. I had to rely on what I could make up to entertain myself.

I sat in my usual spot that evening nestled in the twisted roots of a hundred-year-old Cottonwood about ten feet from the river's edge. The roots and trunk acted as a wind-break, offering a cozy and secure spot to rest and contemplate. Of course, many times I'd doze off only to have my grandmother send my uncle to find me. But tonight, with summer coming to an end, I had lots on my mind.

If I were telling the truth, I would be open and honest about not wanting to go back to school. Not only was it not my fault that I would have to leave, I hadn't done anything wrong; I simply had no choice. My mother died when I was five. I never knew my father. When I got older, I realized that maybe my mother wasn't certain of exactly who my father was. It was rumored that he might have been the surveyor for the county who hung around that summer. Or someone from her school? Was it a classmate or the visiting professor from some ivy league college back East?

I guessed the 'who' didn't matter as much as the 'what.' What was obviously plain to see was that the man had been Anglo, not an Indian but a white man. There were even some who told me as I was growing up that I had such an advantage—a foot in both worlds, so to speak. One well-meaning parent of a friend remarked that I'd probably gotten my smarts from the white side so not to worry. Yeah, no racism there.

Still, these supposedly helpful souls couldn't hold a candle to the meanest fifth grade class known to man. I learned quickly that kids could even be more hurtful than adults. I lived in Utah for most of the year, not in New Mexico where, half or whole ethnic inheritance, these comments weren't even thought of, let alone given a voice. I was simply Benson Pecos from the Jemez area, or Pueblo. But in Utah I was suspect, a foreigner, someone slightly exotic, kept captive in one of those places called a reservation. I could probably talk to animals and pal around with the dead and worship gods that no one there had ever heard of. And, of course, I probably danced around campfires. Sometimes what you don't know becomes bigger than the truth when you can just make up stories.

So why could I only live in my birthplace during the summer months? It was by court decree that I have limited time in the Pueblo. My grandmother had custody but felt that she couldn't give me the opportunities that would be necessary to my success as an adult. Looking back, I could commend her for her sacrifice, but blame her for her shortsightedness. I knew how much I meant to her after having lost her only daughter, my mother. But I would have prospered in the Pueblo. Later in life and with much more knowledge, the result of education and experience, I've come to believe that most children succeed in spite of us.

But on this particular evening as I sat feeling more than a little sorry for myself, something caught my eye. Funny I hadn't noticed it before. I'm trying to not sound like I'm giving it supernatural powers, but I could easily make a case for that just because of the part it played in my life. Even describing it was a challenge. For starters, it was simply a white mound seemingly attached to a rock about fifteen feet to my right. And maybe it was the moonlight that made it appear to glow. I had no idea, but I knew I needed to look closer.

Standing in front of it and looking down, I realized it was a skull. Small, five inches in length and maybe three inches across with some tiny scratch marks around the eye-sockets. My grandmother would later tell me that it had been beetle-cleaned by insects that deftly removed all vestiges of fur and flesh. I didn't know exactly what it had been in life, but the teeth, a hefty mouthful, were comprised of fangs. Yeah, actual fangs —canines in two sets, top and bottom, that curved slightly inward right along-side unbelievably sharp incisors and both premolars and molars. I was amazed and more than a little reluctant to touch it. I'd watched a documentary on the origin of the werewolf fable and the full moon over my shoulder wasn't keeping my imagination in check.

I wanted to pick it up, but hesitated. Then, like with most boys, curiosity won out. I gingerly reached down and lifted the skull up to eye level. The head felt warm to the touch which was strange in itself because the evening was cooling off. Mountain temps could easily be twenty degrees cooler after the sun set. Without fur, I had no idea what it was or had been probably not too long ago. I held it for at least five minutes and then made an interesting decision—I put it in my jacket pocket. If I didn't know what animal it was, I knew my grandmother would. And that was exactly how innocent my finding the skull had been. There were no preconceived ideas of overstepping the boundaries of the dead. No fear of what that bit of bone with the menacing teeth might mean—spells, premonitions, cursed messengers from witchdoctors—none of that even entered my head. I was innocent and not at all prepared for my grandmother's reaction.

The moon was high overhead now. I was late and I knew my grandmother would be worried. The path back down to the village twisted through a wooded patch of dense brush and trees which shaded the back of the houses. The uniqueness of those houses never failed to amaze me. They're attached to one another, actually shared walls. There was never any boasting of 'my house is bigger or better.' There was a forced equality because of how they were situated. And they all looked alike. They were all made of blocks of adobe, that mud and sand and straw concoction that withstood time. Without house numbers or street signs, I'd had to simply memorize who lived where.

I was still shrouded by the woods when I saw something that made me stop cold. Some fifty feet to my right someone was climbing out of the window at the widow Toledo's house. Unless the front door was stuck shut, you didn't leave by climbing out of a window. Then it struck me—unless you were doing something you shouldn't. I stepped back, making certain that I was hidden, and watched this person whose face was almost entirely covered by the hood on his sweatshirt, slide to the ground, look both ways, and take off running toward the road. Weird. It was a kid judging by how fast he could run and definitely male. I waited a couple more minutes before stepping out from my cover. After that bit of excitement, I'd forgotten about my new-found treasure and hung my jacket on a peg by the door when I got back to the house.

My grandmother was a traditional woman. For example, the wall beside the front door had a gaping hole in the two-foot-thick wall. A colony of ants had taken up residence and had to be dug out, contained, and moved to another spot in the nearby woods. Ants were a part of the underworld and, as such, were revered as messengers from that locale. Plus, they were admired for their workmanship. Once while walking to church with my grandmother, she abruptly pushed me off the path and scolded me for almost stepping on a trail of ants carrying food back to their mound. Nature was to be admired, learned from, and protected, never needlessly killed or even have their lives disrupted. Harmony was a word that always had special meaning for me, however difficult it might be to achieve.

I wasn't allowed to sleep in, but I also wasn't expected to get up before six. Imagine my surprise the next morning when I awoke at five—at least according to the windup alarm clock beside me on the floor. The room was in pitch blackness and my grandmother was standing over me. I couldn't see her expression clearly, but something about the way she stiffly leaned forward gave her posture a 'no nonsense' feel to it. When I finally sat up, she simply motioned for me to follow her. No words were spoken.

She walked back to the kitchen where a rough-hewn plank table and accompanying benches sat against the wall. Most people would call it a picnic table, even say it didn't belong indoors, but there wasn't a chrome and Formica dinette set in the world that could mean as much to me. Many a night I sat at that table close to the Kiva fireplace just to stay warm, or on a particularly snowy afternoon, my mother would spread a blanket on the floor and I'd curl up for a nap as close as I could get to the fireplace without getting burned.

This early morning my grandmother had stoked the fire and brought back to life the smoldering embers before placing an oak log in the center. It was late August but in the mountains there was already a hint of fall in the air. The flannel shirt I'd quickly slipped on felt good. I marveled at how easily my grandmother had lifted the log and expertly placed it so that it would quickly catch fire. She was in her sixties then, spritely and well-spoken, a fund of knowledge. She was one of only a handful of Pueblo residents who had gone to college. For a full two years she traveled back and forth to Albuquerque before having to drop out after becoming pregnant with my mother.

She was knowledgeable in many ways. She knew the tribal language, one of the few who were carrying on the oral tradition. No one then worried about what would happen when we lost this generation. She was sought after as a story-teller. The University of New

Mexico required an elective, Pueblo Indian History, and my grandmother was often asked to attend a class or two to talk about the tribe.

My favorite story involved the Navajo. Few today realize that they were known to have raided the Pueblos —not often but enough to become known as enemies. The Pueblo people were farmers—men owning stock and tilling the land. The raids were usually to steal live-stock. So, years after peace had been declared, and a feast day proclaimed to celebrate these new-found friends, my Pueblo got the last laugh.

A stew was prepared for the feast with a savory, thick sauce worthy of being mopped up with chunks of fragrant frybread, and sweet honey-tarts were served for dessert. Sounds delicious until you know that the stew was concocted out of simmering the meat of a black bear—the most sacred symbol of the Navajo. Many were sickened when the truth became known. They had eaten the very guardian of their way of life—their protector, their savior and the soul of their people. It was a story that I'd heard my grandmother share many times and always with just the faintest hint of a smile at the cunning instance of retribution by her people.

I scooted along the bench to get closer to the fire and leaned against the wall. I was having trouble keeping my eyes open. Suddenly, someone began banging on the front door calling out for my grand-mother. The old hook and eye closing gave way and there was the widow Toledo standing in the doorway, mussed hair falling from a knot of twisted braids at the base of her neck and literally wringing her hands. A cotton wrap snug around her ample frame was tied at the waist with a belt of braided cloth. The woman was well known beyond the Pueblo. She was an award-winning potter and had been my mother's mentor.

"They stole my money. A month's work. All gone." At this she began to wail and rock back and forth. My grandmother faced her, shook her gently and then took her arm and led her to the table to sit on the corner opposite me.

"Persingula, take a deep breath. Now, tell us what happened." My grandmother stayed standing with her arm around the woman's shoulders.

"After selling all weekend in Albuquerque, I came home late, after eight. I put my cash box and the pottery that I hadn't sold in my workroom, and I was so tired I went to bed. This morning I went to my work-room to get an early start. And the cash is gone. Other vendors had purchased my change so I had ten one-hundred-dollar bills. The box was opened and emptied. Whoever it was came in and left through the window in front."

I almost choked. One thousand dollars was a lot of money then but what was more shocking? I had obvi-ously seen the thief, hadn't I? I had watched someone climb out of the window of her house. And I froze. No one was paying any attention to me. If they had glanced my way they would have seen my anguish. What should I do? I didn't have a name. I didn't know for sure the person I saw had been up to wrongdoing.

Not really. Would I be believed with nothing to go on but a shadowy figure from a distance? I sat mute.

My grandmother helped Persingula to her feet. "Let's go back to your house. On the way we'll report what's happened to the Pueblo Governor and Fiscal Officer. It will be up to them to lead an investigation."

Still, I said nothing. I watched them go and simply sat there, my mind racing in circles. What was causing my silence? At school I had learned the hard way that being a snitch was asking for trouble. I had lost a tooth, lucky for me a baby tooth, but the punch in the mouth for my indiscretion had left scars. I wasn't going to make that mistake again. I put my head on my folded arms and drifted back to sleep. I woke up with my grandmother standing over me. "We have much to discuss."

I looked up expectantly. Forty-five minutes had passed and it was now six o'clock. "This morning?" I asked. She simply nodded and pointed to a shelf to the right of the fireplace.

I hadn't seen the skull, but now as I looked firelight flickered across its smooth, white roundness. I couldn't help but stare at it and then realized that my grandmother wasn't seated but was still standing over my find. Then she reached up and took it down from the shelf. At last, her eyes met mine and she demanded to know exactly where and how I had found it. I told her and it seemed important that I hadn't dug it up but that it was perched out in the open, on top of a large granite boulder.

This seemed to satisfy her and she sat down on the edge of the bench across from me and placed the skull on the table. Pointing at the skull, she asked, "Do you know what this is?" I shook my head. "I don't mean what animal but do you know its purpose?" Again, I shook my head. I'd found a skull; I brought it to the house, and I wanted to know what kind of animal it was. That was it as far as I was concerned.

She took a deep breath and reached out and took my hand. "This is your spirit animal. I have been concerned that none had sought you out, making known their intent to protect and lead you in this life. You've been on this earth these ten summers now; it was time. I am relieved. It is a good sign."

"Is it a wolf? A bobcat? A badger, maybe?" This had all the elements of something very important to my life.

She paused and squeezed my hand, "It is an opossum."

Before thinking, I burst out with, "I don't want an opossum for a spirit animal. Can't I choose?"

"Never. It is up to the animal to choose you with the help of your spirit guides. They have chosen wisely. They know your needs. When an animal makes itself known to you, like this one did, it's sharing its special mission. I am convinced that its spirit was only waiting for you to appear and claim it. The clue? You didn't have to dig it up; it was waiting to be discovered. "

Opossum. I couldn't get over that. All I knew about them was the fact that they were quirky, little animals with really strange habits. They weren't strong, no one was afraid of them, and they did this fainting thing. How could a spirit protect me in this life if it would fall over and play dead when it thought it was being threatened? I was instantly sorry that I'd tucked it in my pocket and brought it home.

"Let me tell you about your spirit animal. Its name alone has a history rich in the folklore of indigenous peoples. The Algonquin Indians called it *apasum*, or white face. "

"But I'm not an Algonquin. I'm Pueblo and you're wrong. My spirit animal is maybe an eagle—if it's not a wolf." I'd never spoken to my grandmother in this way before. I was defiant, convinced nothing as lowly as this weirdo animal could possibly protect me. Sometimes the narcissism of a ten-year-old can be overwhelming.

But I must give my grandmother credit. She didn't react—no repercussions, no grounding, not even a raised voice. She simply picked up the skull, pulled the bench on her side of the table outward, sat and leaned forward on her forearms. She placed the skull so that it was facing me. I knew she was looking at me but I couldn't meet her eyes. I fiddled with a missing button on the frayed cuff of my shirt. And waited.

"I ask one thing of you, grandson—only one thing. Do not form any opinion until I have finished my story. Will you promise that?"

I nodded. I was getting off easy. It would have been unlike my grandmother, but there wasn't any demand for an apology, and definitely no shaming—blaming my white side for indiscretions. It was common knowledge in the Pueblo that the Anglo was bereft of a true understanding of his surroundings, of nature, and absolutely ignorant of Indian ways. She repeated her question and I nodded. This time I made eye contact. She seemed pleased and patted my hand, picked up the skull and turning it this way and that, placed it back in the middle of the table.

"The spirits have chosen the best animal for you because the Opossum is very complex. This is not a sign that means something straightforward like strength, or cunning, or eyesight that can pierce the dark. Yet, those attributes are also all his. You are being blessed with the animal that calls intuitiveness, problem-solving, awareness of surroundings as a part of his skills. All of the things that allow you to discern danger and protect yourself."

"So, playing dead is smart?"

"I'll get to that. Have patience. First, the opossum will appear to you as a reminder to always protect yourself from others. Do not trust everyone; learn to know who has your best interests in mind and who might like to cause your plans to fail. The world has many bad people. You have a great need to protect yourself. You're smart, an achiever, one who will cause jealousy among those who call themselves friends. I know have been wounded by loss. Your mother had to leave you far too early, and I have not always made the best of decisions."

"Grandmother, do not blame yourself—"

"Hush. There will be time to discuss. Hear me out first."

I nodded and realized that the explanation of the spirit animal was allowing us a platform to visit my loneliness and feelings of abandonment. Was the animal already working his spirit-magic?

"The Opossum is a strong ally for someone just beginning his spiritual journey. I so hope you see how this is the perfect totem for you. The spirits have chosen well, as they always do."

"But a totem?" It was a word I only associated with those decorative, hand-carved poles found among Alaskan Natives.

"Ah, another Indian word, this time from the Ojibwa. *Nindoodem* is Ojibwa for 'my totem.' Their totems had spiritual significance sometimes offering protection to an entire tribe. Our early ancestors were entranced by the opossum. Today we know it's the only true marsupial native to our country."

I must have looked perplexed because she smiled and patted my hand. "Let me ask you what possibly could a kangaroo and an opossum have in common?" I shook my head. "Both give birth and carry their babies in a pouch. When they reach a certain age, the mother opossum gives her young family a ride on her back when she gathers food. They are loving, protective mothers. The young ones stay with her until their eyes are open and they can start searching and finding food on their own. There is a strong familial bond. I believe even now that your mother watches over you."

I didn't know what to say. Did I believe that? Had I not seen my mother shortly after her death appear as a whirlwind, a dust devil twirling across a field? Or was she one of the high-banked, fluffy clouds bringing rain the fourth day after her death? At ten I really hadn't stopped to examine how I believed. And I didn't like to think of a mother who presented me to the world without a father would also protect me. My mother had been unhappy. I know that now. And it was this unhappiness that led to the illness, the times she didn't come home but stayed out at night then sometimes not even coming home the next morning.

It was only at the end of her life that we became close which seemed like a terrible joke to have her so close but lose her. I was only five but mourned her deeply. I refused to eat; I slept only sporadically; I ran away twice trying to find her. I know my grandmother's patience was tried. But she never gave up on me. Looking back, I believe that she sent me away as a diversion. She feared for my health, my very sanity. I grieved with all my heart and at five had limited understanding of why my life had taken such a turn. My grandmother chose to break this cycle and introduce me to another life, a new world—one that would challenge me and help the memories to fade. At a terrible cost to her nurturing and love, she let me go.

"I know this brings back memories. And sometimes this is for the best. Your spiritual animal knows the importance of taking a moment here and there in life to contemplate, to let life carry on around you as you step back to only watch and listen."

That part the opossum had correct about me even down to my slipping away to sit by the river just letting my thoughts go where they wanted. My second-grade teacher used to jokingly call me 'the thinker'.

"The opossum is a true survivor—like you. When the opossum appears to you, it is saying that you will survive, too. Nothing is too big or too threatening for you to overcome. Can you believe what I'm saying?"

"Maybe." I didn't want to give in too soon but she had my interest.

"Then listen to these other attributes. The opossum wants you to be more tactical. Do you understand?"

"No." The word held no meaning for me.

"It means you must learn to plan. Do not move forward with a project that you have not thought through first. Winners plot and succeed because of it. Know the end before you begin. Know how you will win before you engage the enemy. Moving too quickly without first determining a course of action can be your downfall. And, as long as I have mentioned battle, consider this. Your spirit animal is not aggressive. It will avoid conflict if possible. In life this will bring peace. Use your reason to think your way out of confrontation." She leaned forward and patted my hand. "You have been blessed with a good mind, a strong one. There will be many opportunities in life open to you because of it. But you must be able to recognize them."

"And you're saying that my spirit animal will help?"

"Yes, most definitely. The opossum is all about instinct. We mortals call it instinct but it really has everything to do with psychic powers."

"Like a fortune-teller?" My ten-year-old mind had leaped ahead to the time at Halloween when the principal of my school set up a booth. She had a crystal ball which was just an old snow-globe, but she told fortunes and you could ask her questions. The globe, of course, would give you an answer. I remember thinking it was kind of stupid and didn't try it.

"The opossum can help you with riddles—those confusing, sometimes twisted results of something that is difficult to understand. If you listen and remain open to its help, the opossum will often give you a sign—help in deciphering spiritual meanings. Each event in your life has a reason for happening."

"Even the death of my mother?" It was the first time in front of someone else that I had said those words out loud, admitted she had left me.

"Even the death of your mother. She didn't have the strength and wisdom of the opossum to suspect the people around her. She followed where she was led never questioning the intent of others. The illness was the price she paid. The opossum is always alert to traps — people or situations that mean to hurt you. Maybe it will give you a big sign warning you not to do something. More likely, you will just get a feeling, something you can't describe really, a bothersome internal nagging that keeps at you to be careful, do your research, go slowly."

"I don't understand."

"Well, think of it as a little voice inside. Little voices warn us not to step off the curb before we look both ways when we shop in the city. It warns your uncle to go slow at a railroad crossing; your grandmother not to go into the Billy goat's pen." This time she laughed and looked up sheepishly.

I remember how I laughed with her. Everyone knew that of any animal in the Pueblo, that goat was pure meanness. And it had horns. The animal had disappeared after it had gotten out of its pen and cornered a nun in the parking lot directly in front of the village church. I personally think the stew served at the next feast day had the distinct flavor of *cabrito*.

"So, it's a helpful voice?"

"Yes, if you listen. But don't think up excuses for not paying attention to it. Be honest. Is the voice acting in your favor, trying to protect you, keep you from making a mistake? For example, as you grow older, don't be blinded by money and seek it out for itself. Don't trust love without questioning its authenticity. Don't give into emotion without reasoning."

"This is a lot for an animal to do."

"And coming to you as your spirit, it will work for you, *with* you, to protect you always. Now, go get dressed. I think this is enough of a lesson for one day. Remember, you are going with your uncle and cousins to harvest the corn."

I nodded and pushed back from the table, the skull forgotten in the promise of a fun day outside. I don't remember even thanking my grandmother for the time she had taken with me. I was all ten-year-old boy bursting with energy, stumbling over my own feet to hurriedly pull on jeans and lace up my boots.

It was unusual to be harvesting in late summer, August, instead of September, but it already promised to be an early winter. Harvesting began only when the first aspen turned to gold across the mountains. Already bright patches were showing on the slope behind the village. The squash, beans and corn needed to be brought down from the fields atop the mesa and prepared for winter. Crops that had sustained indigenous peoples for thousands of years still provided staples in the Pueblo diet. Nutritionists would discover later that beans and squash together provided all the protein needed to sustain a human being. And if the diet sounded monotonous, pinon nuts and later chilis introduced by Mexican traders added flavor and spice.

Plus, there was never any waste. The corn that they would gather today would hang to dry with husks peeled back and twisted or braided into ropes. Those very same husks could later stuff sleeping mats, or maybe adorn masks—some even being woven into baskets. More than one child's first pair of shoes was made of corn husks. And the cob was fuel or maybe a rattle to be used in ceremonies.

Growing up I never appreciated the food that I ate. Corn was dried and ground into meal for bread or combined with wild honey for a sweet pudding. Dried corn could also be soaked in water containing ash to be used as hominy or posole. But, again, most importantly, it could be easily stored and guaranteed to last through more than one season.

I heard the honk of my uncle's horn. It was amazing to me even then that the old Ford pickup still ran. It was a fossil. Peeling paint, bald patches across the hood, one back fender missing, the front two mismatched in color, and tires that looked smooth without a speck of tread. The tailgate was wired shut and I wasn't sure there was a license plate. When a car or truck never left the reservation, having a license plate was more of an expensive nuisance than something that might be required.

I said goodbye to my grandmother and hurried outside. My uncle had brought his two sons, one twelve, the other fourteen. Roddy and Vicente were in the bed of the truck sitting on a stack of gunny sacks. I hopped up on a now defunct trailer hitch and swung a leg over the tailgate almost losing my balance when it wobbled. As the youngest of the three, I chose to sit in the center of a loose spare tire. At least it was something I could hold onto.

We were probably thirty minutes from the cornfield that we'd work that day. The fields were almost always a distance from the village atop a nearby mesa. And there was good reason for this. The village was backed by the river which twisted its way through a steep canyon. Because of this configuration, sunlight was almost totally blocked in places. There was a need to plant in an area that would receive rain and sunlight and be somewhat out of reach of wooded areas that were homes to bears and deer. And the mesas had an abundance of pumice rock, that porous material that would hold moisture.

In order to get there, we had to cross the riskiest bridge I'd ever seen. I found myself crossing my fingers that we'd reach the other side. But for as much as I might badmouth my uncle's old truck, it ran, climbed, and turned obediently—and even sounded good or, I should say, loud. There was no muffler, but there was also never any sputtering or missing out. I understand now why my grandmother once muttered that he took better care of his truck than his family. At the time it didn't seem strange that he lived with his mother and only visited his wife. Those were grown-up concerns that had nothing to do with me.

By the time we reached the mesa I had been bounced around knocking my head more than a couple times against the cab. But once we'd climbed the gravel path that led to the top of that flat, table-like open field, I was, as always, in awe of being that close to the sky. Didn't they call the Acoma Pueblo, Sky City? When my uncle stopped, the three of us clamored over the sides of the truck and ran ahead. There was something so freeing to be in the open, above the village, letting the sun warm us. My uncle called us back to the truck to help him gather up the sacks and carry them to the edge of the field. He wasn't mad. He seemed to also feel the unfettered freedom that was affecting us.

At ten I didn't call it being close to God. Later when

I would think of a supreme deity, I would imagine being on the mesa. When I visited my grandmother during the summer, I went to mass every morning. Yes, every single day. And if it seems odd that Catholicism established such deep roots among the Natives of the New World, I always thought of Indian stories emphasizing Father Sky and Mother Earth. In concept, these beliefs were not unlike Christian rituals centered around the same—a holy father who dwelled above us and the earthly mother of Christ.

It was still early and the light breeze dried our sweat as we worked the rows of corn. It had been a good year. Plump cobs were swollen with well-developed kernels. Others would gather the squash and beans. It would take several families working together to husk the beans, dry the corn and prepare the squash for storage. The squash was perhaps the most labor intensive. It had to be washed, sliced thinly into strips to hang in the sun or be laid out on top of flat rocks to dry. I have thought many times as an adult how much we miss out on by our itinerant movement—seldom staying in the place of our birth among our extended family.

The morning passed quickly. It had been uneventful other than I was nursing a badly blistered thumb due to repetitive movement removing the corn cobs from the stalks. And I was tired; I'd been up since five. So, when my uncle tossed the truck keys to his oldest son and commanded Vicente to drive back down to the village to unload the half-day's pickings and get more sacks, both boys assumed that I would go with them.

And that's when I heard it. A voice—inside my head? Or something rattling around in my chest? It didn't matter from where, I said no. It commanded me to say no. My cousins started to protest and demand that I go too, they needed my help in unloading the corn. Mostly, they didn't want to see me escape having to work, but their father quieted them and reminded them that I was younger and needed their support and protection.

So, under his breath Vicente called me a 'weenie' and Roddy followed up with 'baby.' Then Vicente added 'suck up' but was overheard by my uncle who cuffed him a good one on his shoulder and admonished him to show some manners and be fair to me. It was difficult to stare at the ground and not look at them and smile from ear to ear.

If the truth were known, I agreed with the voice. I didn't relish riding in the bed of the truck slipping and sliding back down the side of the mesa. I knew Roddy would ride shotgun and the truck's bed on top of the corn would be the only seat left for me. I would have to burrow down among the bursting, overstuffed sacks and my skin would itch for a week. Besides, there were probably bugs. There was not one plus about going with them.

I've given this a lot of thought over the years. Was it just a sore thumb and being tired that deterred me from a trip back to the village? Or was it not trusting a fourteen-year-old driver? Probably not that. I wouldn't have been so knowledgeable at the age of ten and a young teenage driver was not out of the ordinary in the Pueblo. So, it was some sixth sense—some intrinsic, internal signal flashing red, cancelling any temptation to go with them. I couldn't deny it. I heard a warning because what happened next proved that the voice had saved my life.

My uncle and I went back to work but the minute we heard the grinding squeal of brakes, the deafening explosion of metal striking rock and saw the smoke, we simply ran toward the river. From our vantage point above the bridge, we could see where the truck had struck a protruding piece of granite on the right side of the gravel road—the crushed rock underneath it offering no traction. Had a tire blown causing the vehicle to swerve before rolling one full turn to land upside down halfway to the river? The embankment was steep and the truck had crumpled like foil. Its cargo of sacks of corn was strewn everywhere. But my cousins?

By the time we had slipped and tumbled our way down to the road and reached the truck some two or three minutes later, we could hear Vicente yelling for help. He was pinned in the truck's cab, under the A-post on the passenger side. Roddy had been thrown clear but had struck his head and was lying unconscious twenty feet away. We rushed toward Roddy.

"Find something I can use to prop up Roddy's head." My uncle was kneeling beside his younger son. "Hurry. Go now."

I ran the twenty or so feet back to the upside down

cab. Everything that had been inside the of the truck was now on the ground outside— newspapers, a bait bucket, a short-handled axe, two pairs of levis much the worse from wear. What could work as a pillow? Then I saw it. A dark gray hoodie hung precariously from a badly crumpled fender. I grabbed the jacket but in doing so, what had been in the right-side pocket floated to the ground—two one-hundred-dollar bills. I didn't hesitate. I grabbed up the bills and emptied the pocket of eight more. Mrs. Toledo's missing cash. I stuffed them all in the pocket of my own jeans.

I hadn't realized that my uncle was watching me until he grabbed me by the shoulder and reached for the jacket. "Give me that and whatever it was you took. You're stealing from Vicente? He can't defend himself and you piece of shit think you can take advantage?"

"No. It's not like that." I wrenched free and turned to face him but was already backing up. "Nothing I took was his. But I know whose it is." Where did that bravery come from? I also knew I didn't trust my own uncle. A grownup, a relative, but that didn't mean I could trust him. Wouldn't he defend his own son? This time the voice told me to run. I didn't hesitate; I took off down the road, across the bridge. I never looked back. I flagged a family driving toward the fields, explained there had been an accident and that I needed to get to the village and find help; they quickly turned back.

They drove me all the way to the edge of the village and the fire station. A truck of EMTs took off the minute they heard the words 'injured'. I declined going back. I knew what I had to do. I walked quickly to Persingula Toledo's house and knocked on the door. I explained everything from seeing someone exit her house through the window the night before, to finding the one thousand dollars cash after the wreck. I didn't point fingers and say I thought Vicente was the thief. I stuck to the facts.

She only asked one thing of me. She wanted to tell my grandmother instead of me. Because it involved her grandson and possibly her son, she said she felt she owed my grandmother that. I agreed. The money had been returned. My good deed was complete. How members of the tribe wanted to handle the circumstances, well, I didn't need to be a part of that.

Later that evening my grandmother asked me to wait at the table while she cleared our supper dishes. Finally, when this chore was completed, she sat beside me. At first, she shared that other than a few broken bones and a punctured lung, my cousins would mend. But it was obvious she was more interested in my involvement.

"You have grown today. You made the decisions of a man. There is no doubt that your totem gave you the courage and strength to assert yourself and do what was right. We must give thanks." She didn't mention the opossum but pointed to its skull that she'd placed back on the shelf to the right of the fireplace. "It proved its watchfulness today. It kept you safe and showed you the way to help those who needed it. And now, like any talisman, any totem, it must be fed." She placed the saucer that she was holding in front of me. "This corn-meal has been mixed with ground turquoise. Place a small amount in front of its nose."

I didn't ask questions. I did as I was directed. I knew this to be a Zuni ritual faithfully followed by other tribes when honoring fetishes, but in so doing I was accepting the opossum as my spirit guide. Had he strengthened my will to turn down the offer of a ride with my cousins and possibly saved my life? I couldn't prove that he hadn't. But was it his warning for me to run, not listen to my uncle but do what was right and return the money? Yes, and yes, but it was more than that. It was a turning point for me. A time to choose right over wrong and embrace my heritage.

Through the years I have come to recognize the clever, barely discernable but never wavering support of my spirit animal, my totem. I've made better choices because of him.

And I have prospered.

------ ❮•●•❯ ------

About the Author

Kansas native Susan Slater lived in New Mexico for thirty-nine years and used this enchanting Southwest setting for most of her mystery novels. Her Ben Pecos series reflects her extensive knowledge of the area and Native American tribal ways. In 2009, she made her first foray into women's fiction with *0 to 60*, a zany, all too true-to-life story of a woman dumped, and the book was immediately optioned by Hollywood. Her other stand-alone novels include historical book club fiction, *The Caddis Man,* and the spellbinding thriller *Five O'Clock Shadow.* As an educator, she directed the Six Sandoval Teacher Education Program for the All Indian Pueblo Council through the University of New Mexico. She also taught creative writing for UNM and the University of Phoenix. Susan passed away in May, 2023.

Get a free book when you sign up for Susan's newsletter or visit Susan's website at **susansslater.com.** Follow Susan Slater at Amazon, Bookbub, Facebook, and Twitter.

Pound of Flesh

A LOUISE PEARLIE WORLD WAR II MYSTERY

Sarah R. Shaber

"Miss Louise," Dellaphine whispered, wiping her strong brown hands on a dishtowel, "a policeman's here to see you."

"What? Why?" I asked. I couldn't imagine.

"When I got to the Western Market this morning to do the grocery shopping, there was a big crowd in front of the store. Like in one of those crime newsreels, there were flashbulbs popping, cops everywhere, and one of them black police wagons backed up to the rear door."

I felt a sick sensation in my stomach. I pulled off my gloves and hat and tossed them with my pocketbook onto the tapestry chair in the entry hall.

"The policeman's waiting in the lounge," Dellaphine said. "With Miss Phoebe and Miss Ada."

My stomach churned in earnest. I thought I knew what this was about. Though you'd think the D.C. police would have better things to do than run down a couple of pounds of sugar bought without a ration coupon. Best face up to it.

Phoebe, my landlady, never forgot her manners, no matter who her visitor was. Wearing a threadbare Fortuny caftan, she presided over her Limoges coffee set, pouring for the police officer perched on her davenport.

Ada, her platinum hair in crimps and curlers tucked under a scarf, curled up in an armchair.

The policeman rose when he saw me.

"Officer Bennett," Phoebe said, "this is Mrs. Louise Pearlie, one of my boarders."

"Ma'am," Bennett said, touching his forehead.

"Good to meet you," I said, smoothing my skirt under me as I took a seat next to Phoebe.

Bennett sat back down, rather stiffly. He was an older man, with plenty of gray streaking his hair, but his age wasn't unusual these days. The young men were all in the military.

Ada and Phoebe both looked so worried that I felt quite nervous. It was just a pound of sugar. So difficult to drink coffee without it, especially if the coffee was mostly chicory. I had never been able to get used to chicory, no matter how much milk I added.

"Mrs. Pearlie," he said, pulling a notebook and pencil from his pocket. "I need to ask you some questions."

"Officer, I think I know what this is about. I admit I bought a pound of sugar without a ration coupon at the

Western Market last night. I'm sorry, I know I shouldn't have, and of course I will pay the fine."

"What time did you buy the sugar, ma'am?" Bennett asked.

"About nine-fifteen, after the store closed."

"Was there anyone else in the store? Did you see anyone enter after you left? Anybody suspicious loitering outside in the street?"

"No," I said. "I don't understand. What is going on?"

"Dear," Phoebe began.

"Please, Mrs. Holcombe," Bennett said gently, "let me finish. Mrs. Pearlie, do you know of anyone besides yourself who purchased black market goods from the owner of Western Market, Mr. Elmer Metz?"

I tried not to glance at Ada.

"I've already told him, Louise," Ada said. "I've bought three pounds over the last year. That's all."

"No one other than Ada," I said to the policeman.

The words "black market" had such a nasty ring. Surely Metz would be in trouble, not Ada and me. Selling black market goods was a much more serious offense than buying an occasional bag of sugar.

"I'd like you to think again, Mrs. Pearlie," Bennett said. "This is important. Did you see anything suspicious, anything, when you were at the Market? Or after you left?"

I thought back. The café next door to the market had been closed and dark. Of course the windows upstairs, where the café owner, her son, and her boarders lived, were still lit. The filling station on the corner was closed and the nearby movie theatre marquee was dark.

"No," I said. "I didn't see anything unusual."

"Then," Bennett said, turning another page of his notebook, "it looks like you were the last person to see Mr. Metz alive."

"Excuse me?" I wasn't sure that I had heard him correctly. I thought he was investigating black market racketeering. "What do you mean?"

Officer Bennett looked up from scribbling in his notebook. "Mrs. Pearlie, Mr. Metz was murdered last night. His colored boy found him when he came to work this morning."

"Louise, he was stabbed with a butcher knife," Ada said, leaning forward in her chair. "Can you imagine? It was buried right in his chest. Isn't that awful?"

"Oh no," I said, swallowing a gasp of shock, "That's horrible!"

"Poor man," Phoebe said. "More coffee?" she asked the police officer.

"No thank you, ma'am. And please, Miss Herman," Bennett said to Ada, "let me finish here. You can gossip after I've left."

"Of course," Ada said, subsiding into her seat.

"Mrs. Pearlie, it's early days in our investigation yet, but we've gone over the last twenty-four hours of Mr. Metz's life pretty thoroughly. Our doc figures Metz died before midnight. Mrs. Jane Jones, who owns the café next door, was doing paperwork at her desk upstairs when she saw you enter the back door of the Western Market after it closed, right about when you said you did. She saw you leave around fifteen minutes later. She worked for two more hours at her desk and saw no one else go inside, and didn't see Mr. Metz leave. She thought nothing of that. He often stayed late or slept on a cot in the storeroom."

"Someone else must have come later," I said.

"Not that she saw, ma'am. Now, the filling station owner, Mr. Pete Cousins, went into the market by the back door before you. About eight. Several people leaving the café noticed him."

"Really, officer," Phoebe said, "this is uncalled for. Surely someone could have slipped into the store after Louise left. That Jones woman couldn't have been looking out her window the entire time she was working at her desk."

Bennett ignored her. "When Mr. Metz's stock boy —" and here he consulted his notes "—Sid White, arrived at seven-thirty this morning, he found Metz dead."

"How terrible," I said. "But you can't think I had anything to do with this."

Bennett closed his notebook and stuffed it into his pocket. He looked at me with light blue, inquiring eyes. He didn't seem to be accusing me of anything, but he struck me as a man who wouldn't stop asking questions until he got answers.

"Mrs. Pearlie, do you have anything to add to what we've discussed?"

"No," I said. "I don't. I hardly knew the man. I mean, I just bought a couple of pounds of sugar from him."

"I need to collect your fingerprints now. To compare to the ones on the butcher knife. There were several sets."

Both Phoebe and Ada protested.

"Not right here in my lounge," Phoebe said.

"It's all right," I said to them. "I don't mind. I never touched that knife, so this will clear me."

"But you're not a suspect, surely," Phoebe said.

"We need to identify every fingerprint we can on that knife handle," Officer Bennett said. "And you're right, of course. If your fingerprints aren't on the knife, that clears you."

"See?" I said to Phoebe and Ada. "It's okay."

A small black leather case sat at Bennett's feet. He lifted it onto the coffee table. Open, it revealed a tidy collection of bottles, brushes, rollers, and fingerprint cards. Ada and Phoebe couldn't help but lean forward to watch. Bennett rolled my fingers in ink and pressed each finger onto a card, then handed me a cloth to wipe my hands. I didn't tell Bennett that I'd had my fingerprints taken when I swore my loyalty oath early in 1942. I preferred that he know as little about me as possible.

"If you think of anything else, please come around to the station," Bennett said.

"Certainly," I said.

Phoebe showed Officer Bennett to the door.

I wanted a martini in the worst way.

I loved Dellaphine's fried chicken, which was a good thing, since we had it for dinner twice a week. I could live happily with less beef to eat, as long as I could get chicken and plenty of potatoes and vegetables from our Victory garden. Most Americans, like Henry, our male boarder, who sat scowling at his dinner plate across from me, missed fresh beef badly. Tongue and oxtail weren't good substitutes for steak.

It was just the three of us at dinner—me, Phoebe, and Henry. Ada had gone to her gig at the Willard Hotel, where she played clarinet in the house band. Joe, our other male boarder, was in New York City on business.

"You know, Louise," Henry said, spearing a crispy chicken drumstick from the platter, "you're probably the main suspect, being the last person who saw Metz alive."

"Don't be ridiculous, Henry," Phoebe said. "I'm sure the police don't suspect Louise of anything at all. Someone must have gone to the market after Louise left and killed Mr. Metz. The police just want to know if she saw anyone."

It was so stupid of me to have bought that sugar. Because I wasn't just any government girl. I worked for the Office of Strategic Services, America's spy agency, in the Registry, where all the OSS documents were filed. I had Top Secret Clearance and I didn't want to lose it.

Which I might if my name hit the newspapers associated in any way with a murder. I hoped Officer Bennett could solve this case quickly and keep my name out of it.

After dinner Phoebe and Henry went upstairs to their rooms, so I wandered back into the kitchen looking for company. And maybe some gossip.

Dellaphine was drying the last of the dishes. Her daughter, Madeleine, still dressed in the neat blue suit she'd worn to work at the Social Security Administration, sat at the kitchen table reading the evening newspaper. Madeleine was the first colored girl I knew personally who wasn't somebody's maid or cook. I admired her.

"Want the funnies?" she asked, sliding them across the table to me when I sat down.

"Sure," I said, flipping through the section looking for Brenda Starr, girl reporter.

Dellaphine joined us with a tall glass of iced tea adorned with a sprig of mint from our garden. "Miss Phoebe said you were the last person to see Mr. Metz alive," she said. "Except the murderer," she added hastily.

"Looks like it," I said. "The police don't seem to think I'm a suspect, though." I tried to laugh, but the sound emerged as a halfhearted squeak.

"I heard that that butcher knife was real deep into his chest," Dellaphine said. "A woman couldn't have done it."

Madeleine looked up from her newspaper. "You

don't need to worry, Miss Louise. They'll arrest the colored boy, they always do."

"Madeline," her mother said. "I didn't raise you to talk like that."

"Please, Momma, you know Sid was working off his mother's debt," Madeleine said. "For practically no pay. He hated that man. Why look for the real killer when there's a Negro with a motive so handy?"

Officer Bennett didn't seem to me to be the kind of person who'd arrest just anybody to solve a crime, but I didn't like coming between Dellaphine and Madeleine when they argued, so I kept my opinion to myself. "What debt did Sid's mother owe Mr. Metz?" I asked instead.

"He gave credit for groceries during the Depression," Dellaphine said. "Lots of folks would have gone hungry otherwise. They weren't all colored, neither."

Madeline rolled her eyes. "All those poor folks are paying him back with interest now. And then some. When the police find his book, I bet you a Hershey's bar that his murderer is listed right there."

"His book?" I asked.

"He kept a ledger with the names of everyone who owed him," Dellaphine said.

I wondered if that book contained the names of people who bought black market sugar. Like my name. And Ada's.

When I got upstairs, I mixed myself a martini from the pint of Gordon's gin and bottle of vermouth I kept in my dresser drawer hidden under my panties and slips.

Saturday morning after the breakfast rush I pushed through the café's swinging doors and found Mrs. Jones sitting alone at a booth drinking a cup of coffee and scribbling in a notebook. I slid onto the bench across from her. As soon as she saw me, she flushed bright red. She patted her face with her hands, worn from years in the café kitchen, to cool off her cheeks, and then tucked her dyed auburn hair behind her ears.

"I'm sorry," she said. "Don't be angry."

"I'm not," I said. "You had to tell the truth."

She dropped her pencil onto the opened notebook and rubbed her temples. "We're out of coffee. Would you like some tea? Cocoa?"

"No thanks. Have you heard anything more from the police?"

She shook her head. "Not yet. It's all so terrible. Mr. Metz was a good man. After my husband died I didn't know how I'd survive. And I had a son to support. Without the credit for groceries he gave me, I couldn't have kept the café going. For years he wouldn't let me pay anything, just wanted to eat his meals here for free. Now I could pay him in full, but he wouldn't let me. Just said he wanted his meals here every day like always. He sat right at this booth." She patted the bench beside her. "Three times a day."

"I hear not everyone thought so well of him," I said.

She shrugged. "It's hard to like a man you owe money to."

When she reached for her coffee cup I noticed the gold circle on her left ring finger. "When did you get married?" I asked.

She smiled happily. "Just last weekend," she said. "Do you know Tom? Tom Murray? He rented one of my rooms on the third floor. He works for the bus company. We've been keeping company for almost a year, and, well, we're so happy now. And he's good to my son, treats him like he was his own."

"Congratulations," I said. "So I guess you go by Jane Murray now?"

"I still answer to Jane Jones. That's how the customers know me."

On my way back to the boarding house, I passed the rear of the Western Market. The back door was ajar. Curiosity got the better of me and I slipped inside.

"Come to see the blood?"

I started at the voice, my hand over my heart. "You frightened me."

"Didn't intend to," the colored boy said. He was about sixteen years old, I guessed, clad in loose denim trousers and a pressed white Oxford shirt with ragged cuffs. He wielded a mop that had a thick rag head. "You're the fourth sightseer that's snuck in here today.

Sorry, there's no blood, I done washed it away already. Officer Bennett said I could."

"You're Sid."

"Yes, ma'am."

I noticed a dented tin bucket at his feet. The water in the bucket was a rusty brown. I felt my heart clutch.

"Yes, I cleaned up his blood. Hard to believe, isn't it? Every night of the last two years I've prayed to Jesus to be released from this job, and now I'm free, and here I am cleaning up the place." He shook his head and set to mopping the floor again. "It just seemed wrong to leave things such a mess. But after I leave tonight I ain't coming back."

I sat on a crate of cabbages and watched him work.

"Why didn't you quit?" I asked. "There are so many good jobs open now."

Sid stopped mopping and glared at me. "Don't you think I wanted to?" Sid's voice shook with emotion. "I could get a job at a factory and pay Mr. Metz what my momma owed him in a month. But no—he said I had to work it off for ten dollars a week instead. Until her debt was paid." Sid gripped the mop handle so tightly I could almost hear the wood crack. "God, I hated that man!"

"Sid," I said, "you might want to think twice about saying you hated Mr. Metz…."

"Why? Because I might get arrested for murder? Since my fingerprints were all over that butcher knife?" A broad grin split his face. "Ma'am, I got the best alibi in the world. I told that cop and he already checked it out."

"The best alibi in the world?" I wondered.

"Rich white men!" Sid laughed out loud. "I was moonlighting at Mr. Lee Nelson's house on Dupont Circle Thursday night. Fetching drinks and emptying ashtrays for him and his poker buddies. I was there until four o'clock in the morning."

"I'm glad to hear that."

"Mr. Metz's book is missing too," Sid said. "Did you know?"

"The ledger?" I said. "The one that lists the people who owed him money?"

"That's right. Whoever inherits this dump won't be able to collect nothing from nobody."

"I would like to know why this is any of your business." Pete Cousins stabbed a squeegee into the pail of water at his feet. I'd found the filling station owner cleaning his station's front windows. "Why should I answer your questions about Elmer Metz?"

"Because I was the last person who saw him alive, except for the murderer, that's why. Because I bought a pound of sugar from the man and I'm a government girl and don't want my name in the papers," I said. "I don't want to lose my job."

"Oh." He dipped his squeegee into the bucket and drew it over the expanse of glass with long, sweeping strokes. "Well then, I suppose I can tell you what I told the police. Yes, I did go into the market last night, to have it out with him."

"Have what out?"

"For years now, I been giving him free gas, oil changes, antifreeze, because he issued my family credit for a few groceries during the bad times. I got sick of it. I paid him twice over. But he had the gall to take out the ledger and show me what I owed him and there was nothing credited to my account. Said the free gas was just interest, that I still owed him the balance."

He flung the squeegee on the ground and shoved his hands in his pockets "And no, I didn't go back later and kill him," he said. "The police took my fingerprints and they'll find out it wasn't me because I never touched that butcher knife. But I'll tell you something I didn't tell the police. If you mention it to anyone, I swear I'll call you a liar."

"What?"

"I took the ledger. Wrestled it right away from his greedy self. Burned it up in that incinerator over there." He pointed to a metal barrel, singed with black, on the edge of his property. "So no one can say all the folks who paid off their debts in kind still owe any money."

I shook my head, wishing he hadn't done that. I'd hoped to find a clue to Metz's killer in that ledger.

"What's the matter?" he asked. "Everything okay?"

"Sure," I said, collecting myself. I was good at keeping secrets. That's why I'd risen in the Office of Strategic Services from clerk to research assistant. But I didn't see how I could stay silent about this. A man had been murdered. And I suspected who'd done it.

Sunday morning early I knocked on the back door of the café. Mrs. Jones opened it a crack.

"Yes, Mrs. Pearlie? What is it? I'm checking stock right now and it's not a good time for a visit."

"We need to talk," I said, "about Metz's murder."

She shrugged and opened the door. The café's kitchen was spotless. She pulled me up a stool, and I joined her at a wooden table deeply scored by years of chopping meat and vegetables.

"My husband and son are at the fish market this morning," she said. "Tom is going to quit his job and help me run the café."

"That's nice." I ran my hands across the deep scars on the table. "After all these years in this kitchen you must wield a butcher's knife pretty well. As well as any man."

"Sure can," she said, grinning and flexing her biceps like a boxer.

"You know, of all the people I talked to about Mr. Metz, you were the only person who said anything kind about him."

She shrugged. "He wasn't what you would call like-able. But my son and I would have wound up in a hobo camp if it weren't for the store credit he gave me."

"For which you fed him for free every day. Paid him in kind."

"It was the least I could do."

"There's more than one way for a woman to pay a man in kind."

She clapped her hands over her mouth to muffle her shocked cry.

When she could speak her voice broke. "How did you know?" she asked.

"It was a guess, really. I thought of how much Metz's murderer must have despised him, and the filling station guy mentioned paying him 'in kind,' and I realized a woman had more than one way to pay a debt."

"Twice a week I left my bed at night and went to him on that awful cot in his storeroom," she said. "He didn't care that I hated him. After the war started, when the café started making good money, he wouldn't let me pay him back. I had to keep…. screwing him."

I flinched at the nasty word, but she'd had to do a nasty thing. I felt terribly sorry for her.

"I was desperate. Thursday night I confronted Metz with a check in my hand, and told him it was over. He laughed at me. Said he'd tell Tom everything if I didn't keep sleeping with him. How could I do that? Tom would notice if I left our bed."

I reached for her hands and held them. She let me grip them for a second, then pulled back, a defiant look on her face. "I killed him, okay? I'm telling you because I can see from your face that you won't turn me in. The police don't suspect me. They haven't even taken my fingerprints."

She was right. I wouldn't tell on her for killing such a louse. What good would hanging her for murder do? She had a husband and a son who needed her.

"Metz was trimming pork chops," she continued. "The knife was right there on the butcher's block, just like this one." She nodded toward her own knife. "I couldn't stop myself. So many people hated Metz, I did the world a favor."

Then we heard a man clear his throat. We both looked towards the door. Officer Bennett stood there with his small black leather case in his hand. "I'm sorry to interrupt, and so early in the morning. But Mrs. Jones, we're collecting the fingerprints of all Mr. Metz's acquaintances, and I'm afraid I neglected to take yours earlier. Is now a good time?"

Pound of Flesh was first published in *Carolina Crimes: Nineteen Tales of Lust, Love and Longing*, ed. Karen Pullen, Wildside Press in March 2014.

About the Author

Sarah R. Shaber is the author of the Louise Pearlie World War II mysteries published by Severn House. She is also the author of an earlier series, the Professor Simon Shaw mysteries, and was editor of *Tar Heel Dead,* a collection of mystery short stories by North Carolina authors. Her books are available in eBook format at amazon.com and in paperback format at Amazon, Barnes and Noble and many other online bookstores. Learn more at **www.sarahrshaber.com**.

Case of the Prized Pies

A CORGI CASE FILES SHORT STORY

J.M. Poole

"You can keep pointing out other flavors, but I think you ought to know something. You're just helping me make my point. All I'm saying is, well, it's not natural. None of it."

The woman whose arm was hooked through mine turned to offer me one of her million-dollar smiles.

"Oh, Zachary. Don't be melodramatic. Just remember, you volunteered to be a part of this. No one forced you to do anything."

"*Volunteered?* Lady, I was drafted, plain and simple. If I could've made it to the door before they caught up with me, then all of this would be a moot point. For the record, I still say this was Sherlock's fault."

"Just because you got tangled up in his leash does not make it your sweet little boy's fault."

"Sweet? Pssht. What about conniving? Or manipulative? Or...?"

Jillian swatted my arm.

"The bottom line is, you're here *and* you agreed to this. Whether you like it or not, you're going to have to follow through. You wouldn't want to let those little old ladies down, would you?"

"The PV Quilting Club needs to stop taking on the responsibility of judging if they don't have the manpower to do it themselves," I grumbled. "It's not my fault they're short on judges. Why should I have to suffer?"

"You're going to eat some pies, and you think you're suffering? Oh, you poor baby."

I looked at my wife and laughed.

"You know, there was a time when you'd be much more sympathetic."

"Show me a time when you don't feel threatened by little old ladies," Jillian returned, giggling.

"Did you bring it? Tell me you brought it. If not, then I'm making a run for it out the back."

My wife turned to signal the teenage girl trailing behind her, holding a travel mug. This one was the largest I owned, which held just over a hundred glorious ounces of my favorite caffeinated drink.

"Judges to their tables!" a voice called out. "The competition is about to begin. Thank you."

Jillian leaned forward to give me a peck on my cheek as I passed Sherlock and Watson's leashes over to her.

"Good luck, Zachary. I know you'll do great!"

"Oh, man," I whispered, as I again stared at what was waiting for me. "I don't know if I can do this."

247

"Make it through and I'll take you out for a burger and fries after you're done," Jillian promised.

Nodding, I stifled a groan and followed several others to the judges' table at the head of the line. Smiling and giving a little wave to the crowd that was beginning to form, I set my five-gallon bucket of soda on the ground by my chair and looked around. Joining me as a judge was a slim guy over a decade younger than me, whom I knew. Spencer Woodson, or Woody as he prefers to be called, owns and operates a hobby shop by the name of Toy Closet. His daughter, Zoe, was on my somewhat short list of (corgi-approved) dog sitters. Next to him sat an older woman I didn't recognize. Her mouth was set in a frown, and she was wearing a green paisley floor-length gown. Completing that picture was a pink food net covering her hair.

"Isn't this going to be fun?" the little old woman said, as she placed her hand over mine on the table. "Betsy Godel. It's a pleasure, Mr. Anderson. A real pleasure!"

The chair on Betsy's left was pulled out and a second elderly woman sat down. She was wearing a thick wool sweater and a pair of blue jeans. She looked around the table, smiling politely at everyone, until her eyes found me. Both shot open and a hand was thrust my way.

"Zachary Anderson! As I live and breathe! Oh, it's a pleasure to meet you, sir."

I took the hand and was shocked to discover it

heavily callused. This was someone who was definitely used to physical labor.

"Hello. You have the advantage, Mrs.....?"

"Oh, where are my manners? I'm Shirley Baggins."

"Baggins?" I repeated. "As in....?"

"Bilbo Baggins, you'd be correct," Shirley chuckled. "No relation, I assure you. I own a ranch to the south, where I breed and sell horses."

"Oh, like racing horses?" I asked, interested.

"No, nothing like that. My babies are Shires. Draft horses. They are, without a doubt, the most beautiful of all the drafts, and I honestly believe that includes Clydesdales."

Me, Woody, Betsy, and Shirley then collectively turned to look at the empty seat at the end of our table.

"Are we missing someone?" Woody asked.

"You'd be missing two if I didn't get myself tangled in Sherlock's leash," I said, under my breath.

Overhearing, Woody snorted with laughter.

"Ah, here she comes," Shirley informed us.

"She's late," Betsy reported, lifting her nose.

The final member of our team sat down and gave us a sheepish smile. Our last judge was much younger than Betsy or Shirley. In fact, I don't even think she was out of her teens.

"I'm so sorry I'm late, everyone. Wow, were y'all waiting on me? I'm sorry! I just got out of my classes."

"And what's your name, dear?" Shirley politely asked.

"Angela Meyerson. You can call me Angie." Introductions were made, and as expected, when she got to me, she lit up like a Christmas tree. "Oh, I've heard of you! You're Sherlock and Watson's daddy! I love your corgis!"

I gave the girl a smile and inclined my head. "Nice to meet you, Angie."

At that moment, the girl's cell rang. Or, more specifically, the special ringtone she had set for this caller began playing. *Unchained Melody*, by the Righteous Brothers.

"I am so sorry," Angie said, blushing profusely. "It's my boyfriend. Let me–Honey? I'm kinda busy. Call you in just a bit. Love you!"

Now we all heard a loud cricket chirp. That'd be *my* phone. It was Jillian. She said both Sherlock and Watson were staring at Angie, and both were sitting. That was their way of telling me that they had noticed something and were trying to get my attention.

SERIOUSLY?

YES. IDK. TAKE A PIC?

GOOD GRIEF. FINE.

I angled the phone, pretended I was polishing the screen, and snapped a few pictures. I know one of them got her, because Jillian promptly texted back that both dogs were back to ignoring her.

Moments later, without much fanfare, a middle-aged man wearing a bright blue polyester suit selected the first pie from the table and served slices to each of us.

There before me was the first pie I was going to

have to sample. Didn't the rest of my table care that the filling for this pie looked, smelled, and probably tasted, like freshly cut grass clippings?

"Woody? Tell me this is a joke. That we don't have to eat a grass pie."

"It's spinach, you goof," Woody chortled. "Oh, man. I've been looking forward to this. Zack? What's the matter? You don't like spinach?"

"The closest I've come to being able to eat spinach is when it's in a raw form, mixed in a salad. Cooked? Hoo, boy. I'm gonna need my soda for this one."

"They provide glasses of water," Woody pointed out.

I shook my head. "Psssht. That's not nearly strong enough."

"You haven't even tasted it yet," Woody protested.

Small notebooks were handed out. When I opened mine, I could see five printed pages inside, plus an extra dozen or so blank sheets in the back for taking notes. Each pie, it would seem, needed to be graded on four different areas: external characteristics, internal characteristics, flavor, and skillset.

The filling? Well, that was graded, too. It had to have the correct proportions between crust and whatever filling was present. If it was fruit, then it had to be neither dry nor too juicy. And above all, the sheet instructed, there shouldn't be any excessive thickening agent, whatever that was.

I glanced at the what had been set before me and I fought valiantly to keep from groaning aloud. Spinach.

Just the smell alone made me want to gag. I used the fork to get my first bite ready, only I apparently didn't apply enough pressure to cut the crust. Green grass, er, filling, *oozed* out of the shell in great clumps. I swear I could see individual grass blades.

Glancing nervously around my table, I saw that Woody was already halfway through his pie, and Betsy was several bites into hers and taking notes. I took a huge swig of soda and popped the bite into my mouth.

"How is it?" Woody asked, from my right. "It's good, isn't it? The crust is outstanding. I have no idea how they got it so flaky."

Plastering a forced, pageant-like smile on my face, I nodded. "I am in no way a fan of spinach, but whoever made that one did a good job. You're right. The crust is outstanding. It'd be so much better if this was a marion-berry pie."

Woody tapped his notebook. "Better take some notes while you still can."

Nodding, I slid the notebook over and graded it accordingly. I gave it decent marks until I got to the Filling section of the Internal Characteristics part. Good proportions? I honestly thought there was way too much filling for such a thin crust.

"I can't wait to try this next one," Shirley exclaimed, as she pushed her half-eaten slice of spinach pie out of the way. "I was never a fan of cooked spinach. But this one? Oh, I'm gonna enjoy this."

"What's next?" I asked, hoping and praying that it'd be something good.

The next selection was a dull yellow in color, reminding me of a cheesecake at first glance.

"We have a perfect example of a desperation pie next," the announcer informed us. "Originating in the 19th century, these pies were made with staple ingredients. Behold, the pioneer vinegar pie."

Once more, I felt the blood drain from my face. Vinegar? In a pie? Right on cue, my stomach gurgled, and not in a good way.

"It's so good!" Woody moaned, from beside me. "I definitely want the recipe for this one."

Leaning forward, I studied the pie and grudgingly had to admit it looked tantalizing. The crust was baked to perfection. It had a light dusting of cinnamon and sugar on it, and the filling was a rich egg-based custard. Much to my amazement, the pie was fantastic.

"Vinegar is supposed to be in this?" Angie asked, after trying several bites of her pie. "I'm with Mr. Woodson. This is great!"

"It's not bad," I decided, as I picked up my pen and made a few notes. Leaning back in my chair, I watched the plates as the dishes were cleared. "There's something else. Lemon! There's a faint taste of citrus in it."

"You're right," Woody said, giving me a friendly slap on the back. He immediately began scribbling in his notebook. "And I'm stealing that."

I laughed and had a few more bites of the pie before rinsing my mouth with a swallow of soda. All right, I was starting to warm up to the idea of trying these unusual pies. What's next?

Pie number three was presented to me, and I couldn't help pumping the air a few times. Yes! Finally! I get to sample a pie that looks *normal*! However, before I could take a bite, the Fates intervened and brought everything to an immediate and unpleasant stop.

"Omigod!" Someone shouted, from the next table over. "The rumors are true! Stumpy is.... is.... a *fraud*!"

It was then that I made eye contact with Jillian, who was frantically pointing down at the dogs. Sherlock and Watson were on their feet and paying attention to something that I couldn't see. What had the dogs spotted? And who–or what–was a stumpy?

"Did I miss something here?" I whispered. "Why is everyone freaking out about this?"

"You're kidding, right?" Woody stammered. "You're telling me you don't know Stumpy?"

"Never heard of him."

"He's William J. Holden. He's been a farmer for more years than you've been alive."

"Stumpy?" I repeated, confused.

Woody started to laugh, but was able to disguise it as a cough. "Look at his hands."

"What about them?"

"Do you see them?"

"Not from here. What about them?"

Woody shrugged. "He's missing several fingers on each hand."

"Do I want to know how?" I hesitantly asked.

"He was a farmer," Woody repeated. "That means he's had to work around farm equipment. Well, those machines aren't the most user-friendly. And, I'm sorry to say, he's known to be a klutz."

"Yikes. From farmer to baker?"

"He's royalty around here. People have been trying to figure out how he's been doing it for years. Years!"

"Doing what?" I asked.

"Winning, Zack. Stumpy is known for making the best pies you've ever tasted. He doesn't bake many, and those extra he has are sold to a few stores."

"He's a professional baker now?" I asked.

Woody nodded and was silent as he scanned the room. "Hmm, I don't see him here."

"Does he win a lot of contests?" I asked.

Woody nodded. "Every contest he enters."

"Do you think he cheats?"

"I *know* he does," Betsy interjected.

Her soft, grandmotherly features had hardened into a grimace. Surprised by her appearance, I could only stare. Betsy caught me looking.

"Do you have something to say, Mr. Anderson?"

"Judging by your tone, I'm assuming you know this Stumpy person?"

Betsy's frilly white hair bobbed up and down. "He's won the grand prize every year for the past ten years," she reported. "No one is that lucky."

"Maybe he's that good?" I suggested.

"Hmph," Betsy scowled, but didn't say anything else.

"He's favored to win this year, too," Angie piped up. "I've had his marionberry pie. It's my absolute favorite."

Respect for the girl jumped up several notches.

"Everyone always assumes he cheats," Betsy said, breaking her silence. "This would be proof positive that he does. Finally, someone called him out. I should send them a fruit basket."

"Don't be melodramatic, Mrs. Godel," Woody sighed. "Oh, there he is!"

A short, roly-poly balding man, wearing wire-rimmed glasses, was backing slowly away from the angry crowds before him.

"I don't know what's going on!" the poor fellow was saying. "That's not one of my pies!"

"It has your card on it," another voice accused.

"Well, y-yes, but...."

"And that is your writing, isn't it?"

"Y-yes, but it could be...."

Several older ladies broke from the herd and advanced on Mr. Stumpers. Er, make that Mr. Holden.

"Just admit you were finally caught," the first woman insisted. "We all know you're guilty. No one could win as many times as you unless you had found a way to cheat. Go on, admit it!"

"I did nothing wrong," William insisted. "I didn't break any rules."

Moving closer, I finally caught sight of the retired farmer's hands. Woody was right. The index and pinkie finger on his left hand were non-existent past the middle knuckle. On the right, it was the index finger again, but this time, also missing were parts of the middle finger and the very tip of the right pinkie.

"I just *knew* it," a second woman exclaimed. "Haven't I been saying there's no way you could win every contest? No one is that good. Therefore, you *must* be cheating. All your pies should be disqualified!"

"I've done nothing wrong!" William cried.

The angry mob grew larger. One look at William convinced me I needed to intervene.

"Now just stay right there," I ordered, stepping in front of William and holding up my hands. "You're so certain he's cheating? Let's see the proof."

"The crust on this pie is clearly store-bought," one of the female judges insisted. "When you've been baking as long as I have, you just know."

"And you are?" I inquired.

"Mrs. Mildred Turnbuckle," came the curt answer.

"You can say for certain that this crust came from a store?"

Mildred's head nodded. "Without question."

I turned to rotund baker. "William, is that your pie?"

"Call me Stumpy."

My eyebrows shot up. He liked the name? Oh, well, when in Rome....

"Okay, er, Stumpy, is that your pie?"

William was about to nod but he suddenly frowned.

"It's not, is it?" I guessed.

After a few moments, Stumpy shook his head. "I don't know how to explain it. That is not the pie I dropped off yesterday. I mean, parts of it are, but not the...."

"... crust?" Betsy interrupted. "How convenient."

I turned to the senior citizen and crossed my arms. "Innocent until proven guilty. Sound familiar?"

Betsy's mouth became a thin, disapproving line and she promptly returned to her chair at our judging table and sat, clutching her purse in her hands.

I heard a collar rattle nearby. Looking up, I saw Jillian standing on the outskirts of the crowd of onlookers, holding the leashes of two anxious corgis.

"Was that too harsh?" I quietly asked, as Jillian joined me. I gave both dogs a friendly scratch. Sherlock, for some reason, kept turning to the side to look at something on the left, as though someone over there was grilling steaks.

"You were more polite than I would have been," Jillian confided. "Betsy Godel can be an insufferable know-it-all."

"So, William says.... hey, quick question. Do you call him by that name?"

"Who, Stumpy? Of course. He's a delight. He has a sense of humor and is not afraid to make fun of himself."

"Gotcha. All right, let's assume Stumpy is right, and that someone tampered with his pie. Who do you think could've done it?"

Jillian shrugged. "If you're hoping to narrow down

the suspects by determining who might have had a grudge against Stumpy, then you're unfortunately going to be looking at a long list."

I sighed. "That's just great. He's won that much?"

"Yes."

"That doesn't give us much to go on."

Sherlock shook his collar again. Looking down, I saw him staring at me, ears pointed up. He snorted once and then turned to look in the same direction he had looked just a few minutes ago.

"I've been meaning to tell you," Jillian began. "Those two? You'd think you were working a police case. Sherlock and Watson keep trying to pull me over to something on the far wall, but I wouldn't let them. And now? I guess they're trying their charms on you since I wouldn't play along."

I looked at the dogs. "There's no crime here, guys. Well, no *police* crime."

"Awwwoooooo," Sherlock howled.

Several members of the crowd looked over at us and smiled. Fingers began pointing. Sherlock, for his part, ignored them.

"What do you need, pal?" I asked. "Is there something you want me to see?"

Sherlock must have taken the question as permission to go, because he and Watson were suddenly pulling so hard on their leashes that I thought they were going to choke themselves.

"Hoo, boy. Here we go. Pardon me. Coming through. Oh, I'm so sorry about that. Dogs, am I right?

Sherlock, don't.... my apologies, ma'am. Those two have a mind of their own sometimes."

I felt the tension in their leashes lessen as we arrived at whatever I was supposed to see. What was it? A water cooler. Confused, I looked at the dogs, only to see that they weren't staring at the dispenser, but what was sitting on its left.

"It's just a stereo," I reported. "Hear the music? Someone has the radio on, that's all. Now, can we go? Nope, I guess not."

Neither dog budged. In fact, both corgis promptly sat.

"What is it?" Jillian asked. "Watching the three of you wade through that crowd was.... well, *entertaining*. Most of the people had angry looks on their faces, but as soon as they saw Sherlock and Watson, they couldn't get out of the way fast enough."

"Don't I know it."

"So, what are we looking at?" Jillian asked. "A water dispenser?"

Shaking my head, I pointed at the small boombox next to the dispenser. "I think they're looking at that thing."

"The stereo? What about it?"

"I have no idea."

Jillian listened for a moment. "Who's singing? What's the song?"

My eyes lit up and I fumbled for my phone. "*Larger Than Life*, from the Backstreet Boys. Don't ask how I know."

"You like boy bands. It's okay. No judging here. They're sitting. Time for a picture?"

I stared at the corgis, who were now panting. Both looked pleased with themselves.

"Fine. Guys? Here's my phone. I'm taking a pic. Are you happy now?"

The answer to that was a resounding yes. Both rose to their feet and were ready to go.

"He didn't do it," I announced, as we arrived back at Stumpy's side.

Everyone turned to me. I watched quite a few sets of eyes drop down to the ground and knew they had spotted Sherlock and Watson. Soft conversations erupted in all directions.

"They called for a recess," Jillian reported. "We have two hours."

"Perfect. Stumpy? Could we have a few moments of your time?"

"You're Zachary Anderson, aren't you?"

I nodded. "That's me."

"You stood up for me. I can't remember the last time someone did that for me. Thank you."

"You're welcome. Listen, I...."

"Oh, my goodness, it's Sherlock and Watson!" Stumpy interrupted, breaking into a smile.

Upon hearing their names, both corgis started wiggling with excitement.

"You're two for two, pal," I said, grinning.

Stumpy squatted next to the dogs and gave each of

them some affection. After a few moments, he looked up at me. "I'm sorry, did you say something?"

"Could we talk to you?"

"Sure, I guess."

Once we were all seated, and the dogs realized Stumpy didn't have any treats to give them, they visibly relaxed.

"Crazy day, huh?" I began. "Listen, I need to ask you about that pie. It...."

"Someone tampered with it," Stumpy insisted.

"Let's assume you're right. Can you tell me what time you dropped it off?"

"Last night, before they closed up."

Jillian's head lifted. "Pies? Plural? You have more than one here?"

"I submitted a pie to each category," Stumpy said.

I pulled out my scoring sheet so that I could inspect the categories: fruit, apple, sweet, savory, and something called *kitchen sink*.

"Which ones?" I asked.

"Dutch apple, gran's marionberry, campfire delight, bayou, and that one there, the vinegar pie."

My eyebrows shot up. "You made that one?"

"You tried it?" Stumpy eagerly asked.

"I did. It has my vote so far."

"Oh, good. That's so very good to hear."

I held up a hand. "Okay, I gotta ask. Bayou?"

Stumpy nodded. "I decided to think outside the box, so I came up with a new recipe."

"Can I ask what's in it?" Jillian asked.

"Oh, hi Jillian. You've heard of chicken pot pies?"

"Of course."

"Well, I wanted to try making something with more of a southern flair. What are your feelings on gumbo?"

Jillian's eyes widened with surprise. "Are you telling me you made a gumbo pie?"

Growing excited, Stumpy hurried over to the two tables holding the savory options. He pointed at a pie, but then shook his head. He then indicated a completely different pie, but hesitated again. After a few moments, he frowned.

"I don't see it! I dropped it off right here. Where is it?"

"Are you sure it isn't one of these?" Jillian wanted to know.

"I cut a fleur-de-lis vent into the crust, as homage to the French in New Orleans. I don't see it anywhere!"

"Unless it was tampered with," I quietly suggested.

Stumpy moved around the table and stopped at a rather ordinary-looking pie with a generic crust, sitting in a disposable pie tin.

"You're not looking at that one, are you? It looks like something I would bake."

"That's the point," Stumpy was saying, growing despondent. "Do you smell that?"

Jillian and I both sniffed.

"I smell all kinds of spices," I reported, shrugging. "I couldn't identify them to save my soul."

"What about you, Mrs. Anderson?" Stumpy asked.

Jillian leaned forward and gently sniffed for a second time. Her eyes widened.

"Sassafras!"

"Root beer?" I asked. "What would root beer be doing in a pie?"

"That's his gumbo pie," Jillian confirmed. "If you dry and ground up the leaves of a sassafras tree, you'll get filé powder. *That* is a signature ingredient in gumbo."

Stumpy circled the table. "None of them have filé powder but this one. It's definitely mine. Someone got their hooks in it."

Jillian pointed at the other tables. "Check your other entries, Stumpy. Zack? Where's the announcer? I think we need to verify if Stumpy's pies are the only ones that have been sabotaged."

I found the guy in the blue polyester suit and passed on the request.

"Attention. May I have your attention, please? Would those of you who have submitted pies for judging please check for signs of tampering?"

"Awwooowoooo!" Sherlock howled.

I could say his howl wasn't that loud, but the problem was, Sherlock chose to vocalize his displeasure at the exact same time the room fell silent. I heard several people snickering, and saw a few fingers point his way. My little boy was trying to tell me something, and in true bipedal form, I had missed his cues. Catching sight of my dogs, I noticed neither was looking at me. In fact, both were looking at the table with the stereo on it. Again.

"Now what?" Jillian wanted to know. "They're back to the stereo?"

I automatically pulled out my phone and snapped another picture. "Your hearing is better than mine. What song is playing?"

Jillian shrugged. "Bye Bye Bye, by NSYNC."

"Another boy band," I scowled. "What's the deal with that?"

"Have a seat, Mr. Holden," I requested. "They just confirmed your pies have been sabotaged."

"How can that be? And please, call me Stumpy."

"Are you sure?" I asked.

Stumpy held up his fingers and wiggled what was left of them. "Hey, I'm the one who wasn't careful. I made the mistakes. I deal with it by seeing the humor in it."

Jillian nudged my arm. "Told you."

"Yeah, yeah, fine. That's one win for you. Now, er, Stumpy, we need to figure out what happened to your pies. When did you drop them off?"

"Last night. I prefer evenings."

"Do you know of anyone who'd want to set you up?" I asked.

"Yeah, I guess so."

My notebook appeared. "Ready. Fire away."

"Practically everyone. I can only assume it's because the judges always seem to pick my pies."

Jillian nodded. "It's true. He wins every competition he enters."

"I've lost three times," Stumpy corrected. "My first defeat was with my first savory pie."

"What'd you make?" I asked.

Stumpy shook his head and his sighed. "I tried a shrimp ramen pie. I figured, why not?" He saw my reaction and chuckled. "Oh, you're right to be horrified. It was terrible. Turns out I don't have any business using something I've never cooked before."

"How long have you lived in the area?" I asked.

"I was born in Molalla, Oregon," Stumpy said. "I didn't always live in PV, though. My father was British, and we lived in London for a few years. Then we moved here, not long after he changed our names."

I shared a look with Jillian. Stumpy's family changed their names? Both of us sat up a little straighter.

"Was your family's name hard to pronounce?" Jillian asked. "Is that why your father opted to change it?"

"Not really. Ayth."

"It's not too bad," I decided.

"My birth name was Hank."

"Where did you learn to bake?" I asked.

"My father," Stumpy said. "He owned his own bakery."

"Are you married?" Jillian asked.

"Once," Stumpy recalled. "It wasn't meant to be. She left me just over ten years ago."

"I'm sorry to hear that," Jillian said.

I wasn't too sure what to say, so I opted for the first thing that came to mind.

"It's her loss. You've got some mad skills in the kitchen, pal."

"That's very kind of you. Deidra didn't fancy seeing herself married to a baker. A farmer was bad enough, you see."

"Any ideas on what happened to her?" I asked.

Stumpy let out a short bark of laughter. "She ended up marrying a used car salesman. I heard she's more miserable now than ever."

Jillian said, "She screwed up by letting you go."

"Oh, I'm all right. It's been years since I've had to worry about someone else's feelings. Look at those faces. No, don't feel sorry for me. I have my baking and my friends. I'm not some lonely old man who needs your pity."

"I know there are lots of people who'd love to see you lose," I began, "but I have to ask if any of them stand out to you. Can you think of anyone who would have the motivation to pull something like this off?"

"I don't believe so," Stumpy answered.

"You were a farmer?" I continued.

"My farm is about three miles southwest of town," Stumpy confirmed.

"Did you enjoy it?" I asked.

"Not one bit," Stumpy admitted. "After the last accident, with the loss of this finger right here," and held up his right hand, "I decided I shed enough blood. My closest neighbors, the Barnes family, had expressed interest in my land on more than one occasion, so when I mentioned I was going to sell my farm, they jumped at the idea."

I held up a hand. "Just a moment. They wanted, what, the land? The crops you were growing? The farming equipment?"

Stumpy shrugged. "The land, I guess."

"How badly?" Jillian asked.

"Offered full price, so pretty bad, I guess. You're not suggesting....?"

"We know someone sabotaged you," I reminded him. "Your pies were switched out, and...."

"It was more than that," Jillian interrupted. "The pies were dismantled, the filling moved to another crust, and reassembled. Whoever did this didn't want anyone to know what they were doing."

"That's a good point," Stumpy admitted.

"And they did a good job," Jillian added. "You'd never know by looking at them that they had undergone surgery, of sorts."

"You're thinking it could be a fellow competitor?" Stumpy asked.

Jillian nodded. "It's possible. The crusts may be store-bought, but it's still a pie."

"Woof."

The three of us looked down. Both corgis, who had spent just about the entire time snoozing on the ground, were now awake. Sherlock was on his feet and staring off to the left. Again. However, this time, he wasn't looking at the boombox, but instead, at another spot on the table.

"What's he looking at now?" Jillian asked.

I smiled and shrugged. "I really don't know. He's looking at that table again, only I don't think he's interested in the stereo. Sherlock? Watson? Let's go take a look. We'll be right back."

Jillian nodded and turned back to Stumpy. We wandered away before I could hear what was asked. Once we arrived, I saw that I was right. This time, the dogs were focused on the other half of the table, and sure enough, something *was* on the table behind the water dispenser: a half-eaten piece of chocolate cake.

"That? Are you serious? That's chocolate, guys. You won't be going anywhere near it, thank you very much. Don't worry, once we get home, I'll see to it you get extra kibble tonight." I was ignored. Sighing, I pulled out my phone. "Fine. Here we go again. There, the picture of the cake has been taken. Happy?"

Both dogs rose to their feet and pulled me back the way we came, toward Jillian, as though I was the one who was inconveniencing them.

"What was it?" my wife asked.

"A half-eaten piece of cake," I reported. "For whatever reason, the dogs wanted a picture of it."

Jillian looked at the dogs, who returned her frank stare. "Cake? I wonder why."

Stumpy told us he wanted to check the rest of his pies for himself, so he bade us adieu.

"What now?" Jillian asked.

I handed her Watson's leash. "The neighbors. I say we find out what we can."

"The Barnes? Why would you want to know about them?"

"Opportunity. There might be some unspoken grudge between them and, well, it's the only lead we have. We should.... what are you doing?" My wife had set her purse on the nearest table, pulled out a chair, and sat down. Realization dawned. "Wait. We don't need to go far, do we? You know all about them?"

Jillian raised a hand. "Who among us has lived here her whole life? Oh, that's right. That'd be me."

I took a seat next to her. "Ah, got it. What can you...." Just then, I felt I was being watched. And I was. "What are you giving me the stink-eye for? We're on a case, remember? Stop pouting. Since when have I ever given either of you any cake? Pay attention to us, would you, and not the people eating cake."

"And are they?" Jillian giggled.

"Nope. They're staring at that couple over there. Now what? Sherlock? Let it go, pal. I think it's best we.... and I'm being ignored. No, I'm not going to take their picture. It's creepy. Let it go, pal."

Sherlock whined louder.

"Fine. There, happy? I have no idea why you'd want to.... scratch that. I'll figure it out later, when we get around to looking at the pictures. Sorry, Jillian. You were saying? About the Barnes? How many of them are there and how long have they lived in the area?"

"Let's start with the family first," Jillian began, "because they weren't always the Barnes family."

"Huh?"

"The father passed away ten years ago. He was married to Nora and they had three kids: Matthew, the oldest, is now in his mid-twenties. The twins, Mayhem and Chaos are seniors in high school."

"Did they enter this contest?" I asked. "Have they.... what?"

My wife was laughing. She pointed at the notebook.

"You are, without a doubt, a wonderful writer. That didn't even phase you. What was the last thing you wrote?"

"One son, mid-twenties. Two daughters, both in high school. Twins, I'm guessing."

"And the names of the girls?"

"That can't be right. Mayhem and Chaos?"

"Their names are Sherri and Terri."

"Cute. I'm assuming they're identical?"

"Identical, yes. Cute? Physically, yes. Personality? Think older versions of those girls from the Shining."

"You're suggesting they have an evil streak?"

"No suggesting needed. I'm saying it on record: those two girls are the epitome of being entitled. They're so used to their mother catering to their every whim that they've become terrors if they hear the word *no*. They are spoiled brats."

"And this helps us how?"

Jillian took my hand in hers. "They're malicious, Zachary. They could pull this off."

"Would they, though?"

Jillian glanced at the pies. "The fillings were removed and put inside a different pie shell. I'd say so."

"What's the motive?" I asked.

"I'm sorry, I don't have an answer to that. Boredom? Malice?"

"It'd be hard to prove," I said. After a few moments, I pulled out my phone and started a text message.

"Who are you texting?"

"Vance. I want to see if this particular family has any priors."

"I don't remember anything happening," Jillian said.

I looked up after sending the message off to my friend, Vance Samuelson, senior detective with the local police.

WIFE'S RECORD CLEAN. HUSBAND CLEAN. SON HAS HISTORY: PETTY THEFT, AGGR ASSAULT, AND DOMESTIC VIOLENCE.

I held my phone up.

"Nothing on the twins, but the son? He's got a record. These guys live nearby, have a prior history with Stumpy, and from the sounds of things, are capable of pulling this off. But...."

"But *what?*" Jillian asked.

I sighed. "Motivation. Why would they do it?"

Jillian was silent as she considered.

"Do you think there could be a history between the two farms?" I asked.

Jillian snapped her fingers. With an excited expression on her lovely face, she grabbed my hands in hers. "I just remembered something. Before I say what, didn't Sherlock and Watson zero in on a piece of cake?"

"Chocolate," I recalled.

"It just dawned on me. I think one of the twins either has worked for a bakery, or is *still* working for one."

"Locally?" I asked.

"I don't think the one she works at is in PV. Come on. Where there's a bakery, there's bound to be cake. We just have to find the right one!"

"Who would've thought there'd be so many bakeries in the Medford area," I complained, over an hour later. "And at this time of day, they're all the same: practically empty shelves."

My wife swatted my arm. "It's past noon. Most bakeries would have sold out of their best merchandise by now."

Jillian stopped in front of one of the glass display cases.

"What am I looking at?" I asked.

"*Pączki*," a friendly voice informed us. "Like donuts."

We looked up to see a smiling, middle-aged woman behind the counter.

"Would you like a sample?" the shopkeeper inquired.

"You twisted my arm. Thanks!"

Jillian nodded. "Yes, please. Oh, my, these are good!"

The morsel I popped in my mouth had a light, flaky crust and the filling? I had no idea what it tasted like, but it was creamy, with a hint of citrus. Orange? Mango?

"Oh, wow. What flavor is that? You know what? I don't care. They're fantastic!"

"I make a dozen different flavors," we were told. "I only have.... half a dozen tangelo, and perhaps a dozen key lime at the moment."

"I'll take a dozen," I ordered, as I smiled at the proprietor. "Mix and match whatever flavors you have, thanks. Is this your bakery? Are you the owner?"

The woman nodded. "I am. Would you two like anything else?"

I turned to Jillian as I heard the door chime behind me. An elderly fellow entered the store. We gave each other a cursory nod of acknowledgement. I was in the process of turning around when I saw the corgis in my car. They were standing up, on their hind legs, and looking over the seat at us. More specifically, they were staring at the older gentleman who had just entered the store.

"What is it?" Jillian softly asked.

"I'm not sure. I'm going to discreetly take a picture of the guy behind us. Watch the dogs, would you?"

"Okay, Zachary. I'm ready."

As nonchalantly as I could, I pretended to be studying my phone and playing with some of the apps. When the guy wasn't looking, I snapped a photo.

"Both dogs just sat down," Jillian whispered.

"Ah."

"What does that mean?"

"I'll tell you later. Okay, I picked out a few things. Is there something you might like?"

My wife returned her attention to the glass display case and selected a few pastries.

"I love your bakery," Jillian told the shopkeeper. "I've been in here a few times, although I admit it's been too long since my last visit."

"*Dziękuję Ci*. You are too kind."

"J-jay koo-itchee," I slowly repeated. "What's that mean?"

The clerk gave a delighted laugh. "That wasn't too bad. Not many people try to speak Polish back to me. You gave it a good attempt."

I bowed. "Thank you, thank you very much. I'm here 'til Tuesday. Polish? I'll be honest with you, ma'am. I don't recall ever having anything from a Polish bakery, but now? These look great! You've made a customer for life."

"*Dziękuję Ci*. Er, thank you. That's what it means."

"I'm Zack, and this is my wife, Jillian. You've got a terrific store here."

The woman rose up on her tiptoes and extended a hand over the counter. "Ewa Kowalski."

I pointed at the empty racks. "If you don't mind me asking, what was in there? Whatever it was, they seem to be in high demand."

"*Ciastka*. It's my specialty."

I waited a few moments for an explanation of what that was. When it didn't come, I held up a hand. "And that is?"

"You'd call them pastries. They always sell out early."

"I can't wait to try one," I said, smiling.

"Will there be anything else?" the woman gently inquired.

I pointed at the small stack of flat, rectangular boxes waiting for me at the cash register. "I think we're good. How much do I owe you?"

As I was reaching for my wallet, to pay for my purchases, I noticed Jillian stiffen with surprise. Curious as to what had caught her attention, I turned. Outside, a girl was walking toward the door, pushing a small cart. She was tall, slim, and looked to be sixteen or seventeen. What really made her stand out was her hair. It was purple, with yellow highlights. If it wasn't for the unusual color, I wouldn't have looked twice. As the girl approached the front door, she turned around and backed her way through, using her rear to push the glass door open.

"All done, Mrs. Kowalski," the teenager announced, as she dragged the noisy cart behind her. "You might want to call for a dumpster pickup. I think the store next door is using ours again, so we...."

The girl trailed off as she finally faced forward and saw the two of us staring at her, as though a two-headed alien had just appeared.

"Ah, I was wondering what happened to you," Mrs. Kowalski exclaimed. She indicated the two of us. "Would you ring them up, please?"

The teenager nodded. Her eyes flicked over to me, gave me a once-over, and then lingered on Jillian's. "Sure. Will this be everything for you?"

I handed her my card. "I believe so."

"You seem familiar to me," Jillian said. "Have we met before?"

"I'm sorry, ma'am, I don't think so. I don't live around here."

"Have you worked here long?" Jillian casually asked, as she took the receipt that was handed to her and slid it over to me to sign.

"About two months."

About to shake her head, and reach for the boxes at the same time, I watched my wife frown.

"The hair," she was saying. "I didn't recognize you with that shade, and it *has* been a couple of years since you were in my store."

"Do you know me?" the girl hesitantly asked.

Jillian nodded. "It's Sherri Barnes, isn't it? I was beginning to think we were never going to find you. Do you know how many bakeries we've searched? I think this is the tenth, or eleventh."

"Twelfth," I softly corrected.

Sherri took one look at me, then at my Jeep with my

madly barking corgis, and—with a squeal of alarm—darted through the employee-only door. A few moments later, we heard the back door slam. Then, a banged-up VW bus, with a dual-tone paint job, roared by. Well, let's be honest. It *putted* by, probably going as fast as it could.

"Where is she going?" Mrs. Kowalski asked, shocked. "That girl is supposed to work the late shift today. What did you say to her?"

Jillian took my hand. "We didn't say anything. But unfortunately, she just confirmed a few things for us. Zachary, I do believe it's time to go. And perhaps you should....?"

I already had my phone in my hand. "I'm on it. I've got him on speed dial. Vance? It's Zack. Listen, I think our lead suspect just.... what? What do you mean, what suspect? The one who's been tampering with the pies, who else? Yes, *those* pies. Right. You're looking for one Sherri Barnes. She's driving an older white and green VW bus. She'll be coming from Medford. Good. Hmm? Oh, we're not sure yet. We'll keep you posted. Thanks, pal."

"What'd he say?" Jillian asked, once I had finished my call.

"They're going to put an APB out for the van. He wanted to know how we knew it was her. Aside from acting like she's guilty, I didn't know what to tell him."

"You can tell him we found someone with means and opportunity, which were confirmed by her fleeing from us. As for motive, well, we'll have to get back to him on that."

We thanked the store owner and promised to be back. The last thing I said to her was that she probably ought to place an ad in the paper for more help.

As the door swung closed, and we returned to my Jeep, Sherlock and Watson practically climbed into our laps. Both were acting like they had rolled on an anthill. Neither would stay put and they were fidgeting like crazy.

"What's with you two?" I asked the dogs, as I bodily picked up Sherlock and placed him in the back seat.

In less than two seconds, he was back in my lap. This time, he was staring at the bakery in front of us. It was only when I turned to look that I caught sight of the sign: In Cake We Trust. Cake. This must be the first time we hit a bakery with the word *cake* in the title.

Right on cue, the dogs lost interest and returned to their seats in the second row, as if *we* had pulled them up there against their will. That's when thoughts of the half-eaten plate of chocolate cake from earlier sprang to mind.

"Are they trying to tell us about Sherri?" Jillian was asking. "We're on our way back to...."

"Awwwooowooowooo!" Sherlock howled.

Backing the Jeep out of its parking spot, I shifted into drive and pointed at the store's sign.

"Cake. Remember the plate of chocolate cake Sherlock noticed back at the fairgrounds? Just like with any other case, he wouldn't let it go until I took a picture of it. I can only assume he wanted us to come here so that we could make the link to that girl. I just don't know why she'd do it."

"Maybe she's angry with Stumpy for always winning?" Jillian mused, more to herself.

We turned left, onto Crater Lake Highway, and headed toward PV.

"She's Stumpy's neighbor. You already mentioned that this girl is the devil reincarnate. She works in a bakery. She's gotta be the one who tampered with the pies."

"Of course! That must be where she got them!"

"Huh?"

"Sherri. She must've swapped pies from that bakery with Stumpy's."

"Only, it was revealed the filling was the same," I reminded her. "Someone had replaced the crust."

"Oh, that's right."

"Do you think Ewa is in on this?" I asked.

Jillian was shaking her head before I could finish the question. "I don't think so. The owner was too nice. Then again, we know Sherri worked the late shift, which probably meant she had unsupervised time to move the filling from one set of pies to another *and* cover her tracks at the same time."

"Where to?" I wanted to know.

"Let's head to the Barnes' family home," Jillian suggested. "I want to see what the corgis do."

Thirty minutes later, we pulled up to an aging country farmhouse set nearly three hundred feet down a gravel driveway. The screen door banged open and a woman close to my own age appeared. She was wearing a baggy gray sweatshirt, black leggings, and a huge scowl on her face.

"Where is she?" the woman demanded, before either of us had a chance to speak. "What did you say to her?"

I stepped forward and raised a hand. "I'm sorry?"

"Don't give me that malarkey. I know someone spooked my girl. What did you say? If you've threatened her, then I should warn you I have no qualms about pumping your butt full of lead! In fact, where's my gun?"

"Whoa!" I cried, holding up my hands in a timeout. "Look, there's no need to do anything drastic. We don't need to call the cops."

"Yet," Jillian softly murmured.

"You're that wine fella, ain't you? Name o' Anderson?"

I nodded and held out a hand, which was ignored. "Zack Anderson. This is Jillian. I was wondering if we could...."

"I ain't tellin' you nuthin' about my kids," the woman snapped.

"You probably don't remember but we've met before," Jillian soothed, hoping to defuse the situation. "Nora, it's me, Jillian. Do you remember Jillian Cooper?"

"Nope. Whaddya want?"

"Are you friends with your neighbor, Mr. William Holden?" I asked, striving to keep my voice neutral.

"Who, Stumpy? Ev'rybody knows 'im. What do you wanna know?"

"Are you friendly with him?" Jillian asked.

"What? God no! He's old! Ain't you seen 'im before? He ain't my type."

Jillian closed her eyes for a few moments. "Are you and your family friends with him?"

"Nope. We ain't good enough. Whatever."

"Why would you say that?" Jillian asked. "You're a fine family, who...."

"Aww, cut the crap, lady," Nora sighed. "I may be a farmer's wife, but I know a thing or two. It's hard work keepin' up a farm."

"I can only imagine," I said, nodding. "You must do very well for yourself."

"Do I look like I do well for myself?" Nora countered. Her frown deepened. "What do you want? If you don't wanna complain 'bout my kids, then there must be somethin' else buggin' ya."

I let out a quiet sigh. "I'll be honest with you. We need to know if you know anything about the tampering of Stumpy's pies.?"

"Hah! I always knew he was cheatin', only no one could figure out how. No, I didn't do nuthin', and neither did my kids."

We heard a commotion from the barn. One of the four large stall doors, the only one currently closed, suddenly opened. We caught a glimpse of a very familiar VW van when Sherri appeared. She noticed we were all staring at her and yelped with alarm. She ducked back inside the barn and slammed the door closed behind her.

Jillian and I gave Nora a questioning look.

"Like I said," Nora was saying, "ain't no way none of my family is involved. Now, git on your way 'fore I call the cops. I ain't seen my daughter, and have no idea what she's done."

I nodded. "Thank you, we won't take up any more of your time."

"Nora's protecting her," Jillian said, once we were back in the Jeep. "We need to let Vance know they're guilty."

"Clearly. The problem is, we need to prove it. Okay, the text message has been sent. Sherlock? Watson? Are you guys ready to go?"

Before I could shift the car into gear, I noticed both dogs were up on their hind legs and looking out, over the back seat. Glancing in the mirror, I could see that both corgis were now staring down the driveway, in the direction we were about to go. Shrugging, we headed for the highway, only when we got there, Sherlock and Watson turned to look left. For the record, PV was the *other* way. From what I could see, both dogs were looking at a small fruit stand down the road, about a half mile away.

"They want to go *that way*," I told Jillian.

My wife leaned around me to see for herself. "Why

not? Sherlock? Your daddy is going to turn left, so we'll
be able to see what lies in that direction."

As we neared the fruit stand, both corgis became
more and more anxious. Coasting to a stop, we parked
next to several other cars and stepped out. I helped the
dogs down, and before we could take a few steps, Sherlock and Watson veered right, heading for a woman
who had just purchased a flat of strawberries. Unsure
of what I was supposed to be looking for, I noticed the
lady holding the berries had just stumbled a bit, but in
doing so, the leftover wad of bills she was holding, her
change from her purchase, came loose. Being closest to
her, I offered to hold the fruit while she gathered her
cash.

"Thank you so much," the woman was saying, as
she frantically swiped at the fluttering bills. Most were
ones, but I did see a couple of fives. "Serves me right for
holding too much."

"Woof."

I looked down at Sherlock. He and Watson weren't
watching the lady, me, or the berries. In fact, he seemed
to be staring at one of the woman's paper money fluttering about on the ground. Thankfully, there was only
a slight breeze, so while the bills swirled around a bit, it
really didn't go anywhere. Both corgis, though, were
treating it like a train wreck: they couldn't look away.

"Such cute dogs," the woman gushed, as she
retrieved her money. She gave each dog a pat on the
head before taking her strawberries from me. "Thank
you again. Have a nice day!"

Jillian appeared at my side. "What was that all about?"

"I was just lending a helping hand. Her hands were full. Anyway, did you see Sherlock and Watson? They were staring at a dollar bill as though it was made of bacon."

"Did you take a picture?"

I looked down at the dogs. Whoops. I never considered them looking at a one-dollar bill could be considered a corgi clue. Should I have taken a picture? There was one way to find out.

I pulled out my wallet, saw that I had eight bucks in it, and dropped a single. The corgis looked up at me, then Jillian, and then looked at the dollar bill. Both sat. I dropped the five. It was ignored. Sighing, I returned the five to my wallet and snapped a photo of the one.

"Music, boy bands, cake, overweight strangers, and a one-dollar bill. I have no idea how any of that could possibly tie together," I said, as we piled back into the car to head out.

"Overweight strangers?" my wife repeated, confused. "Why would you take their picture?"

"Talk to *your* dogs," I replied. "Take my phone and have a look."

"Do you know these people?" Jillian asked, once my phone was displaying one of the strangers.

"No. You?"

"For this man, no. Let's see. The couple? It's still a no, I'm afraid."

"Same here, but Sherlock and Watson must've

wanted me to take their pictures for *some* reason. You've seen the pics. The couple was at the fair. The guy was at the bakery."

At that moment, my cell rang. I nodded at Jillian, who then tapped my stereo's display screen to answer the call.

"Hey, Vance. Any chance you can tell us what the Barnes girl had to say for herself?"

"I just got in my car," my detective friend reported. "I'm still at their house. She's not here."

"We know she was there," I insisted. "We saw her, pal. She hid her car in the barn."

"Why would her mother lie to me?" Vance asked, growing angry.

"Why else?" I fired back. "She's gotta be protecting her daughter."

"Can you get a warrant?" Jillian asked.

"To look inside someone's barn?" Vance asked. "Based on, what, that we believe she tampered with a pie, of all things? No judge is gonna sign that warrant."

"What do we do now?" I asked.

"We wait for one of them to do something stupid," Vance told me. "The only way I.... is that you guys up there? I think I see a Jeep down the road."

"Yeah, that's us," I confirmed. "We were at the next farm over."

"Why?"

"Because, it's what Sherlock wanted," I answered.

"Hmm. Find anything?"

"Only a lady who dropped a little cash, and then the dogs became fascinated with a one-dollar bill."

"That makes no sense," Vance decided.

"Tell me about it."

"Listen, I'm going to head back to the station and.... huh. I wouldn't have called that one. You said the girl's van is a VW bus? White and green?"

"Yeah, why? Do you see it?"

"It's currently behind me," Vance said. "I can see a young girl behind the wheel. She clearly doesn't know who's in front of her."

"What are you going to do?" I asked.

"Let her pass me, and then I'm pulling her over. Gotta go, buddy."

"What would possess the girl to leave right after Vance did?" Jillian asked, bewildered.

"Guilt," I guessed.

"What do we do?"

"Back to the fairgrounds. I'd say she knows we're on to her. I think she's going to try and cover her tracks. We have to make sure she doesn't have someone already there to do her dirty work."

We hightailed it back to the fairgrounds in time to see Polyester Pants striding to the podium, intent on delivering an announcement.

"Recess is now over. Judges? I believe we're ready to...."

Vance chose that exact time to call back. Twisted Sister's *We're Not Gonna Take It* echoed noisily in the eerily quiet conference room.

"Sorry," I said, as I raised my voice and handed the dogs' leashes to Jillian. "I have to take this. I'll be right back."

Jillian squeezed my hand encouragingly.

"What's up?" I asked, as I stepped into the hallway outside the judging room.

"You called it," Vance said. "Sherri Barnes confessed to tampering with those pies you were talking about."

"That's good to hear, pal. Did she say where she was going?"

"Straight for you," Vance reported. "That is, if you're currently back at the fairgrounds."

"I am."

"She said she had no idea the pies would be discovered and was planning on stealing the ones she messed with, presumably to get rid of the evidence."

"Why did she do it?" I asked.

"Believe it or not, she said she did it to make her mom feel better. From what I could make out, Nora Barnes entered a few pies last year, but didn't place. Stumpy took four of the five categories, and that's only because he didn't enter one."

"Revenge, huh? I guess I can get on board with that."

"I'm not sure what else I can do here other than to check and see if the quilting club wants to press charges."

"Maybe they'll disqualify her? I don't know."

"Thought you'd want to know, Zack."

"I appreciate it. I'm going to go make Stumpy's day, and probably tick off a lot of people."

Vance laughed and hung up. Humming to myself, I started working my way back to the judging table when I felt an arm hook through mine and bring me to an abrupt stop.

"Zachary? What are you humming?"

I looked at Jillian and shrugged. "I was humming something? I have no idea. No, wait. Is this the one?" I hummed a few bars and was rewarded with my wife nodding.

"Yes, that one! Where did you hear it?"

"No clue. What song is it?"

"It's *I Am Henry VIII I Am*. Why would you be humming that song?"

I shrugged. "I don't know. Must've thought about it when I was thinking about that *Ghost* movie earlier."

"What about it?" my wife asked.

"Well, the first corgi clue? It was that song, from the Righteous Brothers. It was Angie's ringtone, if memory serves."

"*Unchained Melody*," Jillian recalled. "And your brain went with.... Zachary? Can I see your phone?"

"I've been over the pictures a number of times," I admitted. "If you're going to tell me that something now makes sense, then I'll.... I'll.... I don't know. Take you to your favorite restaurant and willingly encourage you to order whatever you want?"

My phone was snatched out of my hand. Perhaps that wasn't the wisest of wagers I could have made.

Jillian was silent as she studied the pictures from this strange case. Leaning over her shoulder, I watched her flip through the pictures. Angie, with her *Ghost* ringtone; the two shots of the stereo, with the two different boy bands; the overweight strangers, and finally, the picture of the one-dollar bill. Personally, I didn't see any connection. Then again, anyone who knows the two of us will attest to which one is the smarter partner, and I already know it wasn't me.

"Mr. Anderson?" Polyester Pants called out. "Would you take your seat, please?"

I raised a hand. "Just a moment. I'll be...." Jillian took this moment to whip out her phone and do a few Internet searches. Her eyes lit up. Incredulous, she turned to Stumpy. "What is it?" I whispered.

"Picture one," Jillian began. "The music from *Ghost*. The song you were humming?"

I shrugged. "What about it?"

We were starting to draw a crowd. Since Sherlock and Watson were known to solve mysteries and crack hard-to-solve police cases, our audience grew. Jillian showed me my phone and the picture of the strangers from the fair.

"What was Henry VIII known for?" she asked.

"Being a big dude?" I guessed.

"Uh-huh. Now, the other songs? From the Back-street Boys and N'SYNC?"

"What about 'em?" I inquired.

"They were managed by someone who was arrested for fraud."

My eyebrows shot up. "You're kidding."

"I confirmed it just moments ago. But the one-dollar-bill?"

I pointed at her phone, but not before looking around at the crowd of people silently watching us and gave them a smile. "Look up George Washington. Sherlock and Watson didn't care about the five, so maybe it has to do with the person on it."

Jillian found the answer in less than ten seconds. "Our first president is known for many things," she began. "One of which was his deviousness. He's known for faking out the British army."

"Deviousness," I repeated, thinking. I caught sight of Stumpy. How could I have been so stupid? "Of course! That's what the dogs are trying to tell us! This is all about Stumpy!"

"We already know that, Zachary," Jillian gently reminded. "He was set up, and...."

"No," I argued, shaking my head. "You're not going to believe this but.... Stumpy's guilty! He didn't make those pies! For all we know, he picks them up at Ewa Kowalski's place. How else did he attract Sherri's attention? Sherri must've thought something was up, so she probably staked out Stumpy's place and saw that he was submitting store-bought pies as his own."

"Y-you h-have no proof!" Stumpy stammered, his eyes widening with shock.

I ignored him. "We've been looking in the wrong direction from the beginning!"

"Th-there's *nothing* going on!" Stumpy insisted.

I turned to Jillian. "What was his name again?"

"Stumpy's? William Holden."

"Not that name, the other one, before they moved from England."

"Oh. It was Hank.... no! It can't be!"

"What?" several bystanders demanded.

"Ayth," Jillian breathed. "Hank Ayth! Or, more likely, Henry. Henry Ayth!"

Heads were turning to stare. Blank looks were everywhere.

"That explains the song from *Ghost*, and all the Henry VIII references!" I exclaimed.

"Let me venture a guess," Jillian said, raising her voice. "You said your father was a baker? That part was probably true. What wasn't true was that *you* are also a baker. You've been entering these contests for, what, ten years now?"

Stumpy was silent.

"That must've been when you discovered In Cake We Trust."

Stumpy's head fell.

"Her bakery is tiny," Jillian explained to the crowd. "Ms. Kowalski said it herself. Her specialty are the pies and cakes. They sell out early, so I can only assume she doesn't make much."

"I knew it!" a shrill voice cried. Turning, we all watched Betsy Godel jump to her feet. "I always said he was a cheat! This just proves it!"

Pandemonium ensued. Those who were sitting leapt to their feet, squawking angrily. Those already standing began arguing with their neighbors, regardless if they knew each other or not. And there, rising above all the voices, was the barking of a dog. Sherlock, it would seem, didn't care for all the noise. And poor Watson? She was cowering behind my wife's legs.

I found Polyester Pants and pulled him aside.

"Your hands are full, and I think I've caused enough problems around here. I'll be taking my family home."

The announcer nodded. "You do that, Mr. Anderson."

Jillian and I gathered up the dogs and headed for the door. We weren't notified until a few hours later that, thanks to what's now being called the Stumpy Scandal, the pie judging competition had been canceled and William has been banned for life. And Ewa Kowalski? Well, she was given credit for creating all the tasty recipes Stumpy used over the years.

Having finished reading Woody's text, informing me about the decision, I smiled at my wife and handed the dogs two of their favorite treats. I looked down at the huge, juicy burger on my plate and sighed contentedly. A smile appeared on my face after the first bite. Maybe judging wasn't so bad after all?

———◄•●•►———

About the Author

Jeffrey M. Poole is a best-selling author who specializes in writing light-hearted cozy mystery and epic fantasy stories with a healthy dose of humor thrown in. He began as an indie author in 2010, but now has all 30+ of his titles traditionally published. His series include the cozy Corgi Case Files and the epic fantasy Bakkian Chronicles series. He is a proud and active member of the Mystery Writers of America and the Science Fiction & Fantasy Writers Association. To learn more about the author and his books, please visit his official website at **AuthorJMPoole.com** or follow him on Facebook at www.fb.com/bakkianchronicles.

FIND ME ONLINE

Discover more about the authors at their websites listed after each story and through Thalia Press, the publisher of this anthology. Go to ThaliaPress.com to read about other books and projects from Thalia Press.

Thank you for reading.